Damian McNicholl was born in Northern Ireland and attended law school at University College, Cardiff. His first novel, *A Son Called Gabriel* was an American Booksellers Association Booksense Pick and Lambda Literary Awards finalist. The book is currently under film option with award-winning Director Tom Collins. Damian lives in Bucks County Pennsylvania and is at work on his third novel. He maintains a blog at www.damianm.blogspot.com.

Twisted Agendas

Damian McNicholl

Legend ◗ Press

Independent Book Publisher

Legend Press Ltd, 2 London Wall Buildings,
London EC2M 5UU
info@legend-paperbooks.co.uk
www.legendpress.co.uk

British Library Cataloguing in Publication Data available.

ISBN 978-1-9082480-2-2

1

Edited by: Lauren Parsons-Wolff

Set in Times
Printed by CPI Books, United Kingdom

Cover designed by Yvey Bailey
www.gingernutdesign.co.uk

Author Photo © Megan McLoone

Legend 📖 Press
Independent Book Publisher

Also by Damian McNicholl

A Son Called Gabriel

(Currently under film option.)

Praise for Damian McNicholl

American Booksellers Association BOOKSENSE 'PICK'
ForeWord Magazine Book of the Year Award Finalist
Lambda Literary Award Finalist
Advocate Magazine Top 20 Summer Book Selection
Nominated for the American Library Association
Stonewall Award

'McNicholl is a fine storyteller and, in Gabriel, he has created a convincing, complicated and likable main character.' **Curledup.com**

'It is so well written, and the author's portrayal of Gabriel is so vivid, that readers will be hard-pressed to remember they're holding a piece of fiction in their hands.' **Backspace book reviews – bookblog.com**

'Beautifully crafted, honestly told, and hauntingly heart-breaking with a gentle dash of humor, A Son Called Gabriel is simply one of the best books I've read in years.' **Bookcritics.org**

'McNicholl's descriptions dance and light upon the page, making this a very entertaining read.' **Compulsivereader.com**

'Each character, from Gabriel's girlfriend to his youngest sister Nuala, is so vividly portrayed that their world is all-encompassing, and it becomes almost heartbreaking to say goodbye.' **ForeWord Magazine**

'[A] fine, compassionate coming-of-age story. McNicholl paints a rich picture of Gabriel's life and all its conflicted messages about sex… McNicholl is a graceful writer, and his is a worthy debut.' **Publisher's Weekly**

'McNicholl writes compellingly, drawing his readers deep into Gabriel's … tale of growing up in '60s and '70s Ireland — so much so that I was left thinking about sequels.' **Echo Weekly**

'The author captures the life and times of the Catholic Irish family and community living. We are given a peek at the pressures that are brought to bear on the families through religious and patriotic differences.' **BookIdeas.com**

'... moving reading... [a] touching portrait of one boy's hopes and fears. A sometimes funny, often painful depiction of a young boy's struggles with his sexuality.' **Booklist**

'McNicholl's affable voice captures the wary innocence and budding sexuality of youth with polished and amiable originality.' **Book Marks**

'Damian McNicholl does a marvellous job telling this heartbreaking story of a boy fighting against himself - so good that you will not be able to put it down.' **Wordswordswords.com**

'A beautiful story, wonderfully written, and the top of my list for recommended reading for everyone, gay or straight.' **The Open Book**

'A touching and dark, yet periodically hilarious work on a subject matter often overlooked in Irish literature.' **Irish Connections Magazine**

'A deeply felt and often funny coming of age novel that is ultimately unforgettable.' **Adelante Magazine**

'The complex relationships within the extended Harkin family...are developed with skill and an attention to the minutiae of life in a divided community that easily holds the reader's attention.' **Emigrant magazine**

'A bittersweet coming-of-age tale... McNicholl's publishers are (of course) comparing [it] to *Angela's Ashes*, which is not necessary. This novel, though a bit melodramatic at times, stands well enough on its own.' **Irish America Magazine**

'... the first-person narrative skillfully evokes the feelings of 10-year-old Gabriel, who fears, then knows he is 'different.'' **Lavender Magazine**

Acknowledgements

Thanks to my friends and family for their encouragement during the writing of this novel.

I'm especially grateful to LSE alum Emily Lauren Burg for her help. I also wish to thank Jeanne Denault, Maria Lamba, David Jarret, Chris Bauer, John Wirebach and Russ Allen of The Rebel Writers of Bucks County. And thanks also to my editor Lauren Parsons and Lucy Boguslawski of Legend Press.

For Larry Caban

Breaking free

Sleek and silver-blue, the car was parked under the porch of his parents sprawling red-brick house, its seductive profile gleaming in the rays of the lowering sun. It was breathtakingly gorgeous yet the sight of it enraged Danny Connolly as he returned home.

He strode around to the back of the house and entered through the kitchen where he laid his suitcase down beside the knotted pine table. Theme music heralding the start of his father's favourite nature documentary commenced as he approached the living room.

"Home from the training course, eh?" his father said from the unfurled recliner.

"Hello Mum," Danny said, not looking at him.

"Have you eaten?" she asked.

She was seated at one end of a buff Chesterfield sofa, open scissors in one hand, a spring green spider plant offshoot suspended in the other, the hacked mother plant in a large terra-cotta pot perched on a footstool before her. In a semicircle around the stool were ten tiny pots containing the transplanted babies. His mother was constantly assailing the houseplants, shearing leaves at the slightest hint of brown, as well as over-feeding the scrawny rubber plants in the vestibule.

"I'm not hungry."

"Did they give you a nice certificate to hang up?" his father asked.

Certificates didn't impress Danny. In, fact, they were a cause of monumental embarrassment. After the university forwarded his degree certificate, his father insisted he display it in the company's reception area rather than in his bedroom where Danny deemed it more appropriate. It hung there beside his unduly ornate *Connolly Dairy Management Certificate in Organisational Methodology,* both framed in pretentious baroque gilt frames.

He'd started working in the family business nine months ago at the insistence of his father, a self-made man who'd built a very profitable business supplying supermarkets and corner shops throughout Ireland with milk, cream and cheddar cheese. Danny had graduated with honours in business, and was appointed to supervise a new 'Yoghurt and Soft Cheese' department despite pleading with his father Darragh that a marketing position would benefit the company most because he could immediately utilise the knowledge acquired from pursuing his degree. As part of his training he'd been ordered by his father to a yoghurt-making facility in the Republic of Ireland, Mr. Connelly being the sort of boss who required his future executives to dirty their hands on the production lines. But yoghurt cultures weren't the only thing that had fermented while Danny was at the factory. He'd had ample time to think and decided he was far too subordinate to his father. Things needed to change.

"Dad, they don't hand out certificates for standing in a production line."

Darragh turned away from the television and scanned his son's face, a handsome face, though not classic like his father's. Danny's chin not so precisely chiseled, the upper lip not bowed enough. What they did have in common was height, both men being five-eleven in socks, tanned complexions and crops of wavy jet-black hair.

As Darragh sat erect, the recliner rose obediently to support his back. "That's a shame. Did you see her outside?" His father smiled.

Danny didn't answer.

"I parked her by the front door."

He met his mother's eye. She shrugged before snipping off a tiny shoot that fell to the floor.

"'Metallic azure blue' is her colour," said his father, who peered over at his wife and winked. "Aye, she's a great motor. Very nifty."

"I warned you not to buy it until we'd... "

"Warned?" His father's right eyebrow lifted.

"I asked you not to buy it until we talked," Danny said.

"Any manager working for me needs a better car than that piece of scrap you're driving. You're representing my company." His father laughed unexpectedly. "Wait till you take her for a spin. That'll soon change your mind."

Danny turned to look at the television as a vulture landed on the hind flank of a zebra carcass and placed its bald head inside a gaping, scarlet hole in the animal's underbelly.

"Darragh, how can you watch that so soon after eating?" his mother said. "I thought tonight's programme was about the Thomson gazelle." She snipped another shoot off her plant, inspected it cursorily and cast it into a mounting pile in the nearby wastepaper basket, then looked over at Danny. "Did you do anything exciting in your free time?"

"A lot of thinking and sorting," he said, and looked at his father who was watching the television.

"You two go somewhere else if you want to talk," his father said.

His mother's nose flared when she glanced at her husband. She patted one side of her combed back auburn hair secured with a broad tortoise shell clasp. "I told you to do nothing about that car until he came home, but you never listen to me Darragh, do you?" She pushed the footstool aside, rose and picked up four of the potted transplants. "Danny, will you bring in the rest of those and put them on the kitchen window sill so they'll catch the morning sun?"

"Helen, for Christ's sake," her husband said. He seized the remote and turned up the volume.

She looked at Danny and rolled her eyes.

As soon as his mother left, Danny's father lowered the volume. The pair sat in silence until the programme cut to an advert break.

"Dad?" Danny cleared his throat. "We must talk."

"What, now?"

The tick of the Vienna clock behind him seemed suddenly very loud. "Before I begin, I need you to not interrupt."

Darragh said nothing.

"Okay?"

"Go on."

"I've been allowing you to make decisions for me that *I* should make. This was fine when I was younger. But I'm nearly twenty-one and it's not anymore." He paused and scoured his father's face to see if he was listening. "I'm going to do things differently and need you to understand that so you don't get confused."

"I'm already confused."

"No interrupting."

"Make it snappy. The programme's about to come on again."

Danny took a silent, deep breath. "I need some time away to think things through… where I'm going in life and stuff."

"What's to think through? You've got a job with a future and a fiancée who looks great and has a damned good business head on her shoulders."

He decided not to dilute the conversation by joining the issues of his work and fiancée. Susan was already a member of the family in his father's eyes. His mother was not so welcoming but would not go against her husband's wishes, at least not overtly.

"The job's not giving me satisfaction, Dad."

"Ach, are you going to start up about the marketing job again? You'll get there when I judge you're ready."

"Here you go again. Let me *finish*." Danny paused to allow his command to sink in. "I've decided to leave the dairy for a while to… "

"*Leave?*"

"It's not just the job. It's everything."

"Ah, I see your strategy." His father slammed his palms into the armrests and laughed. "I see what you're up to now. No problem."

Danny's jaw slackened.

"You're slow on the uptake but you do learn, I'll give you that," his father added. "Maybe there's a bit more of me in you than I thought."

Danny wolfed down the compliment. "I thought you'd be angry."

"No way. This is exactly what I want from my managers." His father's eyes glittered and he lowered his head as if it was heavy with wonder. "Tactics are the wheels of business."

"What are you… "

"A sharp man always chooses his moment." His father glanced at the television before turning back to Danny. "Programme's back. Listen, leave it with me and I'll see what I can come up with." He threw back his head and guffawed. "You got me fair and square this time. Wait till your mother hears how you played me to get a raise."

He watched dumb-struck as his father turned away. "This isn't about a raise."

"Shush. A smart man also leaves when he's winning."

"Dad, I'm going to London to do a language course. German." His innards shook like a dangling trout he'd once caught. "Think of it as a mini-sabbatical. Many people take one at some point."

"Interesting."

Like a salesman, Danny moved now to clinch the deal. "You've said many times that you'd like to expand into Europe one day and I'm sure you'd agree Germany would be a brilliant place to start now they've finished absorbing East Germany. It's a huge market and I'll be able to help with the negotiations for leases and supply contracts and stuff." He paused for a response, but his father said nothing. "Well, that's it. I'll leave you in peace to enjoy the programme." Danny walked quickly to the door.

As he touched the brass door handle, his father said, "Help me get this straight, son. You're going to London to learn German?"

"That's it." He pressed down on the handle.

His father was silent for a moment. "Now I might not be a smart man, but would Germany not be a better place to learn German?"

"The school specialises in teaching professional people." Danny opened the door.

"There's also the matter of London itself," his father said.

"What do you mean?"

"Full of degenerates that place. You'll end up using drugs."

"I didn't in Belfast."

"Belfast's different."

"Right, they've only been blowing people to bits for years there."

"Naïve young Irish people get into trouble in England."

A surge of adrenaline coursed through Danny's veins. "It's time you gave me some credit, Dad."

His father tutted. "Going away to think about life. I've never heard of the likes." His father sat up erect again. "You're not leaving here. End of story."

Danny rushed back into the heart of the room. "No matter how I try, you *never* listen. I'm responsible for my… "

"Act responsible then. You'll have a wife in a few months. What's she say about this nonsense?"

Danny didn't speak for a moment. "I need to do this."

His father's cheeks turned purple. "What's needed is for you to help grow my business."

"I don't need your permission."

"A loyal son would be thankful his father's got a viable business that can offer him a future. I had to start from scratch because your grandfather had nothing but thirty acres of heather to… "

"I've heard all this before, Dad."

He looked at Danny fiercely. "I asked you what Susan said about this."

"I'm going to London."

"If you do, it'll not be for a couple of months. It'll be for good because I won't take you back. I'm not paying for you to go on some fool's errand."

"I've got my own money."

"Get the hell out of my sight." His father jerked brutally back on the recliner. "Why can't you be like my other trainee? Aye, that lad knows who puts the butter on his bread." His father's lips puckered and relaxed as he stared at the television. "That new car's going to him first thing on Monday morning if you haven't come to your senses. As well as the raise I was going to give you."

Parrot Talk

His stomach felt as if a swarm of migrating monarch butterflies were inside, their huge wings beating against its delicate lining. He needed to see Susan alone right now. They'd been sitting with her mother drinking tea in the living room for ten minutes, having first discussed the likely value of a crystal bowl that arrived from a relative of Susan's who'd just learned of the engagement, and now were on the list of guests to be invited from his side of the family. The wedding was over three months away, yet Susan and her mother's lives had begun to revolve around the planning. Danny rose and walked over to the window, planted his hands on the mahogany sill and watched a ragged vector of wild geese slicing across the thin blue sky.

"Would your mother be upset if we didn't invite Rita?" Susan's mother asked, her pen poised above the list of names.

His mother and Rita had been friends for years. She was the sister his mother never had. Even her second marriage to a wealthy English dentist and her subsequent removal to Guildford three years ago had not diminished their friendship.

"Mum would mind." He gripped the edge of the sill and pressed down so hard with his thumbs the nails flashed white round their tips. "Susan, do you fancy a ride somewhere?"

"We have to cull this list," Susan's mother said, and she sighed just like his fiancée did when she felt put upon. "It's already over two hundred guests. I feel it's best to keep it to family, and by family I mean only down as far as second cousins."

"That's reasonable," Susan said. "Though we'll have to keep my boss in, Mother. He's sure to give me a decent present."

Three years Danny's senior, Susan was an accountant, but having failed to secure work with a large accountancy firm in Belfast due to the mediocrity of her degree, had had to settle for a position with a solo-practitioner in a nearby town.

"Let's drive to the seaside, Susan."

She came over to the window and gazed out at the landscape of forested hills in the far distance. "It's a bit breezy?"

"You can be silly, Susan," her mother said. "Danny wants you to himself. Off you go. I'll rim the list and run it by you later."

Traffic was light and it took Danny just twenty-five minutes to reach the coast. The sun streamed from between gaps in the clouds, the powdery sand was cold to the touch. Pungent clusters of seaweed, pieces of smooth beach glass and fragments of shells littered the water's edge. A man and young girl sat reading on a checkered rug. Further up the strand, behind a large chunk of silver driftwood, two youths and a collie played with a frisbee. Susan gripped her hand around his forearm and they walked in silence for a minute, Danny observing a man fishing from the seawall, she staring ahead.

"I wanted to see you alone because there's something I need to tell you," he said.

"Is something wrong?"

"This whole marriage thing's happening a bit fast for me."

She unlinked her arm but didn't speak. Her eyes darted from his to a flock of wheeling gulls moving toward the crest of a nearby bluff where the crushed-stone blue coloured walls and white cross of a convent stood sentinel. A shifting breeze pushed the heavy air into Danny's face as he swept his gaze from her to where the sea and sky merged slate on steel.

"What are saying Danny?"

"Remember I mentioned a couple of weeks ago that I wasn't all that happy about my job?"

"Oh, not this again." She laughed. "Everything's going great for us."

"We're very young. Don't you think we're rushing this a bit?"

"We're ready."

He was silent for a moment. "I'm leaving work for a while."

"That's ridiculous." She stopped walking and turned to him. "You're being groomed to take over."

"My brother's still in business school."

"I wasn't going to mention this," she said, and then paused till she caught his eye. "Your father and I chatted after we got engaged."

"You did?"

"He's got great plans for the business and they include you at the highest levels. That's why you can't leave." She squeezed his arm. "You need to be around to make sure the big opportunities come your way. The early bird gets the worm every time. Your brother's got three years of school yet."

Danny stiffened. "I've decided to go to London."

"A holiday? Now?" Her amber eyes reminded him of a lemur's. "There's so many things we need to do for the wedding and… "

"We have to postpone the wedding."

An explosive silence arose, that was punctuated by the reverberating barks of the excited collie as it tried to anticipate the instant when its owner would send the frisbee arcing through the air.

"Postponement's not possible," she said finally. "Daddy's already paid for the reception. The honeymoon package is non-refundable."

His head dipped and he glanced at the ground just like he always did when cornered in an argument. But then he remembered he could allow this no longer. Pushing away his anxiety he met her stony eyes. "I know this is a shock but these things can be changed."

"Have you listened to a word I said? Postponement is not... "

"There's no reason we can't change the date."

"I said, postponing our wedding is not... "

"Susan we can change the date."

"Why the hell are you talking like a parrot? You're destroying my life." She stopped walking and her mouth fell agape. "Oh my God, this isn't about a postponement."

"Both of us rushed into this based on our fathers thinking it's a great thing for everyone concerned. They're talking about financial stuff. Not about love and living together for a lifetime. What's the problem in stepping back to make sure this is right for us?"

"Are you jilting me?"

Her accusation had the effect of a slap on the cheek. Their fathers had contracted business together and eight months ago had arranged a first date between Danny and Susan. The affair was a black tie dinner dance organised by Susan's mother to raise funds for a missionary priest in Lima. That night, Danny found Susan easy to talk to and surprisingly attentive, extinguishing the tiniest lulls in their conversation with questions about his family, his interests, his ambitions. While it was true his father pushed him hard to date her, alluding to her family's two huge dairy farms and Susan's status as the sole heiress, it was Danny who'd ultimately formed a relationship with her.

Like a magpie, Danny had always been drawn to shiny things, and Susan's hair was very shiny. In the fourth week of their courtship, during what he'd expected to be yet another pleasurable session spent necking and running his fingers through her exquisite mane, she encouraged him to go the whole way. That night, sexual attraction galloped to infatuation. He was still infatuated the following morning and would count the hours remaining until they met up again. Danny agreed with his father without reservation when he remarked Susan would be an 'ideal catch' after cornering him for yet another pep talk before he left to go and see her. During more fantastic sex in

Dublin two weeks later, Danny bellowed, 'I love you' amid the ecstasy, Susan admitted she felt the same way, and asked what he felt they should do about it.

His father was ecstatic when Danny informed him he was engaged and immediately set aside a twenty-acre tract of his land for them to obtain a building permit for a house. Almost immediately, Danny began to express the opinion he'd been too hasty but Mr. Connolly countered any reservations with articulate logic as to the soundness of the match. A few months later, when Danny admitted to him that Susan and he were having sex, his father informed him there was now no option but marriage to save the girl's integrity.

Danny gripped Susan's shoulders. "Look at me."

She refused.

"Look at me."

Her eyes cut to an imaginary hole in the middle of his forehead.

"You're not being dumped. This is something I really need."

"How can I believe you?"

He began stroking the back of her head and said nothing.

She sighed, took out a tissue and dabbed her eyes. "I'll resign from my job and come with you. We'll get a flat."

He was conscious now of the strands of her hair rolling and shifting under his fingers like silk. "I have to go alone."

She emitted a strangled gasp, pulled away violently from him and began to weep. Two women turned back to stare after they passed by. Danny felt a familiar urge to apologise and placate her. He resisted and laid his hand on her shoulder.

"Get *away* from me." She shrugged him off, her cupped hands plummeting from her face to regard him venomously. "You've never wanted this. Take me home this minute." She strode toward the car park.

The journey home was silent.

"Let me out *here*," she said when they reached her parent's driveway.

"I'll drop you at the door."

"Stop the fucking car." After climbing out, she held the door and leaned inside. "You've humiliated me and my family. You're not a man. I never want to see you again."

She slammed the door shut.

At the famine house

Since relocating to study in London, Philomena Patricia Harris insisted everyone call her Piper. She'd loved the name ever since she'd first heard it in the eighth grade when a family from Santa Barbara moved to Long Island and their daughter joined her class. It sounded so much better than Phila, the abbreviation her mother used whenever they chatted, which wasn't often now. Her father still called her Philomena when he called. He kept forgetting.

Acceptance of the name change hadn't been automatic in England, either. Three lecturers and her dissertation supervisor regarded her very strangely at the beginning when she'd insisted they call her Piper. They already knew her legal name from the class register, but ultimately had shrugged it off, attributing her insistence to American vanity and its penchant for reinvention, foibles they were used to because of the large number of Americans pursuing a Masters degree at the London School of Economics.

The sound of the car horn blaring pulled Piper out of her reverie. Her driver, a young man called Declan, honked the horn again at a black cow ambling lazily down the middle of the narrow road. The beast stopped and looked back at him, then lifted its tail and urinated before moving to the verge.

"The Glenties sure is pretty," she said in a renewed effort to make conversation as she stared out at the barren, heather-clad hills. "It's how I've always imagined Ireland."

"Americans would like Ireland to stay rugged and poor like this," said the driver. "Nice place for a visit, but not to live."

"Oh, I didn't mean it that way, I know the Irish economy's doing real good. The Celtic Tiger, right?"

"That tiger isn't calling with every Irish family," he said. "Some people are still dirt poor."

She could see another famine house tucked in a shallow hollow. Like the previous one, it was also roofless and constructed of the same fieldstone that formed the crumbling walls enclosing the tiny fields. The abandoned dwellings were smaller than storage sheds in the backyards of Long Island homes.

"Wouldn't care to live out here, though," said Piper. "Life must have been very lonely."

"You're right there."

Wiry, with a pockmarked face, Declan was about ten years older then she, thirty-four tops, and taciturn. This was the most he'd chatted throughout the two-hour ride. Piper regarded herself a people person, good at making folks feel comfortable, but all he'd uttered were monosyllabic answers to her questions. She wondered if he regarded her as a distraction. Or perhaps he was a chauvinist and resented having to take her to the meeting place.

In any event she wasn't going to say anything political and risk antagonising him. She'd networked too hard to commit that act of stupidity, working the telephones for nearly two months as well as enduring a scary interview, before which she'd first been blindfolded, taken to a secret location and then made to sit on an uncomfortable wooden chair looking at a wall with a cheap painting of the Blessed Virgin while two men grilled her. Eventually satisfied she was telling the truth about her objectives, they'd allowed her to turn around.

"Sorry we had to make you face the wall," the older, ruddy-cheeked man with a pure white scar above his right eye had said when they'd finished. "We can't take chances, like."

"Since the split, the Provos have gone to seed but the Brits are still hounding us," said the other volunteer, a slim man with teeth in bad need of flossing. "We had to make sure you're not Special Branch or a Yank in cahoots wey them."

The men were members of the Real IRA and she knew the volunteer was referring to their acrimonious split with the Provisional IRA four years ago at their 1997 General Army convention, the split arising because disaffected volunteers did not want the Provos to lay down their weapons or consent to having their arms dumps inspected and destroyed as demanded by the Belfast Agreement. Though only four-years-old, the Real IRA had already committed significant bombing campaigns and were, Piper was certain, actively seeking recruits and setting up cells in England to ramp up their campaign.

"No problem," she said, and gave him an easy smile. "You gotta do what you gotta do."

Chills of excitement raced up her spine at the thought she'd passed their test and would soon meet a genuine female IRA volunteer. She thought of her late grandfather, of the times she'd sat on his lap as a young girl listening spellbound as he told stories about his attacks on the British Army and days spent on the run sleeping in barns or the attics of sympathisers' homes. Though he'd never mentioned women fighters, as a young girl curled up in bed at night in her parents suburban home, Piper wished she'd been born in Ireland. She'd definitely have joined the IRA to fight the British if she had.

The driver turned into a dirt lane flanked by long brambles that scraped against the sides of the car. Foot-long, silky grass swayed gently in the median. Through gaps in the hedge she glimpsed plump lambs suckling their mothers. After rounding two bends in the lane, the car drew up to another famine cottage. It had a mossy thatched roof, an emerald green Dutch front door and two tiny windows, one with an oil lamp standing on the window sill. A neat stack of peat stood by the side of the gable.

As Piper clambered out, menacing barks from what sounded

like a huge dog started up as the cottage door opened. She retreated quickly inside the car. The driver laughed.

A lean, very attractive woman in jeans and oversized cardigan came outside, immediately followed by a tan and black Dachshund with a greying muzzle.

"I'm Maura," she said, and extended her hand to Piper as she approached. "Karl heard yous pull in before I did."

Her handshake was strong, almost masculine.

"He had me worried for a sec'."

"He's all yap and no bite." Maura patted the dog's head. "Isn't that right my darlin'?"

Recognising the bond between dog and owner and seizing the moment to establish rapport, Piper stooped and ran her hand along the animal's broad back. It was greasy to the touch. Despite his layer of fat, she felt the brute stiffen. "He's a real cutie."

"Real fat, too."

"You need anything from the shops, Maura?" the driver asked.

"A carton of milk." She nodded toward the door when she caught Piper's eye. "Come in."

The dwelling had no electricity or running water, reeked of turf smoke and was sparsely furnished. Informed after they sat at a small dining table that Maura hadn't wanted to meet her, but had been ordered to do so by the Officer Commanding, Piper tried again to establish rapport by explaining her grandfather had been a gunrunner in the Old IRA before he and her grandmother emigrated to America. Omitting her father had refused in the late eighties to offer temporary shelter to a volunteer who'd been sent to America because the British were closing in on him for the murder of a soldier, she ramped up her Irish credentials by saying he marched every year in the annual Saint Patrick's Day Parade in New York City and that he and her grandfather had helped raise thousands of dollars for Sinn Fein over the years.

"What's your opinion of the IRA?" Maura asked.

"Ireland must be united and they're an important part of the solution to reach that goal."

"Why the interest in volunteers like me?"

"Women played an important part in the armed struggle, didn't they?"

"Played? Are you suggesting the struggle's over?"

"No."

"Happy to hear that. It's not over just because George Mitchell, Tony Blair and Bertie Ahern have decided we must disarm."

"Government demands during an insurrection are part of what I'm researching for my dissertation."

Maura's eyes became slits. "Why'd you go to England to study if you're so Irish?"

"That's a great question." Clearly the woman had been informed Piper was doing an MSc. History of International Relations, but was ignorant of the stellar reputation of the LSE. "You know, not everything English is bad."

Maura threw back her head, slapped her palms against the top of the table and laughed. "I hear you." She leaned over the table. "Tell me one thing before we continue. It's been bugging the hell out of us over here."

"What's that?"

"Al Gore won last year's election so why the hell did yous not get him to contest Florida?"

"He should have." Piper smiled. "That's another reason why I left the States."

"What's the other?"

Ignoring the question, Piper signaled her desire to begin the interview by taking out her notebook.

The interview was conducted over tea – the peaty, strong Irish type Piper loved – and buttered digestive biscuits with thin slices of mature cheddar cheese. Her interest in the contribution of female volunteers to the Irish struggle and dislike of the present US administration warmed Piper to the woman. Maura stated her initial reasons for joining the militant wing of the IRA were a combination of romanticism, in that she'd been drawn to the story of a female university graduate who'd become a bomber and been murdered while on a mission, and a deep-seated passion for an independent and socialist Ireland.

"How old was this woman?" Piper asked.

"About your age and a real beauty," Maura shook her head and then readjusted her long hair around her shoulders. She had the type of rich dark red hair Piper saw only on Irish people. "Such warm, big eyes. And you should have seen her cheekbones. A real head-turner, she was. Such a waste."

It was an intriguing comment. Piper made a notation 'Joined out of a sense of romanticism??' in the notebook but then scribbled it out. A revolutionary's personal whims or reasons for joining the IRA would be of no interest to the lecturer marking her dissertation, which Piper had entitled *Ireland at another Crossroads: Can governments broker a durable power-sharing agreement during successful insurrection*?

"Do you think the Provos will disarm as required under the Belfast Agreement?" Piper asked.

"If they disarm, what threat does the minority have to ensure Blair and the Unionists will do what they're supposed to do?"

"So Mr. Paisley's right when he says the IRA is not acting in good faith?" Piper's pen floated above the page in preparation to write.

"Don't get me started on that bastard," she said. "Are you going to interview any politicians?"

"I've already spoken to the SDLP, Ulster Unionists and Sinn Fein's political arm."

"Gerry Adams or McGuiness?"

"Maybe."

"You play a tight hand." Maura leaned over to pat her dog. "What about Paisley?"

"He couldn't see me when I arrived at his constituency office."

"Aye, he's a bit of a slippery customer is the old Reverend."

"I'm planning to catch him at Westminster after my exams are over."

Currently studying for her final exams, the first of which was scheduled to commence in three weeks, it had been inconvenient for Piper to come to Northern Ireland for five days to travel around the province interviewing various political parties. She'd planned to do it after the exams finished because that would have given her over two months to complete the research and write the ten thousand word thesis. However, getting the IRA viewpoint was important and, when they agreed to meet her on a certain date, she could not tell them it was inconvenient. The IRA didn't care about the LSE or her exam deadlines.

Maura laughed. "Would you take him a wee parcel from me?"

"A parcel?" The penny dropped. Piper giggled. "I take it you'd like the armed struggle to continue?"

"Some Provos who won't accept decommission are joining the Real IRA."

"What about you?"

"Ops have to continue. Both here and in England."

Piper watched the dog amble toward the door. "I'd like to ask you something that maybe you won't answer."

"Try anyway."

"How do you join the IRA?"

Maura peered at her hard. "You want to sign up?"

"Signing up. Is that how it's done?"

Running her hands through her hair, Maura said, "Sometimes you're invited, and sometimes you ask somebody you know. Either way, you're interviewed first about why you want to join. If you're cleared, you take an oath of allegiance to the IRA and then you're told to familiarise yourself intimately with some army orders from our Green Book."

"They're called 'army orders'?"

"The IRA's an army, isn't it?"

"What kind of orders?"

"To obey everything without question that comes down, how to execute ops, not to become a rat and the consequences if you do commit treason." A smile formed on Maura's lips. "You still want to join?"

Piper decided to get her interview back on track. "Can you describe how operations are carried out?"

"Boy, with shifts like this, you'd make a good volunteer." Maura nodded at Piper's notebook. "If I were to tell you, would it make its way into this dissertation of yours?"

She considered the question. "It's not really academic enough." Piper set the pen down on top of the book. "Purely out of interest."

"It depends on the situational needs. Shotguns. Revolvers if within range. I've also staged bombs using mix or Semtex."

"Mix?"

"Ground fertiliser mixed with stuff. Semtex is cleaner though. Makes a very nice bang."

A montage rushed through Piper's mind: images of shadowy figures setting backpacks under tables in pubs; ticking packages underneath cars parked in driveways; figures in balaclavas pointing guns at the heads of begging soldiers; the flash and bark of guns; blood spurting from holes in foreheads like a fountain. The montage flashed suddenly to her parent's blazing house. Huge orange flames danced and licked the black sky. Windowpanes in the upstairs bedroom cracked and shattered. Helpless, she watched the house burning, her cat Frisk wriggling in her arms because she was pressing him too tightly to her chest.

"You've gone a bit pale." Maura was leaning over the table toward her. "Are you okay?"

"I'd like a glass of water." Piper took a long drink before continuing. "Can you tell me about your actual involvement in an operation?" She wiped excess water off her lips.

"Is that a roundabout way of asking whether I've ever killed anybody?"

"That wasn't… yes."

"I figured you'd get round to asking and thought I wouldn't answer when you did." She paused. Piper's ears rang with silence. "In war you have to go after the enemy and kill them." Maura picked up her mug, held it before her lips, and then set it down again. "It's that simple."

A strange put-put sound extinguished the momentary silence. Maura cocked her head toward the door. "Shit."

A car drove hastily into the yard and screeched to a stop. Maura ran to the window and looked up toward the sky as Piper's driver burst into the house and slammed the door shut.

"Is it one of ours?" Maura asked, her voice urgent.

"Too high to tell," he said

Piper went to the window. "What's going on?"

"Helicopter," Maura said. "It could be the Brits."

"But we're in Donegal," said Piper.

Maura regarded her as if she were a moron. "Since when has another country's border ever stopped the maraudin' English?"

The sound grew louder and louder until it seemed to Piper it was hovering overhead.

"Maybe it's the Free State boys on a training exercise." Maura peered out the window toward the sky again. "I can't see a bloody thing."

The three stood inert and silent. Piper envisioned the thatch tearing off the roof in clumps and flying through the air. Maura's dog whined and she picked him up.

A few minutes later, the thump of whipped air began to fade. Soon it sounded like nothing more than a bumblebee around a flower.

"Must have been our boys," said Maura, and she set her dog down. "Remind me what we were talking about before?"

London bound

The sea churned in the ferry's wake. The thickly painted banister pocked with rust from exposure to the salty air felt cool to the touch. Danny surveyed the moored ships and tugboats in the harbour. Beyond them, the haze was swallowing the tapering factory chimneys and row houses on the hill. Over the intercom, the captain began apologising for the delay. Danny checked his watch. They were three hours behind schedule. He leaned over the banister and inhaled deeply, breathing in the salty air's invigorating pungency. Two children played nearby on the weathered deck, their shrill excitement causing another wave of joy to surge within him. Something light yet solid splattered on his head. He looked up to see a gull turn like a military jet and head back towards land.

"Shit happens," someone said.

Startled, Danny looked to his left and saw a tanned young woman with spiky hair and a wide smile watching him.

"I got dumped on by a crow once," she added.

Danny noticed a small tattoo of a teddy bear on her upper right arm. He searched his pockets for a tissue but didn't have one. As the woman hunkered and unzipped her rucksack, the narrow strap of her top kept slipping off her freckled right shoulder, obliging her to constantly sweep it back.

She handed him a foil sachet. "I never travel without 'em."

He wiped his hair with the lemon-scented wipe and tossed it overboard when he was done.

"You guys still do that here?"

"Do what?"

She nodded toward the water. "Ain't good for the environment."

"A towelette?"

Her expression looked grave. "Seeing as it eventually biodegrades, I won't file a complaint with Greenpeace this time.

He laughed. "Gee, thanks, I'm Danny by the way."

"I'm Piper."

"Can I offer to buy you a beer for letting me off the hook?"

They made their way to the bar, a cavernous room furnished with pitted black metal tables permanently attached to the scuffed floor, matching chairs and ashtrays with brewery logos. Dust mottled windows afforded patrons a view of the shrinking harbour and passengers strolling on the deck.

"Better make them pints."

He followed Piper's gaze to see a throng of men and women gathered around the serving hatches. "I've got to drive."

"You're a big guy. It'll be out of your system before we reach the other side. You can always eat some fries if you really want to play it safe."

A heavily pregnant woman approached shepherding two youngsters licking ice pops. She glared at Piper, though waited until she'd passed by before shaking her head.

After he bought the drinks, they went outside again. The water was transforming now to burnished copper at the horizon.

"The sea's on fire," he said.

"Yeah, it looks horrible." She turned her back on the horizon. They fell silent.

"Were you on holiday in Northern Ireland?" he asked finally.

"Nah. I interviewed a bunch of people."

They shared potted histories as strangers sometimes do when they chat and find they like each other. Notwithstanding the drinks were pints and she did most of the talking, Piper drank rapidly. She excused herself and went to the bar after her beer was finished, returning ten minutes later with a second beer for Danny as well.

The alcohol quickly made him mellow. Scarcely listening to her, gauzy thoughts billowed like summer clouds across his mind as he glanced about the deck at the passengers. He imagined they were all like him and bound for new exciting destinations. He peered at the horizon to where he imagined London to be, no longer seeing the burning water but the blazing lights of Piccadilly Circus, beckoning to him.

"So what do you say?" she said.

His eyes darted back to her lips, attractive and parted in anticipation.

"I won't take offence if you can't."

Narrow wrinkles appeared on her forehead as she awaited a response.

"Sorry, what did you ask?"

"You said earlier you're going to London and I was kinda hoping I could tag along. The train's hot and takes forever. We can split the gas and driving."

"You don't have to pay. I'm going there anyway."

"I always pay my way." She looked at her watch. "It'll be at least two in the morning when we get into London. You can crash at my place if you like." She tapped the bottom of her glass on the banister to re-froth her beer. "Where are you planning to stay anyways?"

"At my mother's friend in Guildford until I find a place."

"That's a helluva commute. You want to find a place in Zone One or Two."

"Thanks for the tip."

"You're welcome. My grandfather always told me when I was a kid that Irish people... and I'm including myself in the category... have to stick together. He helped anybody from Ireland who was illegal in the States. Got them jobs on building sites."

"He sounds a nice man."

"Was. Gramps was a nationalist. Big time. Didn't like the English."

Danny let her remark pass without comment.

"He's the reason I got interested in my roots."

"Lots of Americans come over to research their roots."

She paused and looked intently at him. "If you're interested, I've got a room with a sofabed you're welcome to use until you find a permanent place."

Danny took a long swig of beer. She seemed respectable, was certainly friendly and open in that manner so many Americans visiting Ireland always were.

"I'll pay you rent," he said.

"It's really a box room. It's gets very warm. I've got a tenant in my other bedroom."

"Oh."

"He's also Irish. But he stays at his girlfriend's place in Battersea most of the time. I hardly ever see him."

"He won't mind me staying?"

"Nah, Pat's cool. I think he rents the room as a kind of safety net. You know, in case they have an argument and she throws him out." Piper tossed back her head and finished her beer in a single gulp. "Anyway, I'm the boss."

Wardrobe Revelations

Fifteen minutes after docking, Danny exited the ferry and followed the serpentine line of trucks, caravans and cars heading toward the exit. The night air was heavy with the stench of oil and decaying seaweed. Two minutes later, the queue slowed to a crawl. He looked out his side window and saw two policemen dressed in fluorescent weatherproof jackets ahead.

"What's up, do you think?" said Piper.

He shrugged.

The queue came to a stop for ten minutes and then began to advance in fits and starts.

"It's a checkpoint," he said. "They're probably checking the MOT."

"What's that?" Piper reached into the backseat and retrieved her backpack.

"It's a car roadworthiness test."

As they drew up to the officer, Danny wound down his window. The policeman stooped and peered inside. "Where have you come from, Sir?" he asked, in a Scottish burr.

"The ferry."

Three police cars were parked along the side of the road, one with its blue lights flashing.

"I know that," said the officer. "Where did you come from?"

"Northern Ireland."

"Where you headed?"

"London."

"Can I see your driving license?"

Danny handed it to him. The officer stood erect as he inspected it, then stooped again and looked at Piper.

"You from Northern Ireland as well, Miss?"

"I'm a visitor."

"American?"

"Yeah."

"Can I see identification?"

"Sure." Piper rooted in her backpack energetically for a moment and then stopped. "I'm not the driver. I don't have to show you my ID, Officer."

Danny's body froze and his grip tightened on the steering wheel. Few in the Catholic minority trusted the British police and military, and many young men including Danny feared being stopped at checkpoints late at night.

He remembered the time he'd been stopped by the police and soldiers, most of whom had Northern Irish accents, when he was seventeen. He'd been with two school friends. They were travelling along a lonely mountain road when he saw someone wave a red light thirty yards ahead. "Where are you coming from?" the sergeant asked.

"A school dance."

"What's the name of the school?"

"Saint Dominic's."

"Let's see your driving license."

As he retrieved it from his pocket, another soldier shone his flashlight into the car and held it on the faces of his friends. After he had given over his license, the soldiers walked over to one of the Land Rovers and stood talking to the others. Movement in the nearby ditch caught Danny's eye. A soldier was watching him, his face painted black, twigs and leaves set within a narrow band of netting encircling his helmet, and pointing a machine gun at his head. The soldiers returned to the car accompanied by a policeman.

"Out of the fucking car, now," one soldier said.

After the boys climbed out, they were spun round, slammed against the car, spread-eagled and frisked. Other soldiers searched his car, pulling out the backseat, opening the trunk and spilling its contents onto the road. Danny was sure they were going to be arrested and interrogated. Or shot. The harassment lasted five minutes and, after they'd tired of it, the soldiers told them to leave quickly and walked away laughing among themselves.

Danny glared at Piper.

"Is that so, Miss?" the policeman said, his narrowed eyes locked on hers. "Pull your car over there." He pointed to the side of the road and then walked away.

Danny's knees trembled as he put the car into gear and began to move toward the side of the road.

"You've made him furious," he said through clenched teeth. "They can keep us here for hours."

"My father's a New York cop. I don't intimidate easily."

He succeeded in not making any kangaroo-like hops as he pulled to the ditch and killed the engine after parking. "Have you got your passport in case he insists?" Danny asked, only barely managing to conceal his irritation. A part of him couldn't understand what the big deal was in showing her passport to the policeman.

"I brought my Irish pass along."

"You've got an Irish one?"

"Americans are allowed to hold two nowadays." Piper looked out to where the officer was squatted, talking to a colleague seated inside one of the police cars. "That cop's not allowed to ask for my identification unless he suspects me of committing a crime." She began to fumble inside her bag. "We have to stand up for our rights. Show these people we know the law."

"Maybe that's the case in America. In Northern Ireland, they can demand identification from anyone as well as search the car."

"Yeah, it's real draconiann over there, ain't it?" Piper took out a notebook and began to flick through it. "Blair's trying to get a similar law passed over here, too."

His anger gave way to reluctant admiration. He looked over at the policeman. The sound of something tearing made him look back at Piper. She'd ripped out pages from her notebook and was calmly folding them while watching the chatting policemen.

"Just taking precautions." She stuffed the notes hurriedly inside her bra. "Should he decide to be an asshole and give us a hard time, it'd be better he doesn't see these interview notes."

The officer returned, stooped and locked eyes with Piper as he handed Danny his driving license. "You can leave."

They arrived in Hammersmith at ten past two in the morning. Following Piper's directions, he turned into a narrow street lit by overhead neon lamps that exposed the peeling paint façades of row houses. Two-foot wide front gardens and triple steps led up to their front doors. At the gables of the end houses on both sides of the street was a diagonal overhead railway bridge. Beyond this was a four-way stop and two zebra crossings and then the street grew wider. Finding no available parking spaces, she instructed him to drive across to the wider section of the street that had an antique shop on one corner and a shabby newsagent's on the other.

He parked between an old Jaguar and a Volkswagen Beetle with flower head motifs on its side that resembled sunflowers. The plangent blare of a siren started up. He looked into the wing mirror and saw a car with flashing blue lights coming toward him. Danny stopped in mid-reverse with the front third of his car sticking out into the road. The police car drew closer and closer until it pulled up alongside them. Piper's face was white as alabaster against the vivid blue of the blinking lights. A policeman looked in but the car continued by, turned right at the intersection and disappeared.

"Someone's in trouble, huh?" Piper said.

A crisp morning breeze cooled Danny's inflamed face when he got out of the car. Not wishing Piper to know he'd been unnerved, he lifted his arms and yawned as he looked around. Though of the same architectural style as those on Piper's section of the street, the façades of these row houses were impeccably maintained, their original, small windows replaced with larger modern ones.

"This is a nice part of the street," he said.

"This section of Chumley Street was yuppified in the eighties apparently," she said. "It was a solid working-class neighbourhood until the yuppies snapped up the properties dead cheap and hired a bunch of trendy architects."

"You don't like what they've done?"

"What gave me away?" She laughed. "Though I've gotta admit, I wish my landlord would paint the interior of my house. The wallpaper's shit."

Piper's house lay in the middle of the block. She hadn't exaggerated about its interior. The seventies velvet-striped wallpaper in the hall was grimy and ceiling plaster bulged precariously in two places. She picked up the post off the floor and began sorting through it as he followed her into a small living room that smelled of cigarette smoke and stale alcohol. Two half-full mugs of cold tea and empty beer bottles were on the coffee table, beside a tin ashtray laden with cigarette butts. Three tabloids and a Sunday broadsheet were scattered on the floor and sofa.

"Sorry about the mess," she said. "I told Pat I'd be away until Friday but I decided to come back early. He's usually quite tidy."

Danny folded the newspapers on the sofa and sat while Piper went into the kitchen to fetch iced water for them. Loose photographs were scattered on the coffee table, many of them smudged with fingerprints. He picked them up and flicked through them. All the shots were of bridges: Tower Bridge and another one he didn't recognise. The most attractive photo was of a galleon with tiers of blazing white sails passing underneath the uplifted arms of Tower Bridge, but most were close-ups of the sides and underbelly of the unknown bridge that had enormous green piers and a pedestrian walkway..

"Are you into photography?" he asked Piper, as she gave him a glass of water.

Her eyes chinked. "Why do you ask?"

He held up the photograph of the ship passing under Tower Bridge. "This one's good."

Piper took the photo. She set her water on the table and beckoned him to give her the rest of the photographs.

"I don't know the other bridge," said Danny.

"It's Hammersmith Bridge. It's just a few blocks from here." Piper tapped the photos on the surface of the table until their edges were aligned. "I'll show you the room now."

When they reached the head of the stairs, Piper pointed to a closed door and told him it was Pat's room. Three more stairs at right angles to the main staircase led to a short landing. "Bathroom's in here… I mean toilet. Keep forgetting that." She pulled on the drawstring to switch on the light. It was pretty, with gleaming white and green tiles and a surprisingly large shower. "Don't flush the john real hard. The handle's loose and the plumber hasn't come yet."

Two more doors stood at right angles to one another. Telling him to go into the first room, she excused herself and went into the second. She returned moments later without the photographs.

"Like I said, it's small."

"It'll do fine."

She nodded at the wardrobe and informed him he could remove some of its contents and put them into her bedroom to make space for his things. "Time I get some shuteye. I've got to go early to the library and catch up on a bunch of stuff I should have read ages ago."

"Running behind, are you?"

"Wouldn't be if they had enough copies of the books on the reading lists at the library." She laughed scornfully. "You have to literally elbow students out of the way at Course Collection."

"That's the way things are here. It was the same at my university."

"It's a cultural thing. The Brits think Americans don't understand irony, and we can't understand why they line up so quietly for everything, even goddamned library books."

After fetching bed linen and a pillow and helping him shift a large cardboard box laden with books so he could set up the sofabed, Piper took her leave. Despite the metal rod in the bed's middle that kept digging into his lower back and ribs every time he shifted on his side, tiredness won out and he fell asleep within half-an-hour. The sound of water gurgling through water pipes awoke him. He put out his hand, fumbled for the switch on a table lamp on the floor nearby and checked his watch. It was already late morning. His joints ached like he was in the preliminary stages of flu.

He pulled himself up on the sofabed and looked around. The room was just a little bigger in dimension than his mother's dressing room. On one side there were boxes and a stack of suitcases with airline tags secured on their handles. A bundle of wrinkled shirts and jeans lay on top of a wooden trunk, adjacent to an ironing board with a heavily scorched cover propped against the side of a single-sized wardrobe that had three more suitcases nested on its top. Behind his head, bookshelves ran the width of the room, extended up to the ceiling, and were laden with bric-a-brac, economics and law textbooks and novels.

After showering, Danny went down to the kitchen where he discovered Piper had brewed real coffee. That was a pleasant surprise. Everyone he knew made the instant kind. She'd also left a key and a note stating where he'd find the cereal, cautioning there was only powdered milk and that, as she didn't have to work at the pub that evening, she'd cook dinner for them. He slathered a brick of Weetabix with strawberry jam and ate it in the living room while peering out the front window at pedestrians. The London accent sounded as he'd heard on the television. He felt lucky. Only hours in the city and he already had the run of someone's house. London was going to be very good to him.

He fetched the rest of his luggage from the car and began to sort through his clothing, removing enough T-shirts to last him a couple of weeks. His suits, jackets, two pairs of chinos, dress shirts and an overcoat needed hanging. He tried to open the wardrobe but found it locked.

Danny searched for the key, trying first in the drawers and then checking under the sofabed even though there was only a tiny gap between its frame and the nubby carpet. Next, he tried the bookcase, searching inside any ornaments where it might have been placed. He ran the tips of his fingers along the edge of the wardrobe's top and then, fetching a chair, stood and searched the entire top of the wardrobe. Before climbing down, more as an afterthought, he stuck his hand between the tiered suitcases and found it sandwiched between the bottom and middle one.

A curious acrid aroma filled his nostrils after he opened the wardrobe door. A black work boot dropped to the floor, a piece of caked mud resembling a miniature portcullis breaking away from the ruts in its sole. Sudden movement above caught his eye and he looked up just as a portion of a down duvet that had been crammed into the shelf slid to the floor.

The wardrobe railing bulged with winter dresses and coats. He removed six dresses and an overcoat and took them to Piper's room furnished with contemporary blonde wood Danish furniture. A replica of Edvard Munch's *The Scream* hung on the wall. The edge of a narrow trapezium of sunlight streaming through the window sliced the photograph of a young boy clutching a cat to his chest on her bedside table, imparting a chiaroscuro effect on his neck and part of his face.

A second purge of the wardrobe still didn't create enough space for his clothes. As he was leaving his room a third time with a larger bundle of dresses, he heard a scraping sound followed by a dull thud. Something had fallen on the floor of the wardrobe. He set the dresses on his sofabed and went to investigate, expecting to find that the brass rack holding the garments had collapsed. Instead, the barrel of a gun pointed at his shins.

A final stance

Agnes Hartley sat on her rocker and gazed at the Queen Mother's photograph hanging on the wall above the fireplace. Flanking its left side was a frame containing a signed sun-faded photograph of Margaret Thatcher. On the opposite side were two framed letters from the Queen Mother – one dating from the mid-seventies, the second from the early nineties – in which she thanked Agnes for various correspondence. Every shelf and wall in the living room was cluttered with photographs of Agnes' family and members of the Royal family through the generations, as well as plates, spoons, ashtrays and other Royalty memorabilia. On a small table, partly pushed into an alcove that had a frayed Union Jack affixed to the wall, was a Royal Navy sailor's hat. A collection of photographs were arranged around it. The photographs were of her late husband Charlie who'd died of a massive coronary nearly one year ago, including a photo of him with their son Keith as an infant on his shoulders, another of Agnes and him on their wedding day and a faded Polaroid of Charlie in gardener's overalls holding a large striped marrow.

Approaching footsteps alerted Agnes to the postman's arrival. She waited for the thud of the post as it hit the floor, but instead the doorbell rang.

"Mornin' Agnes," the postman said. "This needs signing for."

She squinted and regarded the buff coloured envelope. "I'm not expecting anything needing my signature."

"Got your name on it, love."

She signed and took the registered letter into the living room. Her heart missed a beat when she opened it. Fingers trembling with excitement, she began to read:

Sebastian Church & Co.
London ♦ Rome ♦ Paris ♦ Berlin

Discriminating Properties for Discriminating People

Att: Mrs. Agnes Hartley
40 Chumley St,
London, W6

Dear Mrs. Hartley,

Re: Sale dated September 12, 2000 of 42 Chumley Street, London W6 by Edward Williamson to Miss Julia Ralston

Clare Short of our Hammersmith branch recently forwarded your entire correspondence to her in connection with the above-referenced property sale. As you appear unwilling to accept her responses, she asked me to write in order to bring this matter to a satisfactory conclusion.

As you are aware Mr. Williamson listed the property with this agency and I can assure you that it was sold to Miss Ralston in accordance with all pertinent legal requirements. You are misinformed in your belief our client's ex-wife was also a lawful owner and, therefore, her signature was required. The issue of ownership of 42 Chumley Street was settled during their divorce proceedings, at which point Mr.

Williamson became the sole legal owner.

It is not this agency's concern that relations between you and Mr. Williamson were
strained or that he informed you immediately
after the property's transfer that he sold it
to Miss Ralston at a price well below the last
offer you made. Neither does it matter that the
price they agreed on may have resulted from
their having sexual relations, as you allege.
Any prior oral promise by our client that he
would sell the property to you has no legal
validity. Transactions involving agreements to
sell a house must always be in writing
according to the law.

Contrary to your position with regard to any
alleged damage to the wall of your house and
backyard fence caused when the seller was trimming shrubbery etc., I state most emphatically
that this agency had no legal duty to stop or
subsequently set aside the sale for such
reasons. I suggest you contact Mr. Williamson's
solicitor should you wish to pursue legal reme-
dies, though it is my understanding our client
is now returned permanently to Australia. (It
is also my understanding Mrs. Short furnished
you with the full contact details of Mr.
Williamson's solicitor.)

Finally, and once again contrary to your
position, Mrs. Short is a licensed estate agent
and enjoys an outstanding reputation in our
industry. Moreover, she is a valuable employee
whom I know personally. She is not required to
present you with copies of her credentials or
a list of legal actions or complaints against
her or the Hammersmith branch of this company.

Please be advised we do not wish to receive any further correspondence in relation to this sale, nor should you visit Mrs. Short at her place of business again. Our files are closed. Any further correspondence or contact from you will be immediately handed over to our solicitors with instructions to take action against you to the furthest extent of the law.

Let your actions be governed accordingly,
Sincerely,

Sebastian Church
Managing Director

Agnes scrunched the letter tightly in her hand until it formed a ball, took it into the kitchen and tossed it into the bin.

Too close, Madam

It was bizarre to the point of comicality and Julia Ralston, as she watched through her front window, could not understand what her eccentric neighbour could be searching for near Julia's car. She'd caught her acting this strangely twice before. The first time was two months ago, just minutes after Julia parked the Jaguar on the far side of the street across from her house. Realising she'd left her newspaper in the car, Julia had gone outside to fetch it and encountered Mrs. Hartley passing her hand alongside the back bumper of Julia's vehicle before attempting to open one of the back doors. On the second occasion, Julia had been to the off-license to purchase wine for a party she was throwing and on her return came upon Mrs. Hartley, grey-white hair studded with pink curlers, emerging from Julia's narrow strip of front yard. Julia kept her rubbish bin there prior to its collection and she was almost certain Mrs. Hartley had been rummaging through it. She asked her startled neighbour if she could render any assistance, but Mrs. Hartley recovered quickly and mumbled she'd been searching for her cat before walking back to her own house and slamming the door shut.

Julia left the window, took a last pull of the joint and stubbed the spent roach into the half-filled ashtray as she looked about the living-cum-dining room. Jeans, jumpers, and two skirts lay strewn over the sofa and armchairs. A pair of tights flowed like stretched toffee from an upper branch of a tall fichus placed on one side of the French doors that opened onto a spacious garden. The garden itself was girded by five-foot brick walls on two sides, shrubbery and a stockade fence at the rear. CD cases including KD Lang's *Ingénue* and magazines lay scattered on the carpet. Upon the dining room table was a phone and a platter containing a resealable plastic bag of marijuana, cigarette papers and a roller.

Keeping the house constantly in order in case someone called from the advertisement she'd placed in the local paper was more challenging than she'd anticipated. At times of despondency like this, Julia wished her salary was larger and the mortgage payments more reasonable. She also regretted her rush to evict her prior tenant.

Six months ago, she'd purchased 42 Chumley, a cozy terraced house on the well-maintained North section of the street. Spaniel Street bisected the North and South sections, at the junction of which was an elevated railway bridge that served the Piccadilly and District tube lines. It hadn't been love at first glimpse when Julia, accompanied by her estate agent, drew up to the house on that cold October morning. She'd winced at the powder blue façade and instructed the woman to proceed to the next property, but the enthusiastic agent insisted she take a look. Once inside, Julia had been quietly pleased when she saw the house was tastefully renovated and made an appropriate offer for both it and the salvageable pieces of furniture. Within hours the seller's agent rang her agent, and raised the specter of another bidder, thus setting in motion a blitz of counter-offers until the price was within a hair's breath of beyond her means and Julia had had quite enough. She contacted the Australian owner, arranged a clandestine meeting with him and a contract was drawn up and executed next day.

Five minutes later, when Julia came outside to the street, Mrs. Hartley was still standing by her car. She was chatting to Sonia Berg, the German psychiatrist who lived just beyond the railway bridge on the south side of the street. Sonia had stopped her VW Beetle in the middle of the road and was standing half-in half-out of the vehicle, her right foot planted on the tarmac.

"Good morning," Julia said, and nodded at them.

"Ah Julia, it is you," Dr. Berg said. "I have been meaning to ring and thank you for your lovely party. It was so wery fun." She laughed shrilly. "Jean-Pierre enjoyed himself and will pay for the dry-cleaning of your tablecloth. You will give me the bill?"

Mrs. Hartley's face twisted into a grimace.

"Don't worry about it, Sonia."

Having met the doctor's Congolese boyfriend on a number of occasions, Julia had formed the opinion he was socially inept. He made no effort to join in conversation and she figured Sonia was with him only because he was good in bed.

The doctor climbed into the sunflower stenciled Bug and revved the engine so that it hummed in that singular Volkswagony way. "Mrs. Hartley, do not forget to tell your friend Martha it is important she keep her appointments with me."

Her neighbour's face was still pinched with disapproval as she watched Sonia drive away.

"Is anything wrong, Mrs. Hartley? I noticed you examining my car again."

"You parked too close to mine again, Madam."

She found Mrs. Hartley's tendency to address her as 'Madam' quaintly polite. She also felt sorry for the old woman. She'd heard her husband had died tragically. Julia glanced at her neighbour's ancient Morris Minor.

"I don't think it's *that* close, Mrs. Hartley."

"It is."

Julia's mobile rang and she took it from her bag. "There's at least six to eight inches between our bumpers. I'll try to park it further... oh, hello, Clive. Thanks for calling back." She held up her hand to signal to Mrs. Hartley that she wouldn't be long. "Yes, fifty quid will be enough." She laughed. "Of course, I'm worth it. Listen, if you're having it tight this month I understand. I'll take whatever you can afford."

Mrs. Hartley shook her head. "Just see you park further away from my motor next time, Madam." And she walked away.

Lunchtime at The Pound and Penny, a Hammersmith pub serving excellent steak pies and boasting a small beer garden was always packed. As she pushed open one of the narrow double front doors, Julia sent a young woman sipping a pint of lager scuttling into the chest of her male companion. Oblivious to the man's scowl as he brushed beer off his silk tie, she scanned the room for Clive while cutting a path through the throng. She found him bent over the jukebox in the billiard room next door.

"There's never anything decent to play on this thing," he said, and kissed her on each cheek.

"They don't cater to club queens here, Clive."

"Hey, you want me to loan you fifty quid or not?"

"I couldn't resist that."

Clive reached up to the top of the jukebox and retrieved a glass from among the spent beer mugs and stack of whisky glasses. "I got you a gin-and-tonic." He took out a folded bundle of notes from the pocket of his jeans and handed it to her.

"I'll pay you back on Friday," she said. "I promise."

A stocky, hirsute man with a wide forehead, his upper lip partially obscured by a long moustache half-coated in foam, Clive wiped his mouth with the back of his hand.

"Have I got a bit of juicy goss' for you," he said.

"You know I don't like gossip."

"Your boss is definitely shagging that stewardess you think is so good-looking."

Julia sighed. "I don't care who he screws."

As a twenty-five-year-old, pretty immigration officer who'd now worked one year at Heathrow, Julia's objective was to avoid office politics and airport gossip. She wanted only to work her way through the ranks and get promoted as quickly as government jobs allowed.

"Have you asked round the airline if anyone needs to rent a room?" she asked.

"Nobody knows anyone wanting to move. But I'll keep my ear cocked."

"I've had no responses from my ad and it's such a pain having to keep the house constantly tidy." Julia sighed heavily and took a large gulp of gin. "You should have seen me yesterday afternoon. I attacked the living room with a vengeance, dragging the hoover around with one hand and a duster in the other. I need to find someone fast or I'll lose the house."

"Sell the Jag. That thing guzzles petrol. Buy a Mini." He laughed. "It'd make your neighbour very happy by the sound of it."

"Oh, please. Can you really see me in a Mini?"

Peculiar questions

She wondered if she'd made a mistake. Piper thought he was open, honest and very friendly. Certainly he'd behaved that way on the ferry and during the ride to London. She didn't question his integrity. The guy had already paid rent even though she'd told him it wasn't necessary. He'd also chipped in forty pounds towards the purchase of food, something her regular tenant Pat had never offered.

She just didn't understand why he'd become so reserved. He'd hardly spoken the first evening when she'd generously cooked dinner for him, even gone to the trouble of inviting her neighbour Sonia Berg so he could meet new people. And then the peculiar question he'd asked, what she thought about illegally altered guns, while they watched the news this evening. It was very strange. All they'd been watching at the time was the capture of some guy who'd robbed a flat in Knightsbridge.

"Time for me to get outta here," she said.

Danny turned away from the television and looked at her. "I, er, I've been meaning to ask you something else."

"Quick. I'm gonna be late for my shift."

"I found… in my room, there's… " He fell silent.

"What?"

"You were right, it is very warm in my room."

"Are we cool, Danny?"

He nodded.

"Hey, I know you're probably missing home. It takes time to

adapt to city life."

"It sure does."

That must be his problem, she'd forgotten how strange every-thing had been when she first moved here.

"Why don't you drop by the pub for a drink this evening?" she said. "Todd'll be there and he's anxious to meet you. We're going on to a club later if you want to come, too."

"Hmm."

"I'll even buy you a beer."

"I'll come but I won't go clubbing."

"Why not?"

"I've got an interview for a flat."

This was one thing about the guy that Piper really admired. Since the first night, he'd been working feverishly to find himself a place, scouring the newspapers for vacancies even though she'd told him there was no need to rush. When Piper had first come to London, she'd spent the first week sightseeing. Not Danny. He was determined.

"Where's it located?" she asked.

"Peckham Rye."

"I don't think you want to live there. Lots of rough spots and no tube." She went to the door. "See you later then."

My mistake

His father's warning about London reverberated in his head. At first he'd thought the shotgun was a toy because its barrel was too short. He'd thought it was some inferior Chinese replica she'd purchased to frighten off potential intruders. However, after he held it, its hefty weight and the icy touch of the metal, he was convinced of its perverse authenticity and put it quickly back into the furthest corner of the wardrobe.

Guns were taboo in his family. Never discussed. The experience of finding it had been so upsetting, Danny'd spent the night following its discovery peering often at the locked wardrobe, his eyes drawn to the rickety door as if by a magnet. Its presence penetrated deep into his psyche and his mind kept posing a terrible question he couldn't stop. What if it was loaded and he got depressed and used it to kill himself? That's how many suicides happened. He calmed the unease every time by reminding himself he had access to carving knives every day and they were just as dangerous, that he'd never contemplated taking his life. But he didn't want to touch the thing again, didn't even want to share a room with such lethality.

Piper was likeable, a girl he could fancy, but she'd hidden a sawn off shotgun in her wardrobe. He knew from watching documentaries and news bulletins that America had crazies. Everyone over there was permitted to carry guns, and some of these crazies murdered, shooting people dead in schools, offices and on the streets, sometimes without a shred of provocation.

Part of Danny wanted to give her the benefit of the doubt. The other part just kept thinking of the shotgun. If she needed a gun for security, why not a little pistol? Why not mace? She had to know it was illegal to keep firearms. She'd certainly known the British law about search and seizure when they'd been stopped by the police. There'd also been the weird behaviour when she'd ripped pages from her notebook. That was just weird, of course. But weird could overlap with crazy.

He arrived at The George in Covent Garden ten minutes before last orders were called. Piper bought him a pint of lager and guided him to a corner of the bar where her boyfriend Todd was already drinking. He was handsome and cleft chinned. A pair of John Lennon-style spectacles accentuated his intellectual air. After introducing them, Piper left to attend to an impatient customer.

"Ever worked in a bar?" Todd asked.

"No."

"It's nasty, man. In the States, we have bar backs doing the grunt work at least. Over here, you have to do everything and customers don't even give tips... except from visiting Americans until they learn how things work."

Danny watched Piper draw a pint of ale, noticing the tautness of her skin and how the muscles in her upper arms flexed on the downward pull.

"You and Piper study together, don't you?"

"We don't take the same courses."

So she was definitely a student.

Todd swirled the last of his beer to make it froth before looking at him. "So you guys met on the ferry?"

"That's right."

"And she asked you to move in the same day?"

"Yes."

Todd was silent for a moment. "What's your secret, dude?"

"I'm not sure I... "

"I've been telling her we should live together but she won't listen. She keeps sayin' two months isn't enough time." His eyes flitted behind the bar. "Me, I know it is."

"I'm looking for a flat."

"Good to know."

"What do you study?" Danny asked.

"Comparative Politics."

"But she does that too, doesn't she?"

Piper smiled over. It was impossible not to like her. She couldn't be crazy. There had to be a logical explanation for the gun's presence.

"She does Irish stuff as well." Todd turned toward Danny. "You like her, huh?"

"She's smart, and pretty and… "

"You find her hot?"

Danny didn't think it smart to tell him what he thought. "Tell me, whereabouts is the LSE, exactly?"

"I think she's hot. She's also mine. And the LSE's in Houghton Street."

When he got back to Chumley Street after eleven, he found the living room curtains drawn and the lights turned on. Coldplay's *Yellow* belted from a radio upstairs. He opened the living room door and peered cautiously inside, saw a man's lightweight bomber jacket laying on the back of the sofa, its arms outstretched as if its owner had shimmied out of it while still seated. On the coffee table was a duffel bag. Beside it lay a knife, pair of kitchen gloves, a short piece of wood, and what appeared to be a lump of flecked, light-tan coloured putty.

He stepped inside. The door slammed shut. Before he could turn around, an arm wrapped around his neck and squeezed hard while he was simultaneously propelled across the room. To protect his face from smashing into the wall, Danny stuck out his hands. The fingers of his right hand struck the edge of a fisheye mirror above the mantle. It slipped off the nail securing it to the wall and smashed to pieces on the hearth tiles.

"Who the hell are you?" came a Northern Irish accent.

"I'm staying here." Danny tried to pry the man's arm off by grabbing at his wrist, "Piper invited me… "

"She's in Ireland."

"I gave her a lift back." Upstairs, he heard the toilet flushing. "My name's Danny Connolly. I come from Northern Ireland, too."

"Connolly, eh? A fenian." The man released his grip. "I thought you were here to rob the joint. My mistake. Sorry about that." He nodded toward the window. "A place down the street was broken into three weeks ago."

Feet pounded on the stairs and then the door flung open. "Why the hell'd you shut the door, Pat?" A woman came inside. In her early thirties and stocky like his assailant, her small mouth puckered into an 'O' when she saw Danny. "Who's this?" She glanced over at the items on the coffee table.

"He's a friend of Piper's. She's come back early."

"She has?"

"Where you from back home?" Pat asked, his chummy tone in bizarre contrast to the prior ruthlessness.

"Near Strabane."

"Get away," the woman said. "I'm from the Bogside. Who's your people?"

While he explained, Danny massaged the sides of his neck, the harsh shock of the attack weakening to mild queasiness.

"Another fenian living in London," Pat said. He put the putty, knife and other articles into the duffel bag. "The English don't like our type much so we all have to stick together here. Isn't that right?"

The question hung suspended in the thick atmosphere as both watched Danny intently.

"If you say so," he said.

"Bloody right I say so, young fella." Crooked front teeth flashed when the man smiled. "Sorry again. I didn't mean to hurt ye, like."

His expression of remorse intensified Danny's unease.

"I'm fixing a friend's window and came back to get some things I need." Pat tapped the duffel bag and laughed, but the attempt at levity sounded as artificial as his apology. "Tell Piper I'll see her right about the mirror."

"Don't tell me you broke that?" the woman said, glancing over at the fragments. "That's seven years bad luck."

"Aye, but whose?" Pat snorted.

"Was it you broke it, Pat?"

"Technically, Danny here did," he said, as he slipped on his bomber jacket.

"Oh, thank God for that."

Speak of the devil

Her friend's false teeth separated from her gums with a tiny sucking sound every time she chewed on the ginger snap. At sixty-eight-years-old, Agnes was twelve years younger than Martha, their friendship starting because their late husbands had been close friends since their service in the Royal Navy. Agnes' marmalade cat padded into the living room with his bent tail held high. He stopped abruptly as he was passing by Martha and began to sniff, his head lifting higher and higher until it disappeared beneath her skirt.

Agnes rose hastily and brought him back to her chair. She'd just treated Martha to lunch at her favourite café on King Street, a weekly outing both women looked forward to, but it had not been pleasant. Martha smelled and the young waitress made it obvious without actually saying a word that she didn't want to serve them. A proud woman who'd always been fastidious about her appearance, Martha had begun of late to forget to bathe and her clothes reeked of stale perspiration. It pained Agnes to see this and decided she must come over to Martha's flat more often and help her out.

"You're ever so lucky to be living across the river now, Martha. Things have changed on this street and not for the better. That hussy next door is forever entertaining and she's so noisy. The council won't do a thing when I complain."

"Young people today have no respect."

They fell silent, the ticking clock and Martha's moving teeth the only noises in the room.

"You need to keep your appointments with Doctor Berg," Agnes said. "She works for the National Health Service and could report you as a no show and you know what kind of trouble that might bring." She sipped her tea. "They could send out a social worker and they do like to interfere."

"Why does Blair allow doctors that don't speak like us to work over here?"

"It's all to do with the European Economic Community." Agnes recalled what her husband used to say, how the Germans lost the war only to get their companies and people into England when it joined Europe. "Charlie and your Norm always said we should never have joined the E.E.C."

"Poor Norm," said Martha. "I always thought I'd be first to kick the bucket."

"Women last longer." As she leaned toward her friend, she caught a whiff of body odour. "You know what, Martha? I'm in the mood to reset that barnet of yours."

"Nothing wrong with my bleedin' hair."

"A new do will be as good as a tonic."

"Not today."

"Why not? We're not doing anything. What I'll do is go upstairs right now and run you a nice hot bath. After you've soaked, I'll nip in and wash your barnet. And while I'm at it, I'll pop your things into the washing machine because I'm just about to do a load."

As the silence stretched, Agnes wondered if Martha'd guessed what she was attempting to do. A car drove up quickly outside. The driver began to park in the vacant spot beside Agnes' house. She approached the window and drew back the net curtain half-an inch with her finger.

"Speak of the devil and she appears." Agnes drew the curtain back a fraction more. "She's got three with her today. A blonde woman I've been seeing a lot of lately and two blokes."

"Who, dearie?"

"That Ralston slag."

As she watched Julia take a case of beer from the car and hand it to one of the men, Agnes wondered how she could ever have considered the tart a match for her son and make his dream of combining both houses a reality. The sale of the house devastated him, reopening the festering wound of his having been passed over for a funeral director position at his job and the catalyst resulting in his hastily leaving Agnes to take a position at a funeral establishment in a bleak South Yorkshire town.

Journalist in training

She hadn't needed to use the fake journalist's pass she'd tucked in the pocket of her skirt to get into Westminster Palace. Security hadn't even inspected her backpack. Having once served as a Congressional page while a high school student, Piper had experienced negotiating political establishments albeit the workings of Westminster and Capitol Hill very different.

Locating Paisley's office wasn't as easy. When she arrived at the bustling Central Lobby, the tall arched hallways of polished marble ran off in several directions. Clusters of people were gathered chatting spiritedly to Members of Parliament and their staff. She asked an old man dressed in a cute, old-fashioned uniform, who turned out to be a member of the Commons security, and he'd helped her.

Before she entered Paisley's office, Piper whipped out the journalist's pass and slung it around her neck. A member of his staff sat at a desk in the reception area, his face and pristine white shirt striped like a zebra from the rays of sun streaming through the adjacent venetian blinds. He looked up as she approached.

"Sheila Doughty, *New York Times*." She held out her hand. The aide shook it very tenuously. "I'm here to see Mr. Paisley."

"Doctor Paisley's not expecting any reporters," he said, in a nasal Northern Irish accent, the kind she'd used to think was Scottish but now knew as Ulster Protestant. "The procedure is to call and request an interview. Even for American journalists."

She let the sarcasm slide. "I've been here interviewing another MP and thought I'd drop by on the off-chance."

"I take it 'off-chance' is part of your journalistic armoury, Miss Doughty."

"Exactly."

"What's the member's name?"

"Excuse me?"

"The member you interviewed."

"I don't disclose that kinda information until my story's in the can."

"Quite."

He was a cold fish. Changing tactics, Piper flashed him a bright smile. "Is it really not possible to ask if Doctor Paisley would see me for a few minutes, Sir? I'd be really grateful."

"Nothing I can do."

"I tried to meet with him when I was over in Northern Ireland but he had to cancel." She smiled again. "Please."

The aide sighed. "I'll see what I can do. He's leaving in an hour to catch a flight back to Belfast. I'm sure you know Doctor Paisley's busy dealing with issues relating to the upcoming elections." His eyes narrowed. "I'm assuming that's what you want to talk to him about?"

"Of course."

Telling her to take a seat on one of two chairs placed adjacent to the door, the aide disappeared down the nearby hallway. Dust motes agitated by his departure floated in the shafts of sunlight. Down the hall she could hear phones ringing and people talking. Her own mobile phone rang. She fished it out of her pocket.

"Can't talk for long, Todd." She kept her eyes on the hallway entrance. "I've bagged him. You owe me big time."

When she'd told Todd about her plans to get an interview with Paisley by posing as a journalist he'd said she didn't have the nerve to pull it off, even bet her five pints of the most expensive draft beer that she wouldn't go through with it. She knew now how real journalists in the field felt when they got a scoop. It made her think she should more seriously consider becoming a journalist, either here or on her eventual return to the States.

If she did become one, Piper knew she'd work only for a prestigious outlet. One of the big networks if television or *The New York Times* if print. She could never do the regional beat with its incessant flurry of shootings, road accidents and fires. Her mind's eye skipped to her *New York Times* job interview and she pictured herself revealing the ruse she'd played to get to Paisley, backing it up by handing the interviewing editor a copy of her dissertation containing his comments as the evidence.

Footsteps started down the hallway. "Gotta go."

The aide approached. "Doctor Paisley will see you shortly."

"Thank you so much."

Minutes later, a middle-aged woman whose glossy smile proved incapable of extinguishing her natural frown lines appeared at the opening to the hallway. Her head jerked back slightly as she scrutinised Piper, taking in her face, clothes and backpack in one incisive sweep. She turned to the aide, said she needed to speak to him immediately and walked away.

Alert to the sinister vibes, Piper rose and watched them pass along the corridor and go through the second doorway. She sneaked down the hall. The first office was empty, as she heard the woman's urgent voice in the next office.

"My instinct's never wrong," the woman said. "I've dealt with too many media types to know that woman's no reporter, never mind one from *The New York Times*.

"She did seem a bit young," said the aide.

"She could even be dangerous. Didn't you see her rucksack?"

"Security would have checked that."

"Security here's not like in Stormont." A phone rang. The woman answered. "Make it fast." The receiver slammed down on its cradle. "The police are on their way to question her. Go out and stall her till they get here. Tell her… "

Piper fled down the hallway and out the door as fast as her six-inch heels and pencil skirt would permit. She ripped off the journalist's pass as she scuttled along the outside corridor, expecting at any moment to hear the screech of alarm bells, a security code or even an alert blared from the banks of latent speakers she knew must be mounted within the building's nooks and crannies. Arriving at the stairs, she attempted to negotiate them in twos but couldn't. Two policemen came up the last flight of stairs, one carrying a walkie talkie, the other a machine gun. Her heart stopped but her feet clicked onward and she whipped out her mobile and pretended to take a call. Affecting an English accent as the policemen drew closer, she said, "It's simply got to be struck from the bill. It's got to. If it isn't, Tony won't be happy when I talk to him, believe you me." She nodded perfunctorily as they passed by, cringingly aware of her grimy backpack. The men nodded and continued up the stairs.

The policeman's walkie-talkie crackled to life just as she exited the stairs. She walked at a brisk pace, the back of her heels on fire because the thin leather ankle strap had rubbed her skin raw. She hoped she was headed in the right direction. Moments later, she arrived at the hexagon shaped Central Lobby and threaded her way through knots of people toward the Saint Stephen's entrance. A group of school children, the girls in grey pinafores and boys in shorts, shuffled in pairs toward the exit. Piper joined them. Someone touched her right shoulder. She spun round to see a liver-spotted hand with a shiny wedding band.

"Ma'am, do ya know how we get to the debatin' chamber that's on C-Span?" A man in pointy-toed cowboy boots asked, his wife in a pink tracksuit standing beside him.

"No clue." She turned back toward the vacating line of children. "Wait for teacher, please."

Outside, three policemen stood chatting near the vaulted entrance, their Victorian-era helmets and submachine guns they carried a study in contradiction. She passed them, looking straight ahead. Deciding it prudent not to use the nearest tube station, Piper limped off at a leisurely pace bound for Waterloo station that lay across the river. Though she removed her shoes, hoisted her skirt and jogged across Westminster Bridge as soon as she reached it.

Offbeat places

Piper cooked what she referred to as 'comfort food', a batch of minced beef shaped like a loaf that she served with buttered sweetcorn and mashed potatoes. Her lodger Pat was also present. Now they'd spent some time together, Danny found him friendly and intelligent though the circumstances of their introduction were never far from his mind.

After eating, they went into the living room to watch the news. Following a segment about a proposed congestion charge for central London, a report followed about a security breach at Westminster. With the parliament building serving as a backdrop, a Metropolitan police inspector stated they had no further information about the identity of the woman who'd come to Doctor Paisley's office masquerading as an American journalist. When probed further by the journalist, the policeman admitted it could have been an assassination attempt by the Real IRA.

"The Provos should have got him years ago," Pat said, his lips curled in disgust. "With the elections looming, I bet Paisley's blowing this whole thing up just to get out of living up to his part of the bargain once the IRA decommission their arms." He sat back on the sofa. "The Provos should never have agreed to disarm."

A crude sketch of the suspect with slicked back hair, pert nose and a sullen expression flashed on the screen. Piper edged forward in her seat and peered intently at the screen.

"That doesn't look like me, right?" she said.

Pat laughed.

"I'm serious. It's me who went to see him."

Pat slapped his thighs. "You're quite a joker."

Danny smiled. "You know, there is a similarity." He winked at Pat.

"Are you serious?" Piper asked, her face full of concern.

The phone rang, and Danny answered it. "It's Todd." He held out the phone.

"She's a card, eh?" Pat said.

"She is that."

As they watched the rest of the news, Danny heard Piper say she was going to dye her hair as a precaution in case the sketch appeared in the newspapers. Pat's brow furrowed and he looked at Danny.

"You weren't coddin'," Pat said, after Piper hung up.

"No, but offing him wasn't on the agenda."

Danny couldn't believe what he was hearing. Just when he'd decided his imagination had been running riot about Piper, that his father's warnings had made him paranoid.

"More's the pity," Pat said.

As Piper explained what had occurred, Danny was incredulous.

"With that sort of nerve, you'd make a hell of a volunteer," said Pat. "Wouldn't you agree, Danny?"

"I don't know anything about that sort of thing."

"Nor do I." Pat paused and looked at the television. "Yer tone seems very anti, though." Pat's eyes flickered with annoyance or menace. Danny wasn't sure which.

"Don't you approve of what they've done through the years?"

Danny's instinct was to be silent but also felt he was every bit as entitled to state his opinion as Pat. "I think it's moot, Pat."

Pat's eyes changed to slits. "What's 'moot' mean?"

"Pointless," said Piper.

"Why would you say that?"

"The fighting's over now. It doesn't matter what my opinion is... "

"You fucking hear what this man's sayin'?" Pat said.

"Don't get all bent out of shape," said Piper. "He's only saying what people are thinking."

"What kind of man are you anyway?" Pat said, turning back to Danny.

As he rose out of his seat, Danny raised his hands but Pat snatched his jacket off the armrest. "Is the tricolour flying from Belfast City Hall yet?" he asked. "Last time I saw, it was still the bloody Union Jack.

Pat reminded Danny of some of the bullies at his school. They were so pugnacious, so quick to take offence.

"Hey listen Piper, no more visits to parliament, at least not for a wee while." He hugged Piper and then smiled at Danny. "That was some dinner she made, wasn't it?"

Danny couldn't answer, he was so amazed at how quickly Pat's mood had changed.

Though he'd vowed not to look at the shotgun again, Piper's escapades at Westminster brought Danny's uneasiness about her back and he wondered if there'd been a sinister reason for her going there. He knelt and stretched his hand toward the far right corner of the wardrobe where he'd placed the weapon, hoping his fingertips would feel its smooth metal snout. He felt nothing but the rough grain of the wardrobe. He shifted the bottoms of the dresses, trousers and coats and peered inside. The gun was no longer there.

Saying she needed a break from her revision and as his German course hadn't yet begun, Piper insisted on taking Danny on what she'd called a 'tour of London's offbeat places.' After calling at the US Embassy to renew her passport, they'd visited Saint Giles, a quaint church where Oliver Cromwell was married, and paid two pounds apiece to climb to the top of the Monument so he could see out over the city. They were now standing in front of a three-storey house in Craven Street where the statesman Benjamin Franklin had lived for sixteen of the eighteen years he'd spent in London.

Throughout the tour, Danny wondered how to bring up the anxiety he felt without insulting her if he was wrong. Standing before the old house afforded him an opportunity.

"Franklin was a revolutionary, wasn't he?" he said to Piper, who'd now dyed her hair a colour she described as 'Irish red'. To Danny, it looked the same colour as an aubergine.

"I think of him as an inventor first."

He pretended to mull. "Pat a bit of the revolutionary, eh?"

"Hmm. I read in a magazine back home they're planning to open this house to the public at some point."

A squadron of pigeons passed over the rooftops on their way to nearby Trafalgar Square.

"I think Pat supports terrorism judging from last night's comments."

"Franklin was very friendly with the landlady's daughter Polly. Apparently he treated her as a second daughter while he lived here. They remained lifelong friends."

"Do you support terrorism?"

"Polly was at his bedside when he died in Philly."

"I mean, could you shoot anybody?"

Her deflections were as rude as they were admirable. He'd always found it difficult to turn a tricky conversation, especially with his father. Unsure now how to proceed without getting angry, Danny glanced across the street while he considered his options. A man in a beautifully cut denim shirt with a yellow Venetian lion on its breast pocket was at the bus stop. He'd seen the tourist at Saint Giles taking photographs. The man looked up from his newspaper and their eyes locked for an instant, before Danny turned back to Piper.

"You're avoiding my questions, Piper. Why?"

Her eyes remained fixed on the shiny black front door of the house. "One person's definition of terrorism is another's definition of war."

"Is that something you learned on your course?"

"It's what I believe."

"How come you believe that?"

"Well, seeing as we're at Franklin's old pad, let's consider the case of the American patriots first. They didn't jump on some ship and sail to England to *ask* the King for independence. They knew they'd get their asses thrown in jail. Instead, they raised an army and used guns to fight and make the English understand the colonies wished to be free. That was war. And it worked. But to the English, it would have been terrorism, except it was called rebellion back then." She looked about as if checking to see if anyone was listening, then took a step closer toward him. "Now let's consider the British occupation of your homeland. The British have tried for years to make the public believe the IRA are terrorists. But they're not. They're a legitimate, disciplined army. They've used their guns and bombs to bring the British to the negotiating table." She paused and looked hard at him. "And to answer your other question, I'd have no problem shooting somebody in that kind of situation. I think anyone who cares about freedom and justice would agree with me." She paused again. "What's your thinking here?"

He wondered now if she might be in the IRA. There'd been Americans in its ranks in the past. She'd stuffed writings into her bra that she didn't want the police to see. She owned a gun. She'd gone to Westminster in search of Paisley. Did he dare ask if she was an IRA volunteer? Did he really want to know? Was he just being paranoid? If he shared what he was thinking and he was wrong, she'd laugh. He'd be utterly humiliated. Worse, she'd think he was ungrateful, and taking advantage of her kindness.

Horns blared from the traffic circling Trafalgar Square. Two could play the avoidance game.

"My thinking's you made your hair a bit too red."

"Who's avoiding now?"

"You need to tone it down."

"Opinion or hair?"

After they'd eaten lunch, Piper suggested going to the Three Tuns, a student pub that looked seventies institutional.

"I've had class in here," Piper said, as she set two pints on the table.

"I figured that was a tutorial going on over there." He nodded toward a corner where five students and a man with silver hair were gathered around two tables.

Five minutes later, Todd entered and walked up to them, his eyes fixed on her hair. "Didn't recognise you for a sec'."

"You like?" Piper touched her hair self-consciously.

His eyes cut to Danny and then he turned back to Piper. "I thought you were studying at home today."

"I needed a break."

Todd set his satchel on the table. "Thought we had a deal, dude."

Danny looked at him nonplussed. "I'm not sure what you mean."

"Weren't you supposed to let me know when you were stopping by here and she and I'd show you around together."

"I'm not showing him round here today," Piper said, before Danny could reply. "I took him to a few spots round the city this morning and came here for a drink as an afterthought."

"That's why you took the day off. Sightseeing?"

Piper sighed. "No."

He turned to Danny. "How's the flat hunt going?"

"I've been looking hard, believe me."

"You wanna beer, Todd?" said Piper. "My treat."

He ignored her. "Tried any agencies yet? They'd find you something real quick."

"Danny's welcome to live with me as long as he likes," said Piper.

"Live with you, huh?" Todd laughed, but it was hard and sharp. "How come you've never made me that kind of offer?"

Window shopping

Notices were posted all over the dusty window of the corner shop and Danny stopped to read them when he came out from buying the milk. They were the usual assortment of temporary work positions he'd seen before, ads from carpenters and plumbers, housewives offering their services as a babysitter and an old handwritten plea for information about a lost two-year-old calico cat. The words 'SHARE HOUSE WITH FRIENDLY OWNER – IMMACULATE CONDITION' jumped out at him as he came to the last row of ads. Posted eight days ago, he assumed the room would already be rented, but memorised the telephone number and called when he got home.

An answering machine picked up. The female's voice very posh. He didn't leave a message. His father, an expert salesman, taught him leaving messages was the hallmark of an amateur, ceded unnecessary control to the other person who might never return the call. The post dropped with a clatter through the letterbox. He found the local newspaper among the pile and scanned the accommodation section, immediately spotting the same ad among the classifieds. Now nervous the owner would be inundated with responses, Danny called again, blurting into the answering machine he'd recently moved to London, that he was solvent and leaving both Piper's landline and his mobile number.

For an hour, he lay on the couch willing the phone to ring like a lovesick teenager. It rang just before eleven, but it was only his mother who'd confused the week his course was scheduled to begin. By twelve, the woman still hadn't rung. He went to Oxford Street to buy a pair of trainers. On his return, a light was blinking on the answering machine.

"Hello, this is Julia Ralston calling for a Danny Connolly," the voice said. "I've had a large number of responses, but if you're still interested I'll be at home until three."

He checked the time and picked up the phone.

"Ralston, hello."

"Danny Connolly here. I left a message that I'm looking to rent."

"You sound Irish."

Her statement made Danny's heart skip a beat. Some English people, especially the posh ones, didn't like the Irish. "I'm from Northern Ireland."

"With that accent, I'd never have guessed." She laughed. "I'm just showing someone around the place now."

He wondered if he was being given the brush-off. "When can I see it?"

"I'm making a decision soon. Can you hold a minute?" Without waiting for his reply, he heard a thud as the receiver was set down, then heard her call out to someone to go out and take a look at the garden. "Sorry about that, when can you come over?"

"Right now."

"I'm leaving for work in five minutes."

"When, then?"

"Eight tomorrow morning."

When she gave him the address, Danny couldn't believe it. The house was also on Chumley Street.

He waited ten minutes until he was sure she would have left and then went in search of the house. A woman wearing sixties-style, pitch-black sunglasses came out of a house and climbed into an old Jaguar as he was crossing underneath the railway bridge. Unsure if it was the owner, he crossed the street to the antique shop. He checked out the displays until the car drove off and then made his way to the address he'd been given. It was the right house and he was surprised. The home looked bizarre, its brick façade was painted powder blue, the front door dark purple.

An eight-inch gap in the net blinds on the front window proved too tempting. He took the two strides comprising the width of the front garden and drew up to the window. Unlike Piper's home, the interior was open plan. An oversized sofa and two large armchairs occupied nearest the window, and just beyond was a dining table and chairs, in front of a set of French doors through which he could see part of a large garden and an ornate wicker chair.

"You looking for something?"

An old woman stood on the pavement watching him. She wore a gingham nylon housecoat and gaudy headscarf. Part of a fat pink hair curler peeked from underneath. Danny blushed.

"No-one's home."

"You just missed her."

Danny came out to the street.

"I'm Julia's neighbour." The woman nodded to the house next door. "You can give me a message and I'll make sure she gets it."

"There's no need." He started to walk away.

"Fine, I'll just tell her an Irishman was lurking at her door."

Danny stopped abruptly and turned round. "She's looking for a tenant and I'm meeting her tomorrow about it."

"You're wanting to rent from her?"

"Aha."

"Last one got thrown out on her ear. Blimey, such a row they had." The woman clamped her mouth with her hand. "Goodness, I shouldn't have mentioned that. It's just you seem like such a nice young man."

Crap humour

The house was untidy and she felt exhausted. Julia wished she hadn't spent the night at Katie's after her shift had ended. She should have come home. Her girlfriend's mattress was unbearably soft and Julia always slept with one eye open because Katie's children might burst into the room in the early morning and catch them in bed. The relationship was totally inconvenient. And yet every time Katie rang and said her husband was going out of town, Julia couldn't resist and made the forty-minute drive to her house in Godalming.

After forcing her coat into the stuffed cupboard and yanking out the hoover, Julia began to vacuum until she realised it wasn't sucking up any dirt. The red light was blinking. She opened the canister and had taken out the bag when the doorbell rang. She stashed the hoover and bag behind the sofa and waved her hands about to dispel the cloud of dust. CDs were scattered on the floor beside the stereo and she considered swiping them underneath the cupboard with her foot but then figured there were too many.

Her face smacked into an invisible wall of cologne when she opened the front door. He gripped her hand more firmly than a secondhand car dealer.

"Gosh, this is really lovely," he said, as he crossed the threshold.

Julia made a mental note he might be a liar or just desperate to move. His inability to keep his eyes fixed on hers suggested reserve or shyness. The smile was broad and engaging, so engaging she'd returned it before she remembered her strategy to keep everything formal until the interview concluded.

"Let me show you around and then we'll have a chat," she said.

After a tour that didn't include her messy bedroom, she took him out to the garden, fragrant with the perfume of jasmine. Shrubbery, including two wine-red Barberry bushes and hydrangeas, was in urgent need of trimming. A portion of the trellis running along the wall jutted out at an angle where it had broken away from the post. He followed her to an elevated brick patio in the garden's middle furnished with a wrought iron table and pair of fan-backed wicker chairs. Julia had bought the chairs on impulse, fancying the idea of sipping ice-cold wine during hot summer evenings. Flanking each chair were five-foot rubber plants still in their original plastic nursery pots.

"These are lovely." Danny reached out and gently touched one of the leaves. "My mother loves plants."

"They don't need any attention, which I like."

"I hope you don't mind me saying but they're root bound. They need to be transplanted." He looked around the garden. "Your grass and shrubs could do with fertilising as well."

"Really."

"I'd be glad to do that if you... if we decide I should move in."

From the other side of the wall Julia heard a noise. Her nosy neighbour was in her garden.

"It's much hotter than I thought," she said. "Let's go inside."

She invited him to sit on the sofa, excused herself and then went to her bedroom where she rummaged energetically through her bedside drawers until she found a notebook. As she was coming down the stairs she saw him slam her novel shut. He slid it back on the coffee table so hurriedly it continued to glide and finally dropped on the floor. Julia picked it up without comment.

"I couldn't resist looking to see what you're reading," he said, the attractive hazel eyes much more noticeable now his face was scarlet.

Julia set the notebook on top of the table. "Do you like the room?"

"Very much."

She disliked Irish accents but, now they were talking in person, his accent was not as harsh as it had sounded on the telephone. And he was meeting her eyes now.

"The rent's £320 due on the first of every month."

"Inclusive?"

"Except for the telephone, which we'll split down the middle."

"I have a mobile but I'd like to be able to use the landline, too."

His sense of fairness was appealing.

"Do you need a deposit?"

"Oh I… one month's fine." She picked up the notebook and wrote 'deposit' and 'will split phone bill'. "How long is your course?"

"Five months."

"I was looking for someone to take the room for a year, minimum."

He shifted and crossed his legs. "There's a chance I'll stay longer. It all depends."

"On?"

"I'm sorting some things out at home."

He averted her stare and rubbed the tip of his nose, signs her training indicated he might be hiding something. Julia underlined the words she'd written in the notebook and began to doodle directly underneath them.

"Where are you living now?" she asked.

"Down the street."

"Why are you leaving?"

"It's a box room."

"Have you got a reference I can ring?"

"Would my mother do?"

"Conflict of interest, wouldn't you say?"

"What about her friend in Guildford?"

"What's your current landlord's number?" As he tendered it, Julia considered if she'd maybe been too direct, a result of her work training. She also wondered if she was being tough because he was Irish. Julia didn't consider herself prejudiced but knew the tendency lay just beneath the surface. She decided a joke might set him at ease.

Raising her eyebrows so they formed perfect arches, her way of conveying exaggeration or leg-pulling, she said, "Best I find out if you're in the IRA before I let you move in, eh?"

His face turned scarlet again. He unclasped his fingers and laid one hand on the armrest as if in preparation to leave. She'd miscalculated, angered him and she didn't have anyone else. She'd lied when she told him she had others interested, a ruse Clive suggested to make the house appear more desirable. The only other person she'd interviewed was a middle-aged woman and Julia terminated the interview when she'd offered her a glass of wine and the woman declined saying she was Plymouth Brethren. She would have to begin the entire tedious process again. Advertising and keeping the house obsessively tidy.

"I meant that as a joke."

He laughed as he eased forward on the sofa. "No offence taken."

"Room's yours."

He made no attempt to leap at the offer.

"You don't need to sign a lease and I'll even skip the deposit."

"That's very nice of you." He placed his hands on his knees. "If you don't mind, I'd like to ask you a couple of things."

"Of course."

"Did you have a prior tenant?"

"Yes."

"Why'd she leave?"

"How did you know it was a woman?"

"I came by yesterday to check out the house and bumped into one of your neighbours. I didn't get her name. She was old."

"That'll be Mrs. Hartley. What'd she say?"

"That you threw the last tenant out."

It was Julia's turn to blush. She laid the notebook on top of the novel and began to align the books' edges. "I don't know how Mrs. Hartley would know that. She's a lovely old woman but a little strange also."

"She heard the two of you arguing a lot."

"The woman renting from me last was a piece of work. It's true, I did ask her to leave. But I gave her notice and she didn't take it."

It was her turn to squirm. His eyes riveted on hers like he was trying to determine her veracity.

"That sounds fair," he said. "I had to ask."

"Absolutely." She felt it safe to arch her brows now and smiled. "Danny, there's no need to worry. We'll get on, should you decide to move in. I hope you will."

Once Danny had left, Julia knocked on her neighbour's door and rang the bell twice. The old crow didn't answer. About to leave, she happened to look toward the front window and saw the lace curtain move. She waved. A moment later, the door opened.

"Yes," Mrs. Hartley said.

"I've been interviewing tenants and… "

"Is that what you call it?"

Julia regarded her angry face. "I really don't know why but we seem to have got off on a bad footing."

Her neighbour folded her arms and peered toward the sky. "My son's moved away for starters."

Julia tried to make sense of her neighbour's remark. "I'm not sure what that has to do with me."

"I intend to get him back."

She wondered if her neighbour was perhaps mental and not just eccentric. "Mrs. Hartley, I'll come to the point. You informed someone I threw out my previous tenant."

"I wouldn't rent to any bloody Irishman if you want my advice. They're all terrorists. Look what they did to poor Lord Mountbatten."

Julia ignored her outburst. "I dislike it when people say things about me that aren't true so I'd appreciate if... "

"My tea's getting cold." Mrs. Hartley went inside and slammed the door shut.

A letter to Ma'am

40 Chumley Street
London, W6

Dear Queen Mother,
 It's been a little while since I last wrote. I sincerely hope your collarbone is mended now from the fall and your leg is also feeling better because I noticed you was wearing a heavy bandage in a photograph I came across recently.
 Before your accident, I was ever so glad to read you were able to visit the Queen Mary Clothing Guild. You have been such an inspiration to us knitters through the years, Ma'am. Martha, my friend, who's doing poorly, was saying she'd love to do a bit of sewing for the Guild again but her fingers are just not up to the work.
 My late husband's first anniversary is just around the corner. I'm sure you still miss your husband, our dear departed King. Don't you find nighttimes worst of all? My cat Percy is such a comfort.
 Not much has changed in this part of London since I last wrote. Well, except I've got

an Irishman living next to me now. My opinion of the Irish is the same as Princess Margaret's, Ma'am.

Well, that's all my news for now. I look forward to seeing your smiling face on the telly again soon.

With loyalty and affection, I remain yours,
Agnes Hartley

Settling in

The guests were all Julia's friends. He'd invited Piper, but she'd arranged to study at Todd's flat as her exams were starting the following week.

"You must return to the gym, Julia," Sonia Berg said, as Danny refilled her wine glass. "You will get more thick around the middle."

"*More* thick, Sonia?" Julia said. Her eyebrows arched in the manner Danny now knew conveyed fake annoyance. "Is this your way of saying I'm already fat?"

"Sonia, make sure you close the front door on your way out, will you?" Clive said, a man whom Danny thought seasoned his conversation with too much double entendre.

The doctor's eyes crinkled in befuddlement. "But I am not leaving yet," she said.

"Could have fooled me, darlin'," said Clive. "You just insulted the hostess."

"This was not my intention. I do not mean you are fet in the middle, Julia. I meant you will get fet. You comprehend now?"

"But working out's so bloody boring," Julia said.

"This Burgundy *schmeckt*, but so many sugar grams." As if to underscore her point, Sonia held her glass up to the overhead light. After she set it down again, she looked over at her boyfriend, a hospital porter who kept leaving the table between courses to wander about the room and look at things. "Jean-Pierre, you must return to the table, please."

Fine-featured, with a haughty air and kneeling beside a stack of CDs on the floor, he glanced at her and then shrugged. He turned away and continued reading the CD booklet he had in his hand.

"Sonia, will you speak German to me after I begin my course?" Danny asked.

"Why is this?"

"I'd learn faster."

"This is not so possible. I am looking always to improve my English."

Danny concluded that her directness, although perfectly logical, might be to do with her German culture. Certainly, she wasn't a typical psychiatrist, revealing as she had over dinner that she supplemented her modest National Health Service income by conducting a psychotherapy practice from her home. Danny wasn't even sure what a psychotherapist was or how it differed from a psychologist.

"I want to play this now." Jean-Pierre held up an Elton John CD.

"That's fine," Julia said, and she turned back to Sonia. "I think I will go back to the gym after all."

Jean-Pierre turned up the volume and began to dance.

"You must not play it so wery loud, *Lieb*," Sonia said. "It's late."

"The volume's perfect," Julia said. "What a great idea, Jean-Pierre. Let's all dance."

Julia, Clive and Danny formed one cluster in the small empty space between the living room and dining area, Sonia and Jean-Pierre another. Possessing no sense of rhythm, Danny shuffled his feet and tried to copy Clive's movements. He hoisted his hands above his head and shook them. After the second song, Jean-Pierre left the dance floor and went into the kitchen. Sonia sashayed over to Danny, eyes misty from drinking too much wine, and grabbed the sides of his hips. Using his body as if it were a tree trunk, she lowered her own in a bizarre squat-like dance until she was almost on her knees. Loud thuds commenced from the wall adjacent to the stairs.

"What's that noise?" said Danny.

Everyone fell silent. He could feel the pressure of Sonia's nose pressing against his mid-thigh.

"It's nothing," Julia said, as the next song began to play. "Just the water pipes."

Fifteen minutes later, Sonia announced it was time for her to leave. The others left, too.

"I'm knackered," Julia said, as she shut the front door.

"Me, too."

He collected the glasses and dishes off the dining table. The kitchen was a mess, its floor tiles sticky and the side piled with dirty pots, pans, knives and measuring jugs. He decided he'd do the washing up and Julia could dry. After he'd finished two large pots and a roasting pan, there was no longer any space on the draining board to place any more items. He looked to see what she was doing and was glad to see her approach.

She came to the kitchen threshold and stood clutching her shoes in her right hand. "We'll have to do dinners on a regular basis."

"That'll be fun."

She yawned. "See you in the morning, then."

"What about the dishes?"

"I'd let them soak overnight if I were you." She yawned again. "Good night." She stopped at the bottom of the stairs. "Don't forget to put the lights out in here before you go to bed."

A strange emergency

He was sweeping crumbs into a mug of unfinished tea Julia had left sitting on the coffee table for two days, when the front door was flung open. Julia rushed inside, tossed her linen jacket over the chair and crossed to the dining room table where she began searching through the pile of books and magazines laying upon it. Not finding what she was looking for, she peered about the room.

"Have you seen the phone book?" Her plumy voice was unnaturally shrill.

"No."

"Help me find it?" She fell on her knees and began searching in the CD cupboard. "I need the nearest FPA fast."

"What's that?"

"Family planning clinic."

He began to search the shelf underneath the coffee table. Now she'd misplaced something she desperately needed, he seized the opportunity to indirectly highlight her untidy nature. "We really need to keep things in their proper place, don't we? That way... "

"The damned condom burst."

He stopped searching and gaped at her.

"Shit, I just saw it the other day."

"You've got a boyfriend?"

"An American I just met." She moved to another cupboard. "I was processing passengers coming off a New York flight yesterday and this bloke just started flirting with me... ah, here it is." She flicked through the yellow pages and then began to run her finger down a page. "Long story short, I ended up spending the night at his hotel." She picked up the receiver and dialed. "We fucked again this morning but the condom tore and I need to get the morning after pill... Oh, good morning... " She brandished her hand like a traffic warden.

Danny couldn't have spoken anyway. The words 'tore' and 'fucked' were still ricocheting around his head.

Canapés at Tiffany's

The staircase was slick with city grime turned muddy and it was raining heavily when she emerged from the Underground. She had six minutes to get to work or she'd be late, her progress impeded now by having to dodge people grasping umbrellas held inches above their heads. Piper found London and Manhattan similarly unpredictable this way; one could leave home with not a rain cloud in the sky, take the subway downtown or travel on the tube into the West End and emerge into a deluge that would often end as quickly as it'd begun. True, London got a lot more rain than Manhattan, the one downside of living this side of the pond.

Working a catering job wasn't what she'd wanted to do tonight. Her first exam had gone well and she'd have preferred to stay home and revise but she needed the cash. Notwithstanding she'd got a partial scholarship from an organisation in the United States as well as three small British grants and occasional cheques from her father to help pay the tuition that ran to nearly $4,000, she'd had to take out a loan to cover the balance. On top of these bills came the rent and living expenses, which took a huge chunk out of her budget. Living in London was far more expensive than Manhattan.

Piper considered flagging down a black taxi but one glance at the slow-moving traffic along Piccadilly made her realise it would be futile as well as expensive. Her mobile rang as she turned into Old Bond Street. She checked the number, hoping to call the person back later, but saw it was her father, Kevin.

"Hey, Philomena. How's it going?"

"It's Piper now. Remember?"

"I don't see why you gotta go changing your name."

"Whatever."

"You done something illegal I don't know about?"

"You're hilarious, Dad."

"I can't get used to the name, honey. Sorry."

"I'm gonna legalise it."

There was a silence. Other than a note and enclosed cheque for $400, it'd been six weeks since she'd heard from him. That wasn't unusual. When she'd been at NYU, they'd met only once or twice a month even though he worked at a midtown precinct. Piper knew it was his way of giving her space and appreciated it.

"Todd got me a catering gig so I can't talk long."

"You still seeing that guy, huh?"

"Yeah."

"That's a record for you, ain't it?"

There was dead air, as if he expected her to agree or protest.

"I'll have to meet this guy. Give my seal of approval."

"It's early yet."

"I've got news."

"Oh yeah?"

"Your mom's demanding I sell the house."

Piper stopped abruptly. Though her mother Philomena Kathleen and father were married nearly 26 years on paper, they'd actually separated eight months after her brother's death. Piper remembered the evening her mother left as vividly as the night five years ago when her brother died. It was during her last week of high school. She'd come home high after being out late with her friends and found her father hunched at the kitchen table. He was still in his NYPD uniform, a crumpled sheet of paper in his hands.

Without speaking, he handed over the sheet of paper. It was a note from her mother stating she didn't love him, hadn't for years, that their marriage was a shell but she'd stayed. She went on to say Piper was going off to NYU, that she'd done her 'duty by our daughter even though she's selfish and forever getting high,' and she was leaving him to find whatever happiness a forty-two-year-old single woman could find in Manhattan. The words brought Piper down instantly. She didn't know if her parent's marriage had turned bad while she and her brother were children or who exactly was to blame. Certainly there'd been horrid arguments, but there'd also been good times. Her eight-year-old brother's death had been a catalyst. Or was she the true catalyst? The word 'duty' had stung most even though she'd always been much closer to her father.

"Sell our home, for real, Dad?"

"She says the market's hot and it'll go fast." There was a slight pause. "You know anything I don't?"

She checked the time and began to walk briskly. "She and I hardly ever talk."

"I'm gonna list with a broker next week." He sighed. "I'm real cut up about it."

Piper knew it was not the prospect of leaving his house, a home he'd restored after the damage caused by the terrible fire that hurt her father. It was the reality that any hopes of reconciliation he'd been harbouring were irrevocably dead. She also knew her mother hadn't pushed for a divorce because Piper's maternal grandmother and her father's family came from strict Catholic backgrounds, the sort that believed marriage really did last till the death of one of the spouses. Piper resolved quietly to spend more time with her father when she planned to visit New York in late July.

"I'm so sorry, Dad." She arrived at the entrance to Tiffany's but couldn't bring herself to cut him off.

"One good thing is, I might make detective at last," he said. "A buddy who knows what I'm going through is going to put a word in for me with some people. That's important to me.

Real important."

Her father had been working to make detective for years without success. "Got my fingers crossed for ya. I gotta run, Dad. See you real soon, okay?"

"Love you, hon. Wish you were here now."

A lump formed instantly in her throat. She swallowed it away.

"Where've you been?" Todd said, when she came down the stairs to the basement.

Young men and women dressed in black and white attire were forming two lines across the room. Chefs were slicing meats, chopping vegetables, whipping sauces and adding garnish to items that had been prepared beforehand. The aroma of roasted lamb and fresh oregano made her ravenous. After she gave her name and signed the staff register, they were told to join the lines of waiters and await instructions from the event manager.

Five minutes later, an effete, narrow shouldered man came down the stairs and walked up to them. He clapped his hands for silence before announcing they'd be serving the cream of London society, possibly even a member of the Royal Family. A lecture on politeness and unobtrusive efficiency ensued as if they were morons.

"Any wannabe actors and pop stars, be warned," he said. "You'll be sacked on the spot *without* pay if I see you loitering near the likes of Judy Dench or George Michael."

"George Michael is *so* eighties?" said someone behind Piper.

There was a ripple of laughter.

"You people mean only one things to these people," the manager said. "Drinks and food. Is that understood?"

No-one spoke.

"Is that understood?"

A grudging 'Yes' went round the room. Piper was appointed to drinks. Todd was too, though only for the first hour. Thereafter, he was to move to canapés because he had experience weaving through a crowded room with a large platter.

"Okay people." The manager clapped his hands. "Let's get this show on the road."

It was a groupie's paradise. Famous and wealthy unknowns were packed in like sheep in a shearing shed. Two British sitcom actors chatted to a female MP and an American film director. A gay British actor and his companion reached out and lifted drinks off Piper's tray as she passed by, even though their first ones weren't finished yet. His friend was dressed head-to-toe in a red tartan suit and tam-o-shanter. Now used to the British penchant for drinking as much free booze as possible at events, it didn't surprise Piper that famous personages did the same.

It struck Piper as ironic that the displays of outrageously expensive commodities on the shelves had the same disconcerting sparseness as a Soviet era supermarket, the sparseness for diametrically opposite reasons admittedly. She threaded diligently through a coterie of power women, their husbands and toy boys, navigating the silver tray back and forth as skillfully as she could.

"What are you doing here?" The manager approached with his palms out and rising slowly. "You're supposed to wait in the diamond launch room."

"No-one said anything."

"We really must listen more carefully, mustn't we?"

"Dude, no-one told me. Okay?"

She was rewarded with 'What an obnoxious American' look. "*Go.*"

"Where is it?"

He scrutinised her drinks tray and ordered her downstairs to replenish the champagne. Piper longed to sit. Downstairs, she dropped her tray off at the bar and headed to the makeshift kitchen while the barman swapped her empty flutes for new ones. She hovered, one eye on the table laden with food and the other on her drinks tray. When the chef turned his back and began to garnish a platter, she devoured two canapés, caviar and crème fraîche on sliced French bread, as payback for the manager's rudeness.

"How's it going?" Todd asked, as he set his serving platter down on the table to be refilled. He ran his hand up and down her back.

"Can you do my feet, too?"

He nodded at the caviar. "Hope there's some of these left to take home."

"Fat chance. Eat now."

"Been doing that," he said, and winked.

"Oi," the head barman called over. "Yeah, you. Think you're a bleedin' guest or what?"

As she made her way upstairs, Piper quenched her thirst with a flute of champagne, finishing it just as the manager appeared at the top of the stairs.

"You're not in diamonds yet?" he asked. "What's this?" He retrieved the empty flute with his long, skinny fingers.

"Bar guy must have missed it."

"Your job's also quality control." He sighed as he gesticulated to his left. "*Go*."

A European ex-supermodel remarried or divorced from a New York tycoon (Piper couldn't remember) and her equally stick-thin sidekick were standing just inside the room as she entered. They were chatting to a local evening news show anchor who looked decidedly healthier on television. Both women were in their early fifties and wore pancake concealer. The hemlines of their flouncy party dresses stopped just short of the globes of their asses. The ex-supermodel was holding court and ignored Piper as she held up the tray. Piper walked away.

The flawless profile of a woman seated on a stool to the left side of the bar made Piper stop abruptly. In her early thirties, she had high cheekbones and gleaming raven hair cut in a bob. Dressed in a snug, jet black dress, long matching satin gloves, she wore a long rope of pearls around her neck and posed with an upward tilted, fourteen-inch ebony holder containing an unlit cigarette. She looked like a flapper out of a 1920s *Harper's Magazine*.

Piper was equally intrigued and unsettled by the woman's svelte femininity. Despite her best efforts, as Piper moved about the room, she could not peel her eyes off the stranger's face. A man to her left touched her arm lightly for some champagne. The glasses on her tray were empty and she needed to go downstairs again for more. The quiet animosity she felt toward the man surprised her.

When she returned, a handsome, young man in a caramel-coloured linen suit was talking to the beautiful woman. After serving the man his drink, Piper approached the couple.

"Sir, would you like some champagne?"

"Lovely." He looked Piper up and down as he took a glass off the tray. "I watched you in the other room earlier. You're very good at your job."

The woman remained frozen, her face a mask, the exaggerated cigarette holder pointed toward the ceiling as if she were a mime artist.

"Ma'am, some champagne?"

The woman's head turned instantly. Her liquid eyes fell to the tray. "Oh, why not," she said, in a cultured English accent. "It's pretty decent stuff." As she put the flute to her lips, she held Piper's gaze to the cusp of brazenness. An unexpected electric shock whipped through Piper.

"We own a private club in the West End," the man said. "We're always on the lookout for pretty waitresses."

Piper's instinct was to set the record straight and inform him this wasn't her regular job until she remembered her place in the pecking order and didn't speak.

"Don't you think she'd fit in nicely, Annabel?"

When the woman looked into her eyes again, another electric shock darted through Piper. It was bizarre. She needed to get away.

"You're very attractive in a pixie sort of way," the woman

said. "Our members would love you serving them drinks."

"Is my waitress disturbing you, Lady Annabel?" the manager said, as he approached.

"On the contrary, actually, we've been detaining her. You're awfully lucky to have her."

Attractive in a pixie sort of way. The woman's words circled in Piper's head as she went downstairs, simultaneously welcome and unwanted.

"Almost over," Todd said.

"I can't wait to get outta here."

Piper put her tray on the counter and looked at Todd. They'd been dating for nearly three months and he'd been patient.

"You wanna eat the leftovers at my place?" she said.

"Fine by me."

"You can… you can stay over too, if you like."

His eyes shot wide open. "For real?"

"I'm ready," she whispered in his ear.

"I thought you wanted to revise."

"I'm assuming that's a yes?"

Honey bunny, now

"That was awesome." He looked into her face for a few seconds before easing himself off her body. A trickle of sweat ran between her breasts. Propping his head up by his right arm, he looked at her lovingly. "Champagne, caviar and you."

"In that specific order?" she said, her mouth still dry from drinking the bottle of champagne Todd had smuggled out from the event.

"Was it for you as well, honey bunny?"

She wondered how many pet names were made post-coital. "It was good."

"Just good?" The Bambi stare transformed to one of concern. "What do I need to do to make it great next time?"

"It was great."

He smiled like a goofy teenager, reached out his hand and began to stroke her cheek with the backs of his fingers.

"I hadn't put you down as Mr. Insecurity."

"This is just so unexpected. I've wanted this for weeks. And then you just decide it's happening tonight. How come?"

"Is that a complaint?"

He moved to kiss her on the mouth. She offered the cheek.

"I need to get some shuteye," she said. "I've got to study. You, too."

"Let's cuddle."

"It's too hot."

"Aaw, come on honey bunny."

She relented. They lay in silence, the dusky orange light from the outside street lamp piercing the loose curtain weave. The adjacent yellow bookcase glowed and cast a sharp shadow over the bed.

"I like you a lot, Piper," he said, kissing the nape of her neck.

She didn't answer, just lay with her eyes wide open.

"You awake?"

"Against my will." She gave him a mock nudge with her elbow. "Go to sleep."

He pressed his naked body closer and cupped his hot hand over her left breast. A moment later, he put her nipple between his fingers and squeezed.

He cleared his throat. "I'm glad Danny's gone."

"Oh yeah?"

"I admit now I was jealous of him. He could be here with you and I couldn't." He kissed her neck again. She felt his penis stir against her leg.

Sliding her hand underneath the sheet, she pulled his hand away from her breast and moved to the other side of the bed.

Surprises

Two short cries emanated from Julia's room as he came out of his bedroom. Danny stopped and listened. There was another cry. He walked along the landing to her door and gently knocked. She didn't respond.

As he opened the door, he said, "Julia, is everything… "

"Don't come in!"

The harshness in her tone caused Danny to freeze with the door still ajar. He stared at his hand on the brass door handle until his muscles caught up with his brain and permitted him to obey the command. Halfway along the landing, he heard Julia talk aloud. It dawned on him what he'd heard. His face burned with mortification.

Ten minutes later, Julia came down dressed in her shabby robe. She was as unkempt as the house, tufts of her hair standing on end, waxy face and a love bite at the base of her neck.

"Did you make tea?" She headed toward the kitchen.

"Coffee."

"That'll do."

He watched from the sofa as she lit a cigarette, eased back her head and blew smoke at the kitchen ceiling. Upstairs, a door creaked open. A moment later, the bathroom door closed and was immediately followed by the metallic gurgle of the water pipes inside the wall of the kitchen.

"Sorry for bursting in on you," he said.

She peered over the top of the magazine. "No problemo."

She turned a page and reached out for her mug on the coffee table. As she did, the front of her robe parted and exposed her right breast. A chunky silver earring was attached to the nipple. She eased back and readjusted the robe.

Danny's eyes remained fixed on the spot where he imagined the ring.

She looked over and caught him staring. "What's the matter?"

"Nothing."

"You've seen a tit before, haven't you?"

"What's on it?"

Her lips curled into a sly smile. "It's a nipple ring." She laughed. "Clive got one and I liked it."

"Looks heavy. Isn't it painful?"

"It's great for sex." She arched one eyebrow rakishly. "You should get one. Lots of men get their nipples and dicks pierced these days."

Danny's scrotum crawled. He became aware of his shirt pressing against his nipples. Her overnight guest crossed the landing and started down the stairs. About to take a sip of coffee, Danny peered expectantly at the staircase. His coffee mug pinged hard against his front teeth as a woman, slender and petite, appeared at the doorway.

"Julia, you don't happen to have a spare toothbrush, do you?" She smiled at Danny.

As Julia introduced them, Danny rose automatically, shook her hand and sat again. A lull in the conversation occurred before Katie and he spoke simultaneously.

"You go first," Katie said.

"Would you like a coffee?"

"Lovely."

When he returned Julia and Katie were entwined on the sofa. Julia nibbled the woman's ear lobe. Their blatancy astonished him. He set the mug down quietly on the table and went to his room.

Bunting, as in bunting

Wide carrara marble steps, concaved in the higher trafficked areas by two centuries of visitors, swept up to the modern plate glass entrance doors of the *Kant-Institut* a three-storey former residence adjacent to a German art museum. Once inside, however, the sumptuous classical interior Danny expected had been sacrificed in favour of German practicality; a glittering chandelier in the foyer had been replaced with parallel rows of recessed lighting, the marble floor blanketed with tough industrial carpeting and the beautiful oak staircase was embellished with a garish fire red metal banister. A large sign in the middle of the foyer performed a triple function, greeting students, advising the whereabouts of the finance office and stating any course fee balances were to be paid on registration.

A friendly German woman helped him complete the enrollment documentation and told him to proceed to Classroom three on the second floor. When he got there, fourteen people, including two Chinese gentlemen and a woman in her sixties who looked like Dame Edna, but dressed in a business suit, were already seated at flimsy desks arranged in a semi-circle around a chalkboard and slide projector. Some students had fat dictionaries and notepads on their desks.

He spotted an empty desk next to a young woman on the other side of the room and started across. Her elbows were planted on the desk's surface and, as she read, she supported her face by pressing her fists against the sides of her cheeks.

"Is anyone... "

The woman jerked back abruptly. She lifted her hands with the palms facing out as if they were shields. Her right wrist was swathed in a bandage and she had a small cut in her forehead, just beneath the hairline.

"I didn't mean to startle you."

She lowered her hands again and the terrified expression softened to one of neutrality. "It's my fault. I never hear a thing when I'm reading."

A long slender neck ascended to an oval face housing a defined chin, straight perfect nose and intelligent eyes. Her hair was luxuriant and glossy, so glossy it sparkled in the overhead light as if dipped root to tip in a pot of varnish.

"I'm Danny Connolly."

"Nice to meet you." She began reading again.

Danny thought he heard a faint whimpering but couldn't tell where the sound came from.

"Is anyone sitting here?" He nodded at the vacant desk when she looked up.

"I... yes... no-one,"

He heard another whimper.

"Did you hear that?"

"Hear what?" She leaned quickly over to the far side of her desk and thrust her hand into a large bag at her feet.

"I didn't get your name," he said, when she sat up again.

She extended her slender hand. "Finty Bunting."

The hand was freezing to the touch. "Did you say 'bunting'?"

"Bunting, as in bunting."

Her tone sounded jaded, as if she'd heard the question many times. "I wasn't trying to be funny. It's just, I've never come across the name."

She smiled. "You said you're 'Connolly'?"

"Aha."

"That's Irish Catholic?"

He nodded.

"I met another Irish chap called Connolly a few years ago. "He was an inmate at the jail I used to work at."

Her remark implied he should know the man. Danny wondered if this was what the English always thought when they met an Irish person; whether Irish people with the same surname were related, whether all Irish Catholic were in the IRA or just sympathisers, and whether they would do them harm.

A tall man with a blonde-grey imperial moustache came into the room with a bundle of papers he set on top of the projector.

"Good morning, my name is Alfred Fehler," he said in a German accent, "I'm your teacher for this course."

His gaze moved from face to face, as if he were burning everyone's features into his memory. When he was finished, he muttered, "*Na schoen*" and began to discuss the course content. Next, he distributed the stack of papers that turned out to be vocabulary lists. The remainder of the lesson was dedicated to introductions, each student stating their name and discuss the extent of their knowledge of Germany and its culture. The next lesson ran consecutively. Halfway through, Finty excused herself to the teacher, picked up her oversized bag and hurriedly left the room. She returned ten minutes later.

"Would you like to go for coffee?" Danny asked, after the lesson had ended and they were making their way out to the street.

Hilary, the Dame Edna look-alike, came down the steps toward them. She spoke with the same BBC accent as Julia, was a Magistrate and lived in West London.

"I say, Herr Fehler covered a lot of ground this morning," she said. "I think we'll learn quickly if we apply ourselves."

"That's the general idea," Finty said.

The older woman peered over the top of her black-framed glasses, as if trying to decide whether Finty was being acerbic or witty. She half-turned toward Danny. "I took a Portuguese course a year ago. Damned tricky language." She brayed like a donkey. "Herr Fehler's supposed to be a baron, you know?"

Danny was skeptical.

"Anyway, must dash," she said.

He watched her stride down the street, her head held high and the sun making her lilac-rinsed hair very vivid. He turned back to Finty but she was already walking away.

When he arrived home late that afternoon Julia was stretched out on the sofa reading a romance novel, a genre he'd been surprised to discover she liked until he asked her about it and she explained she could polish them off in three to four hours. On the carpet between the sofa and coffee table was a hillock of newspapers and magazines.

"Hello," he said.

She didn't answer.

"I'm going to really enjoy the course."

There was still no response. On two occasions since he'd moved in, she'd behaved this coldly. The first time he'd been hurt, his hurt turning gradually to worry that he'd perhaps unknowingly offended her as the silence stretched. When he asked her about the churlish behaviour after she'd returned to her usual good spirits the following morning, she informed him she was like this occasionally and to just ignore her when it happened. Though he was getting used to the moods, he didn't like them because the atmosphere in the house was so thick and uncomfortable.

The coffee maker was still switched on, its carafe stained brown because the coffee had evaporated. The kitchen side was littered with the trimmings of raw chicken amid puddles of pinkish water. Nor had she cleaned up her breakfast or lunch dishes.

"I need to ask you something," she said, as she walked toward the kitchen, a menacing tone in her voice he'd never heard before.

"What?"

"You seemed disgusted when I introduced Katie to you."

"I don't know what you mean?"

"Don't insult me any further."

"I really don't know what you're talking about."

"How'd you describe your attitude?"

"I didn't have an attitude."

"You looked disgusted."

It crossed his mind she'd been too busy nibbling on her girl-friend's ear to have noticed his reaction. "You misread."

"Why'd you go to your room so quickly?"

He hesitated. "Okay, I was confused."

"About?"

Her absurd question rendered him momentarily speechless. "One day you urgently need the morning after pill, the next you're with a woman. That's confusing."

"I like men and women. What's so confusing?"

"Well, I don't like men that way."

"It's not contagious."

There was a flash of rust-red as a robin landed on the window ledge. It cocked its head and peered in with shiny, beady eyes.

"I was also shocked. Now please don't take offence... and I don't think it's a sin like I was brought up to believe as a Catholic. It's just I don't really understand homosexuality. I don't understand why Clive is attracted to another man. And I don't understand why a woman would like another woman. I never knew any gay people until you two."

"Gays don't go around wearing signs, you know?"

He looked at the sink full of dirty dishes. "Can I ask you something personal?" He took her silence for implied consent. "Are you a lesbian or bisexual?"

Julia pushed away from the wall and stepped down into the kitchen. She took a glass from an overhead cupboard, turned on the faucet and allowed the water to run for a moment before filling the glass. "I prefer women."

"So you're lesbian?" Articulated, the word sounded harsh. It was not a pretty word.

"It's more complicated. I have urges to be with men some-times." She laughed. "As you've already found out." She paused and her brow furrowed in thought. "I get more from a woman emotionally. With men, the sex is great, but overall it's unsatisfying." She shrugged. "Does that make me bisexual? Or a lesbian who fucks men? I've never really worried about labels."

"Do your family and friends know?"

"Yes, and some of my work colleagues as well."

He admired her courage and would have hugged her to show his acceptance, but it didn't feel appropriate. "I take it Katie's your girlfriend?"

"You could say that. She's married with kids, which makes it bloody tricky."

Danny kept his smile to conceal the horror of her revelation.

Julia set the glass down. "So I'll assume you have no problem with my sexuality."

"Live and let live as the man says."

"Good to hear because this woman says this is my home."

As she looked at him, Danny understood how immigrants coming to live illegally in London felt when they had the bad luck of Julia scrutinising them on arrival.

Smoking trains

Pat and the woman sitting beside him whom Danny had never met before were already there when he arrived. So were Sonia Berg and her boyfriend. He'd moved out only three weeks ago and already Piper's living room felt dowdy and cramped in comparison to Julia's spacious open plan design, though he missed her fastidious tidiness. No matter how often he led by example, hoovering the carpets, mopping the kitchen floor, dusting and washing the dishes when Julia was around, she made no attempt to muck in. It seemed as if she was oblivious to the dust and domestic chaos around her. Countless times, he'd had to ask her to hang her jackets and not air dry her tights and knickers on the backs of the dining room chairs. She never refused, even apologised sometimes, but after a few days she'd forget and the room would return to its depressingly cluttered state.

"Hey, Danny," Todd said. He rose off his chair and shook hands animatedly. "Great to see you again. Piper and I have been looking forward to having you over tonight."

His enthusiasm caught Danny off guard, though he concealed it by handing Piper the bottle of red wine he'd brought as a hostess gift.

"How's about ye', young fella," said Pat.

Danny nodded.

He placed his hand on the thigh of the woman seated beside him. "This is my girlfriend, Anne Marie."

"It is so good to see you again, Danny," Sonia said. She

pushed a pair of oversized turtle-shell spectacles up the bridge of her nose. "Last time we were all very influenced by the wine, I think." She chuckled as if recalling the dinner at Julia's when she'd done the crazy squat dance. "The German course goes good for you?"

"*Sehr gut, danke*," he said, and kissed her cheek. He turned to greet Jean-Pierre whose handshake was as tenuous as Todd's had been confident.

"Ah, you speak already German," Sonia said. "This is good."

"We've got red and white wine and beer," said Todd. "What'd you like?"

"Red wine'd be lovely."

"Comin' right up."

"I'll get it, Todd." Piper started toward the door.

"No, honey bunny," he said. "Todd's got it under control. You stay here and chat to our guests."

She smiled and handed Todd the bottle of wine Danny had brought. "Todd's a doll," she said, after he left the room. "I had an exam today so he did all the cooking."

"You are now Todd's honeyed rabbit," said Sonia, her eyes glinting mischievously. She turned to Jean-Pierre. "*Liebchen*, I would like it if you would find something nice like this for me."

Jean-Pierre took a swig of beer.

Sonia turned back to Piper. "You have progressed further in the relationship you are holding with Todd?"

The doctor's stiff sometimes comical way of expressing herself in English made Danny wonder if his German would also sound like that.

"Not quite getting what you're asking me, Sonia," Piper said.

The doctor cocked her head. "You have moved forward. Todd is living here, now?"

"No, he just spends more time here, is all."

Sonia winked at Danny.

"Did I hear somebody talking 'bout us?" Todd handed Danny a glass of wine.

"I was just telling people we're beginning to write our dissertations soon." Piper started toward the table. "Let's eat, folks."

Because he was from San Francisco and wanted the guests to sample that city's fare, Todd had baked sourdough bread, which Danny thought judging by its name alone would taste vile. It was one of the most delicious breads he'd ever tasted. Sonia was clearly of the same opinion, devouring three slices slathered in butter before the main course, fresh scallops that still tasted of the sea, and prawns in a pink vodka sauce over angel hair pasta. After dinner, Piper suggested they go to the living room. She put on a CD of baroque music while Todd fetched dessert.

"Your new house is pleasing to you?" Sonia said.

The dessert looked like wedges of a spongy apple cake they used to serve at Danny's old high school.

"I love living there," Danny said, as he took a plate of dessert.

"Julia is also wery pleased," Sonia said.

"How do you know?" Danny asked.

Piper assumed the lotus position in front of the television and began to eat.

"She said this was so at the gym," said Sonia.

"I didn't know she was working out," he said.

"It has been a long time for her." Sonia laughed. "During the buttock tightening exercise in the aerobics, she was puffing so hard like... oh, how you say the train that makes much smoking."

"A steam train," Piper said. "Jeez, what a visual."

"And Katie finds you handsome." Sonia winked at him slyly.

"You know about her girlfriend?"

"It is not so wery serious, I think. The woman has childrens and Julia is not so fond of childrens."

"Wow, it's all happening in Chumley Street," Todd said.

Sonia moved to the edge of her seat. "You do not approve, Danny?"

He looked about the room and saw everyone was watching him, Piper very intently.

"I don't care if Julia's involved with a woman, but it's not right for her to have an affair with a married woman with kids."

"What if Katie's relationship with her man is not satisfying?" Sonia asked.

"Sexual problems can be worked out, can't they?" Danny asked.

"Bad sex is not always the ground," Sonia said. "In Bonn, for example, I have counseled many womens who have all kinds of relationship problems with their mens. Sometimes the mens are too controlling. Sometimes it is the money. And yes, sometimes it is the sex."

"And I always thought it's only bad sex that destroys relationships," said Todd.

As Danny shifted in his seat, he saw Piper look at Todd with a peculiar expression on her face.

"Katie's responsibilities are to her children and Julia should tell her that," said Danny.

"I agree," said Pat.

"Women with women is dead disgustin'," said his girlfriend.

"Hey, anyone up for some more of Todd's awesome cobbler?" Piper asked. She sat beside Todd on the couch and began to run her fingers through his hair.

A man wearing a navy baseball cap stood on the bottom step leading up to Piper's front door when Danny left an hour later. The stranger turned around and started hurriedly down the street. There was something familiar about him but Danny couldn't remember where he'd seen the man before.

Danny started walking slowly. The man was now thirty feet away. He was tall, about six foot, with a neck as muscular as a rugby player's. A car engine started up ahead. The passenger door was flung open. The stranger ran across the street, climbed inside and the car swiftly pulled away from the kerb. Danny watched it speed down the street and turn the corner toward central London.

Only after he'd climbed into bed did it occur to him where he'd seen the stranger. An icy chill froze Danny to the bed and held him prisoner. He was the tourist, the man in the handsome denim shirt with the lion motif he'd seen that day at Saint Giles church and later again across the road near the house where Benjamin Franklin had lived. Was someone watching them?

Puppy *non grata*

It was a mewl, the same sound he'd heard five minutes earlier.
It was the same mewl he'd heard on the first day of class. Danny
looked around the room. No-one looked guilty. Nothing seemed
out of place. Most of the students were still focused on Hilary,
the rest staring at their textbooks. Finty was searching for something in her bag at the far side of her desk.

"Your sentence and pronunciation is good but 'table' is a
masculine noun in this case," Herr Fehler said. "It's *der Tisch*
not *das Tisch*."

"It's all so terribly complicated," Hilary said. She pushed a
wayward lock of lilac-coloured hair behind her ear. "It's an
object. How can a dining table be masculine or feminine?"

"You must not think this way," said Herr Fehler, toying with
his Prussian officer moustache.

Another mewl occurred, more plaintive this time.

"Who is making this hound noise, please?" Herr Fehler
asked.

Out of the corner of his eye, Danny saw sudden movement.
Finty gasped. A fluffy white ball of fur scampered out from the
left side of her desk.

"Rexie!" Finty lunged but missed.

The puppy raced into the middle of the room. It stopped
abruptly, squatted and began to piddle. A chorus of coos swept
around the classroom.

"Rexie, come here at *once*."

Finty moved slowly toward him but, like a precocious child, the puppy did not intend to surrender the limelight. He scampered, yapping underneath an empty desk. She scuttled over. Before she could reach him, he bolted to the next desk where he lay down behind the woman's crossed feet and peered out at her with big dark eyes.

"I'm so sorry, Herr Fehler." Finty wiped her forehead with the back of her hand as she squatted. "Come here." Her face began to flush.

Danny rose and went over to where he could see the puppy's black eyes peeking out at him. He assumed a position between the woman's desk and the adjacent one, knelt and attempted to coax him out by pretending he had a treat concealed in his outstretched fist. The woman, a dour executive at a private bank, tried to assist by gripping the sides of the desktop and raising her legs. Enjoying the game of hide and seek, the puppy broke for the next desk occupied by one of the Chinese Embassy employees.

Danny lunged and scooped him up, encasing his hands around the puppy's tight tummy. His coat smelt of shampoo and was silky to the touch, but the skin underneath was surprisingly elastic, as if already fully formed and just waiting for the puppy's body to catch up. Danny planted a kiss on his head before handing him over to Finty. Taking a tissue, he then cleaned up the puddle of urine.

"Class, we might as well learn the German for dog is *Hund*," said Herr Fehler. "Puppy is *Huendchen*. Now *Hund* is masculine which means the definite article is… "

"*Der*," the class called out.

"Exactly so."

Hilary sighed loudly.

Herr Fehler turned to Finty. "Your dog is very nice but he is also not allowed to come to class again."

"Shall I leave?"

"That would be fine."

She placed the pup carefully into her bag and left.

"Finty, wait for me," Danny called down the hallway.

She stopped and glanced over her shoulder. "Please go back. I don't want you to miss anything."

"It's nearly over and besides… " Danny nodded toward the tiny head peeking out at him from a corner of the bag. "We've learned a new word we're not supposed to know yet so I'm way ahead of the game."

She laughed.

Danny scratched the puppy's head.

"I can see you really like dogs," she said.

"Mine died when I was seventeen."

"I'm sorry."

"I was so upset Mum let me take the day off school. I even put my school tie around his neck before I buried him."

"That's sweet."

"I loved him."

They walked toward the stairs. "I had someone looking after him but she found a permanent job just as the course started. I don't like to leave him alone. He's only four months old."

When they got outside, Danny checked up and down both sides of the street to see if he was being followed again. He scanned the entrances to two side streets and a line of people standing at a bus stop. His eyes returned to an athletically built man standing beside a mailbox who seemed to be looking over. The man took a bundle of letters out of a satchel, dropped them into the box and walked away.

"Do you want to go for coffee today?" he asked.

"Somewhere nearby."

"And *Hund* friendly."

"Is something the matter?" she asked, as they started along the street.

"Why do you ask?"

"You keep looking over your shoulder."

"Habit. Sorry."

They found a coffee shop two streets south of the *Institut*. As it had rained while they were in class, it was hot inside and a sour odour of damp woolen clothing hung in the air. Over coffee at an unsteady table commanding a full view of the street, Danny talked about his family. He decided not to mention he'd had a fiancée. Finty explained she'd taken German for a year as a schoolgirl, that she'd paid for the course at the *Institut* two years ago when her work had been steady and she was flush with cash, but had had to drop out after the second week. Although she didn't say why.

Taking out an unfiltered cigarette and lighter from her jeans, she patted the puppy's head to calm him because he was growing restless. A silence arose. Danny grew uncomfortable when it began to stretch. He hated these awkward moments in the company of others and always felt tongue-tied. He tried to think of something interesting to say.

"What sort of work did you do at the prison?"

"I was still a psychology student and had to do field work as part of my course."

"So you counseled this Irish guy called Connolly?"

The waitress arrived with Danny's ham sandwich. Finty stopped talking until she left.

"We became friends eventually," she said. "I wasn't supposed to. It's considered unprofessional. But I liked Seamus. He had backbone. Took no shit from the prison officers." Her lips were full and he liked that she didn't wear lipstick. She opened them to permit the smoke to curl lazily from her mouth. "Poor guy was in for murder."

She'd said the word 'murder' so casually. He'd never known anyone who'd killed another human being. Danny looked instantly about the café. No-one had heard.

"He killed a cop."

The crash of breaking crockery rushed from the kitchen. The café went quiet. People turned to look at the swing door leading to the kitchen.

"Whatever she broke'll be deducted from her wages."

"Is that what happens?"

She nodded at the window. "You're doing it again."

"What?"

"You've checked outside at least six times and you look at the door every time somebody comes in."

"I wasn't aware."

She took a long pull of her cigarette. "Seamus got me in a lot of trouble with the authorities." The puppy began to whine. "Quiet, Rexie." She looked about the café. "He asked me to do things for him and I wasn't experienced enough to realise I was being used."

"What kind of things?"

"I smuggled in a penknife for him." She didn't speak for a moment and looked past Danny's face, her gaze suddenly introspective. "He was dead artistic. Some of these IRA men make fantastic Celtic crosses out of mahogany. He gave me one." She took another drag and allowed the smoke to curl from her mouth. "I also smuggled letters out for him and got caught when the prison authorities did a spot check on all personnel. Special Branch got involved. It was a bloody nightmare." She shivered. "In the end, they realised I hadn't meant anything and let me go."

The puppy mewled again. Opening the lid of his sandwich, Danny took out the thin slice of ham and looked about the café. "He might be hungry."

A look of intense horror crossed her face. "Don't! Rexie's vegetarian."

Nanny's mistake

Traffic on the A3 had been light and she'd made excellent time. Sonia Berg's advice to drink bitters before retiring to bed had been sound. Though she still had a hangover, its effects were negligible, reduced to a slight headache that bothered her only when she flitted her eyes too quickly. Her spirits had improved throughout the drive too, partly on account of the magnificent beauty of the Surrey countryside and partly because she'd managed to expunge the residue of guilt about leaving the house in such an untidy state for Danny. He was a good sport about it, but still it wasn't right. Julia resolved to change her ways. She just hadn't had time the previous night. Sonia had stayed very late. Then Katie rang just as she'd been about to start the washing up, to invite her down for the weekend because her husband Harry was going off to scout locations in the north of England for a production of *Wuthering Heights*. Before Julia realised it, they'd been chatting for over an hour.

She turned into a gravel driveway flanked on one side by a high hawthorn hedgerow and white paddock fencing on the other. Three sleek horses and Charlotte's piebald pony stood within the shade of the weathered barn. As she rounded the driveway's only turn, she held her breath and strained to see if Harry's Range Rover was parked in the yard. She didn't expect to see it but caution was always wise. With the car's absence she could breathe normally again.

"Aunt Julia, you're here," Charlotte cried, as Julia entered the kitchen.

She was sitting at the table on top of which was a wicker picnic hamper. Her brother Rupert was seated directly across from her, the pair of them sipping homemade lemonade through fat straws the colour of peppermint. Tresses of platinum blonde hair framed Charlotte's cherubic face. Rupert didn't greet her, just watched without blinking as he sipped.

Every time she first saw the children on these visits, Julia experienced an unsettling feeling, the feeling she was equally licensed and illegally on their property. She couldn't shake it. Katie told the children to call her 'Aunt' despite Julia's mild protestations. Rupert never did. At eight, he was as sharp as Julia had been at his age, undoubtedly figuring out there was no blood relationship and therefore no reason to indulge his mother's ridiculous fantasy.

"Where's your Mummy?" Julia said, as she set her overnight case by the door leading to the hallway.

"Upstairs," said Rupert. He sucked the last of his lemonade.

"She's searching for our pretty red and white tablecloth," Charlotte added.

Julia nodded at Mrs. Ratcliffe, a local woman who came in daily to do light housework and mind the children. "I'm Julia, a friend of the family."

"Pleased, I'm sure," she said, though her face didn't reflect it. She turned back to the sink and began to scrub the cooking pot with increased vigour.

Katie came into the kitchen carrying a folded tablecloth. "What great timing. I was about to take the children to the river."

Wearing tight, cut-off denim shorts and a royal-blue top, her nipples jutting beneath the thin cotton, Julia had an urge to kiss her wide sensuous mouth. Every time she saw Katie, it constantly astonished her that such a petite, fragile-boned woman could be so passionate and demanding in bed. Of course, it bothered Julia that Katie might be just as demanding, just as energetic, with her husband, but she tried not to think about that.

"Sally, would you take my friend's things up to her room, please?" Katie said.

While the woman had been in the family's employ for years, Katie told Julia she knew nothing of her affairs with women because she was very discreet in her presence.

"Certainly, Mrs. Bennett." She began to dry her hands on her apron.

The most direct route to the river skirted the old barn. When they reached it, Charlotte's insisted on petting her pony. Julia and Katie set the basket down. While they waited, Katie's mobile rang.

"Annabel, marvelous to hear from you," she said, and then walked away toward the barn's main entrance door.

Her voice lowered. Charlotte called Julia to come and feed the pony with clumps of grass. She reluctantly obliged, immediately disliking the waxy feel of its facial hair on her fingers. Its teeth were enormous. She whisked away her fingers every time the pony's muzzle jerked upward. She strained to overhear Katie's conversation but only heard fragments because of Charlotte's prattling.

The call ended and Katie rejoined Julia. "Charlotte, that's enough. Come along, darling."

Julia and Katie picked up the picnic hamper and began to walk towards a stile that led to a gently sloping meadow with a copse of oaks and thick undergrowth in its middle.

Unable to contain her curiosity while at the same time hating the urgent need to know, Julia asked who'd called and was told it was an old school friend.

"We were really close."

Julia pondered. "Close, as in… "

"Exactly."

They climbed over the stile and walked into the meadow. The grass was interspersed with fragrant clover and daisies and felt springy underfoot. The sensation evoked a hazy memory of being in a similar field with her father when he took Julia bird watching in the countryside as a girl. A sudden rush of elation at being among nature engulfed Julia and she pushed the petty jealousy out of her mind.

As they drew near a copse of oaks, four Jersey cows sheltering from the hot afternoon sun walked out in single file from a clearing. Moments later, a massive rust-coloured bull emerged. Its hair was beautifully curly. The beast stopped. His ears flicked back and forth. He stopped chewing and watched the party advance with what Julia was certain was an irritated air. She stopped abruptly, causing Katie to lose her grip on the handle of the picnic hamper. It fell lopsided and a plate of sandwiches wrapped in cellophane and an assortment of oranges, pears and apples tumbled onto the grass. The bull jerked his monstrous head up and down. The thick brass nose ring glinted in the sunlight. He snorted, the reverberation filling the distance between Julia and him, and then he started to advance.

Julia let go of the hamper and began to walk briskly toward the stile, frequently peering over her shoulder as she made her way. The bull began to canter. Shrieking now, Julia started to run. Katie and the children didn't move.

"JULIA, STOP RUNNING," Katie called. "Bruno's friendly. He's testing you."

"Aunt Julia, don't be scared," Charlotte said.

She heard Rupert's high-pitched laughter, looked over her shoulder again and saw Katie, still clutching Charlotte's hand, shooing the bull away. It turned around and began to walk back to rejoin the herd of bemused cows. Rupert sprinted toward her.

"It's all right," he said, and held out his hand for her to take. It felt clammy, just as a little boy's hands would feel. "I'll guard you. You're safe now."

Katie burst out laughing as they walked up to her.

"How was I supposed to know he wasn't dangerous?" Julia said. "It's not *that* funny."

"It's very funny," said Katie.

"I don't understand animals like you country people do."

"You run really well, doesn't she, Rupert?"

He made an attempt not to giggle. The shock having passed, Julia was unable to quash her own smile. It blossomed into a chuckle and then outright laughter, which the others interpreted as an open invitation to join her.

"It's so beautiful here." Julia lay beside Katie, her mind suspended between the alcohol buzz and lull of the trickling water.

Katie squeezed her arm gently.

Julia finished her Pimm's, immersed her thumb and fore-finger into the glass and fished out a slice of apple which she popped into her mouth. Stalks of tender grass pressed pleasur-ably against the back of her neck. She set down her glass and began to lazily explore a dock leaf, sliding the pads of her fingers first along the glossy surface and then its rougher under-side. Nearby, a bumblebee moved about a clover flower collecting pollen. Further away, she could hear Charlotte calling to her brother as they played hide and seek within the ash thicket near the riverbank.

They stroked one another's forearms for a while and then clasped hands and squeezed tightly. Charlotte finished a twenty count.

"It'd be hard for me to live here like you do, Katie. The quiet's a pro and a con."

"The children love it here... and so does Harry." She took a deep breath. "As you've found out, he likes to play gentleman farmer."

Julia lifted her head slightly, squinted and peered up at the sun. "I'm a city girl. Through and through."

"I could live in town again, just not now. Maybe when the

children go off to boarding school."

She pondered her lover's words. "Does Harry know you're planning to pack them off to boarding school?"

"We make these decisions together." Katie fell quiet for a moment, then squeezed Julia's arm. "Did you bring the cuffs, darling?"

"Aha."

"And the rope?"

"You are so bloody kinky." Julia rolled on her side and propped herself up with an elbow. "Are all suburban house-wives like this or is it just you?"

Katie giggled.

Leaning over, Julia kissed her fully on the mouth. The wide plump lips were velvet and yielding. She drew back and peered down at her lover whose hair was fanned about her head like a splayed peacock tail. Katie raised her arm, cupped her hand around the back of Julia's neck and pulled her down toward her again. They kissed more urgently.

Julia heard the gasp before comprehending what it was she'd actually heard. She sat up instantly. Rupert stood in the gap between an alley of brambles, his eyes enormous, right hand clamped against his mouth. Instantly, Katie pushed her aside like an unwanted toy.

"Where... where's your sister?" she asked.

"Mummy, why are you *kissing* her?"

"We weren't kissing, darling."

"You were."

"Something bit me and Julia was sucking the sting out."

"You were kissing like Daddy kisses you."

Julia couldn't help bristling.

"Where's Charlotte?" Katie said.

"She's looking for me."

"Fetch her at once. We're going home. I need to tend to my lip."

He made no attempt to move, just stared at them sullenly.

"Do as I say, Rupert. *Now*."

He turned and sprinted through the shrubbery. While they waited, they frantically discussed the options. Julia thought Katie needed to be honest, but also state it'd been for a lark. Katie disagreed.

"He's clearly upset," Julia said.

"Ironic, isn't it?"

"What do you mean?"

"When he's a man, he'll fantasise about two women kissing. All men do."

The children appeared around the bend in the river.

As they wended their way across the meadow, Charlotte, who'd run ahead to be with her pony, stopped and called to them her father was home.

"Don't be silly," Katie called. "He's not back till Sunday."

"She's right, Mum," said Rupert, his high-pitched voice too dangerously animated for Julia's comfort. "His car's parked beside *hers*." He tossed Julia an evil glance.

Shading her eyes with her hand, Julia looked over to where she'd parked. Something glinted above her car's roof, but it was too blurry and formless to determine if it was the Range Rover.

"Oh, Daddy is home," Katie said, after they got to the stile.

Julia and Katie traded glances.

When they reached the paddock gate leading to the lawn, the kitchen door opened and a man stepped out. He waved as he walked toward them.

Charlotte yelled excitedly and ran to her father. He scooped her up in his arms and kissed her.

Over six-foot tall with artistically unkempt hair, tanned forearms protruding from the rolled up sleeves of his faded denim shirt and sporting a thick, highly polished wedding ring on his finger, he was precisely what Julia imagined a television director should look like. He was also at least ten years older than his wife. But neither his age nor the ludicrous idea of someone so tall making love to Katie was what surprised her most. What surprised her most was his unclipped salt-and-pepper beard. She'd always assumed Katie disliked body hair. She'd once complained about Julia's unshaved underarms when she'd put on a sleeveless T-shirt.

"Aunt Julia's afraid of the bull, Daddy," Charlotte said. "Isn't that right, Rupert?"

Her brother didn't answer. His eyes darted from his mother to Julia.

"We meet at last, Aunt Julia," said Harry.

"We do," she said.

"Dad, I saw something very naughty," Rupert said. He shot his mother a sly look.

"Rupert, Charlotte, go to your rooms and wash your hands," Katie said.

"What naughty thing did your brother see, Poppet?" her husband asked.

"Julia ran away from the bull," Katie said. She glared at her son. "Isn't that so?"

"Yes, but… "

"And you were very brave and came to my rescue," said Julia.

"Well done, sport," his father said. "Helping the ladies, eh? That's my boy."

"Rupert, Mummy wants you and your sister to wash your hands and arms right away," Katie said. "There's nightshade where you were playing. If you touched it, your skin will blister."

"Both of you go and wash up," said Harry, as he put Charlotte down.

"Did something happen?" Katie asked her husband.

"We've postponed until early next week. I called your mobile."

"I didn't have it switched on."

"I also called here and left a message with Mrs. Ratcliffe." Harry smiled at Julia. "I was beginning to think you were a figment of my children's imagination. You're only ever here when I'm not."

"Julia's staying for a few days."

"I know." He turned to Julia. "Mrs. Ratcliffe put your things into our bedroom by mistake."

Amorphous shapes

The girl seated diagonally across from her began to pack her books, photocopies and pens into the clear plastic bag all the students brought with them to the library. When she'd first started at the university and learned she was forbidden to bring her backpack and snacks into the library, Piper had been blown away. Back in the States, college libraries were social centres, places where you gathered to chat with friends as well as do research. Here students had to suffer the huge inconvenience of checking their belongings into a locker that lay underground. Way underground. The basis for the crazy rule was just another one of a score of cultural habits and customs the Americans had to master when living on this side of the pond. Another was trying to figure out the rules of British politeness.

Piper looked at the clock on the wall above the librarian's desk. The afternoon revision session had passed quickly. Arriving at the library at ten-thirty that morning determined to catch up with reading for her final exam, she'd read large chunks from books kept at Course Collection and made lots of notes. By lunchtime, she was so pleased with her progress she agreed to go to a nearby café on Kingsway with Todd where she drank two cups of espresso, hoping the caffeine would focus her concentration for the next three hours after her return to the library.

Only a handful of articles remained unread and she wondered if she should track them down and at least skim through them to ease her conscience before setting out for Todd's apartment. As she deliberated, she caught the delicious tang of banana from somewhere nearby, evidence that a student was breaking another regulation in some hidden nook. Feeling hungry now, she decided to leave.

It was raining when she got outside, one of those early summer rains with heavy drops that refreshed as they smacked into her face and bare arms. Not having brought an umbrella, her muslin blouse was soaked through and clung to her shoulders and chest by the time she reached Todd's flat. His eyes zoomed in on her breasts like a heat-seeking missile.

"Stop checking me out, pervert."

"Me? Not guilty."

"Are too, perv." While intended as a joke, Piper realised it had come out a little too harsh.

He stepped aside to let her in. "I suppose this perv had better fetch you a sweater then."

He disappeared down the short hallway to his room and returned with his sky-blue Berkeley jumper that he gave to her. She dried off in his tiny bathroom and hung her blouse on an ice-cold radiator. A glass of red wine on a side-table sparkled in the soft glow of a lamp when she returned to the living room. Todd was cooking in the kitchenette. The aroma of soy sauce wafted toward her. Approaching the gas stove, she picked up a morsel of chicken and blew on it before popping it into her mouth. "Yum."

After dinner, they went directly to his bedroom where they sprawled on his double bed and began to study. Piper wanted a third glass of wine badly, but knew she couldn't. It didn't take much alcohol to fog her concentration. She peeked over at Todd prone on the bed, a full glass of wine on his bedside table.

"How can you drink wine and still cram?"

"Shush."

"But doesn't it... ?"

"Hello! Trying to work here."

"That's it," she said, a few minutes after ten o'clock. She slammed her notebook shut.

Todd gathered his notes and set them on the bedside table, stretched out and yawned. He rolled over on his side and looked at her. "Come here, magpie."

Piper ran her fingers through her hair self-consciously. "I hate it when you talk about my bad dye job."

"It's nearly grown out. Come here."

She sidled over and they kissed. Quick as a flicked whip, Todd pushed her gently onto her back and climbed on top. Piper's instinct was to push him off but instead she closed her eyes. He removed his glasses and laid them on his heap of study notes on the bedside table. They kissed again. His lips left hers and she felt the tip of his tongue trace along her neck. She let out a little moan. She wasn't sure why. He thrust his tongue into her mouth. His breath grew laboured. He began tugging at her clothes. She assisted him, arching her torso off the bed and lifting up her arms so he could peel off her jumper. He fell down on her and began to suck her breasts, commuting back and forth between them.

Moments later, he leapt off the bed and tore off his clothes. She rose also, took off her jeans and panties and fell back naked on the bed. His tongue flicked over her body, licking her cheek and down the right side of her neck. He sucked on one of her breasts while firmly kneading the other. His mouth left her breast and he zigzagged his wet tongue down her tummy. It dipped into the shallow well of her belly button as his hand gently pried open her legs. His mouth moved again and she felt his hot breath against her skin, and then his tongue was inside her. Piper experienced a strong urge to stop him but she resisted. Why did she always feel this way? Why could she not relax? She shut her eyes tighter and tighter until a roaring started up inside her ears. It sounded like the sea crashing against rocks. Loud and furious and sinister. Amorphous yellow, blue and black shapes smashed against the backs of her eyelids. Todd stopped probing abruptly, slid back up the bed and turned himself awkwardly upside down so his rigid cock was fully in her line of vision.

"I... I can't do that."

"Aw, please, hon."

"I don't give blow jobs. Sorry."

"I did it to you."

"I didn't ask." Piper wondered why she drew the line at fellatio. Was it to do with perceived submission or a warped sense of feminism? She didn't know. In any event, it didn't matter. "I can't, Todd."

"Hey, no problem." He righted himself and climbed on top of her. "I'm sorry."

"It's fine. Another time, okay?"

She didn't reply. He kissed her and pushed his tongue deep inside her mouth. A moment later, he was reaching inside his bedside table drawer for the condoms he stored there, at the same time pushing apart her legs to signal what he now wanted. It was as if there'd been no rejection. Piper wondered how men could be so different to women in this regard, how they could move so easily from one kind of sex to the next. Was it something they learned in boyhood? As she relaxed her body to accept him, she hoped it would be different this time.

After he began thrusting, she closed her eyes tightly and willed herself to enjoy the experience. The amorphous shapes loomed again. Big and yellow. She felt his every thrust and withdrawal. It was neither pleasurable nor uncomfortable. She was just not engaged. The bed springs creaked. She dug her heels into the bed and began to grind against him.

Moments later, she found herself wishing it was over. She began to consider her excellent day's work at the library, the notes awaiting attention on her desk at home and how it all might be tackled. She saw herself seated in a lecture theatre. The face of one of her lecturers rushed forth, swiftly followed by another. A change in his breathing brought her back to him, but it didn't last. The stir-fry he'd cooked came to mind next. Piper wondered why Chinese food was always so quickly eaten, why MSG made her mouth so dry? She'd have cooked it differently to Todd, with a dash more soy sauce and lots of fresh ginger. Definitely lots of fresh ginger.

Todd began to breathe heavily. It would soon be over. She moaned, not too loudly in case he became suspicious. Moans always sped things along at this point. She emitted another tiny moan two seconds later, followed by two thrashes of the sides of her head against the pillow. The bedsprings began to creak satisfactorily loud. He gasped. She let out a throaty moan, followed by some rapid panting.

"I'm gonna come," he said.

She let loose a storm of high-pitched moans, backed up with head thrashes and finally dug her nails into his back. All she could think of was his sweaty chest against her skin. She didn't move a muscle.

"That was fantastic, hon," he said.

"Sure was."

He rolled onto his back, reached over and began to twist a lock of her hair between his fingers. They lay in silence, she listening to the tick-tock of the clock. She counted one minute, another and then another. After five minutes, she eased away from him to the side of the bed, swung her feet to the floor and began to dress.

"Where you goin', honey?"

"Home." She lifted her right foot and forced on the sock.

"Aw, spend the night."

"Can't. My notes are at home."

News from home

Subject: Hi
From: Philomenaharris234@aol.com
To: PIPERalways@aol.com

Hey Phila,
  Hope this finds you well and your course is going fine. Been a while, but then I don't hear from you either. Have you decided what kind of job you want after you're through with college? I hope it'll be something useful connected to your diploma and that you're really over the writing kick you were on a while back because I met some folks in publishing recently and they told me the majority of book authors make no money.
  BTW, I'm working at a law firm now. It's banking and securities law with a bit of white-collar stuff like DUI thrown in, but only for existing clients. They like my research skills and said they'll pay for law school because I got accepted to Fordham. My LSAT score was 180. Columbia accepted me, too. Yeah, Columbia!
  I've been seeing a guy called Juan. In fact, we've been living together for a while now. He's Puerto Rican and also a cop, which I know will annoy the shit out of your father. He hated it when the NYPD changed their height requirement so minorities could qualify. Juan's recently made detective and works at the Port Authority. We're getting married end of August so I've filed for divorce. I know what you're

thinking. Well, it doesn't matter how long you know someone in my book. Juan makes me real happy. I haven't felt this good since before Rory died. You know, I visit Rory's grave every month. When I'm with him, I pray for you, too. He was a special little guy, and smart, and I know he'd have made something of himself if he'd been given the chance. But he didn't get the chance, did he?

Your father will be all bent out of shape. He needs to get real. Separation doesn't work anymore. Our marriage wasn't good for years. I'm sure you can relate to what I'm saying because Rory and you couldn't stand all the arguing. Especially Rory.

Juan wants to meet you. If you're gonna be stateside this summer, I'd like you to be a bridesmaid or at least come to the wedding. It's not going to be a church affair. Been there, done that, got the T-shirt! We're exchanging personalised vows in the Conservatory Garden at Central Park and then we'll have the party at Juan's sister's home. She's married to some rich corporate guy and they own a brownstone on the Upper West Side.

I'd love someone from my side to be there. Nana Rose isn't coming. What a surprise, huh? I know it's because Juan is Hispanic. It's got nothing to do with her not believing in divorce.

So Phila, please call or email and let me know if you'll come. If you decide to be a bridesmaid, we'll need to get together and go shopping for dresses, etc.

That's it for now.

Love,

Mom

Piper set the print out down and went upstairs, almost wishing she hadn't checked her email account. She lay on the bed, curled into a fetal position with her eyes open wide and visualised her mother standing alone at the graveside, the polished black headstone with Rory's photo and short life span etched in gold leaf at its centre. In the dusk, the whites of her brother's eyes glowed in the photograph on her bedside table.

She recalled that December evening her mother, brother and she had gone into the city so he could see the tree at the Rockefeller Center. Afterwards, they'd gone to see the *Rockettes* Christmas Show at Radio City Music Hall. Her brother's hand clung tightly to hers as he eased back his head to take in the art décor splendour of the Hall's interior.

"Mom, how can they make their legs lift so high?" he said.

"Shush, hon," her mother said. She looked over his head at Piper and smiled. "We mustn't spoil the show for the other people."

But it was the nativity scene that blew him away. When he saw the camels led by the three kings walk across the stage, he'd jumped off his seat and stood rigid, his hands gripping the top of the seat in front of him.

"Wow," he said. "Wow." And then he turned unexpectedly in the midst of his huge joy and searched deep into Piper's eyes to see if she was equally enthralled. The sacred connection between them had been over in a flash, but everything innocent and beautiful in her brother had been seared forever into her brain. Moments later, like the impish boy he was, he laughed raucously when one of the donkeys urinated on the stage.

Tears coursed down Piper's cheek. In jer thoughts she was catapulted now to her old home in Hempstead. She felt the wall of heat searing her face as she turned and ran out the front door, felt the cat's stiff body against her chest.

She took the photograph of her brother and traced the outline of his skinny body with her fingertip. Impulsively, she kissed the surface of the glass above his happy face. She placed the frame on her cheek. It felt cold against her skin. Drawing the frame close to her chest now, she lay in the dusk with her eyes wide open. Seeing and not seeing.

Staying the course

Agnes watched Keith pick a photograph off the table, the one of him as a child on his father's shoulders. He turned the frame around and inspected its black velveteen back.

"That was taken in Blackpool," she said. "You were two then."

"You've told me the story, Ma."

A wiry chap in his mid-thirties with a long neck and shallow chin, her son put the photograph back on the table.

"Put it back exactly where it belongs next to the one of your father holding the marrow. And you should be glad to hear my stories because the day's soon coming when I won't be around. *Then* you'll be sorry."

"It can't be healthy having this shrine in your living room."

"It's *not* a shrine." She paused. "You still think about your father, don't you?"

"Of course I do... just not all the time. He's nearly gone a year... "

"Are you coming to visit him on his anniversary?"

His momentary silence was answer enough. "Ma, you need to get on with your life. Dad would want that."

Agnes ignored him, eased back the net curtain and peered out. "There she comes with that Irishman. She's... "

"You need to stop watching her, Ma. Let it go."

"That's not what you said when she came to live here."

"It's over." He crossed to the window.

"She's a slag. Blimey, you should see how many… "

"Stop, Ma."

It was always like this on the final day of her son's visits. What was playing out was just a part of the essential ritual. There were his bed linens, the lightweight ones now because it was mid June. They were waiting for her. She'd go upstairs after he left, bury her face in them and inhale his scent. She could never let him know she didn't wash his pillowcases for two weeks after these visits. It calmed her.

Another part of the ritual was the argument they were now having, an argument always beginning with his criticising her for displaying so many photographs and calling it a shrine. And now she'd ask the question to maintain the status quo.

"You wouldn't have left to go live in Barnsley if she hadn't got the house, would you?" She turned away from the window to scrutinise his expression.

He tut-tutted. "You know that's the case, but it's all… "

Status quo maintained, Agnes said, "Things can change. You just never know, do you?"

All's forgiven

Having got a first in his business degree, Danny knew how to work hard. He was also very disciplined and used the same approach to tackle German. Now a month into the course, he was pleased with his progress. Having internalised both the vocabulary contained in the lists distributed by the teacher as well as additional words he took upon himself to learn, he was already able to converse in grammatically perfect but simple sentences. He could talk about food and describe his fellow students eye and hair colours. A few other students could also form perfect sentences, including Finty who'd studied basic German, Hilary now receiving extra tuition from Herr Fehler and the two Chinese students.

Learning German wasn't the only reason Danny looked forward to classes at the *Institut*. On those afternoons when she didn't leave immediately after class to fetch her puppy from the sitter or work a shift at the juvenile detention center where she was employed part-time, Danny and Finty went for coffee. Or they'd have lunch in a nearby pub, though her menu selections were always confined to lackluster garden salads or overly spicy vegetarian chili.

Danny had also invited her to his home twice so they could study together for class tests. She'd come but vexed him by never reciprocating and asking him to visit her flat in Elephant & Castle.

The answering machine was blinking when he returned home. Two telemarketing messages preceded a call from his mother saying she'd been 'working subtly on his father' and felt she was 'making progress' because he'd asked about Danny for the first time since he'd left for London. Another telemarketing call preceded a call from Julia. His face tightened as he listened to her insincere apology about leaving the place in such a mess for him to clean up that morning. She'd overslept.

"Danny, hello," the next message began. "I hope all's well. I bet this'll be a surprise… " A peal of high-pitched giggling ensued. He'd never liked the way Susan laughed. "God, I hate talking to machines. Where are you?" There was a silence, as if she expected him to pick up. "At class, I suppose. You'll never guess, but I bumped into your father the other day completely out of the blue. He told me you're doing well. He's looking forward to having you back in September." The line crackled for a moment and she breathed heavily into the receiver. "And so am I. Listen Danny, I've been thinking about you… about us a lot." Another pause. "I'm missing you very much. I didn't mean it when I said I never wanted to see you again. I was just so angry. But I forgive you." She sighed. "I'm okay about the postponement now. It's taken until now, but I fully understand. You were right when you said time would pass quickly. It's going so fast. I was silly, I suppose." There was another silence. "I wish you were home. I really hate talking to this damned machine. Anyway Danny, I want you to know I'd taken off my engagement ring because I was so mad at you. But I'm wearing it again. I'm looking at it right now in fact. It's gorgeous. Nothing's changed. Don't think my family still hates you, either. Daddy's been feeling ill recently. We don't know what's wrong with him. It's a pain around his heart. We're hoping it's just a bit of indigestion. He's fair going through the anti-acids, I can tell you. Gosh, I hope your machine's recording still." He could hear some background chatter, and then she said, "No, he's not at home, Mammy. I have no idea. Probably at his

German class." Susan's voice grew loud again. "Mammy told me to say hello. Danny, please call me. We need to talk. I love you. I can't wait till you come home and we can get married. Bye."

He checked his watch. It was quarter past eight. She'd most likely be at home. He fetched a beer from the fridge and returned to the dining table. He picked up the receiver and started to dial.

A call to arms

The discarded summer jackets thrown over the back of the sofa, the towers of CDs on the floor next to the stereo, the curdled cold tea in the mugs on the dining room and coffee tables, the grimy bathroom, all of it screamed disrespect. And cleaning up after Julia made him feel like her skivvy. At first, he hadn't really noticed, or more truthfully avoided noticing. He'd been settling in, wanting to make a good impression, wanting them to be friends. When Julia told him she'd broken up with Katie after her husband discovered their affair, the untidiness worsened but he hadn't made a fuss. He'd felt sorry for her. But no more. What he needed now were permanent changes. He hadn't broken away from his father to become a lesbian English woman's patsy.

When he heard the key inserted in the front door, he lowered the television volume and picked up a magazine. He peered at her under his eyes as she entered.

"I've had one hell of a shit day, my dear," she said. She set her briefcase by the foot of the stairs, took off her jacket and tossed it on the back of the sofa. Her eyes skipped over the CD piles before darting to the kitchen where the sink was still full of dirty dishes.

"Oh," she said, a puzzled expression on her face.

"Yes?"

She didn't answer and sat on the armchair. "I thought today would never end."

"So you said."

"I had to detain three illegal Jamaicans and process them for deportation."

He didn't speak.

She eased her legs up on the coffee table. "I'd love a cuppa if you're making."

"I'm not."

She met his eye. "Is something wrong?"

"I need to talk to you."

"I'm sorry about the mess."

"I'm doing all the work, Julia." His voice sounded quivery. "It's not on."

She swung her feet on the floor. "Why don't I make us a lovely cup of tea?"

"Tea won't fix it. We need to discuss this."

"What's to discuss? It'll not happen again."

"You always say that."

"Now's not a good time." She looked at him soulfully. "Really."

"Yes, now." His resolve amazed him.

"You're being inconsiderate, Danny." She pushed her head back on the chair and closed her eyes as if to convey the depth of her exhaustion.

"I'm tired of living in a sty. The bathroom's crap. I'm tired of doing all the hoovering."

Her eyelids popped open and she looked up at the ceiling without blinking. The fridge started up with a shudder, followed moments later by the phone ringing. He made no attempt to answer it like he always did.

"Aren't you going to get that?" he asked.

"It's probably Katie calling again and I don't want to talk to her. We're done."

Both of them waited for the answering machine to pick up, which it did after the fourth ring. It was his fiancée to say she was shocked she hadn't heard from him.

"You haven't told her yet?" Julia asked.

"Are we going to discuss who cleans where in this house?"

Her neck turned the colour of claret. She laid a hand on the armchair rest and began to drum. "I'm not the tidiest person in the world. I admit that. But I'm *not* dirty and I resent the accusation. If you're not happy here, you should leave."

Her gallop to sanctions stunned Danny. Rational, assertive people discussed problems and devised with solutions.

"You've misunderstood me, Julia. I'm not calling you dirty."

Her mouth became a grim line. "We're not working out. You need to go."

Her invitation to leave was now a requirement. He was homeless. It was Sunday. He'd have to find a hotel. First, he had to pack, then ring to find an available hotel and finally move his belongings. It would take hours. Danny sprang from the sofa and went to the bottom of the stairs.

"Your ad read 'immaculate condition'. That was fraudulent."

"So sue me."

"I should."

"We're not in a relationship, you know?"

"True. I don't have breasts."

"Get out of my house, you fucking Paddy."

Her insult was worse than a slap in the face. He mounted the stairs two at a time and went into his room, taking care to slam the door behind him. A picture fell off the wall on the landing. Sitting on the edge of the bed, he stared out the picture window at the darkening sky above the rooftops.

Five minutes later, he heard her coming up the stairs. He rose, seized a suitcase from the top of the closet and began to hurl T-shirts into it. She passed by without hesitating.

"Bitch," he muttered.

He snatched a shirt from the wardrobe, laid it on the bed and started to fold it. The shoulders wouldn't line up symmetrically. Every attempt was deformed. He tossed it into the case and fetched another shirt.

He'd progressed to trousers when he heard her come out of her bedroom. She walked across the creaky landing, came down the three stairs and stopped at his door. A silence preceded two quick raps.

"Can I come in?"

He made her wait five seconds. "Enter."

The door opened and she peered inside. Her puffy eyes darted from the open suitcase to the elephant cord trousers he was folding. "You don't have to leave."

Her tone was a hybrid of empathy and control. He placed the trousers in his suitcase and took a pair of chinos from the wardrobe, holding them by their bottoms and shaking them until the sharp creases aligned.

"Until the next row?"

"I shouldn't have insulted you. I apologise. It was unwarranted." Her lips twitched. "I've also taken you for granted."

How often he wished to hear these words from his father. Danny tossed her a bone, laying the folded chinos on the bed rather than putting them in the suitcase.

"Let's work something out," she said, her gaze travelling from the trousers to his face.

Pretending to deliberate, he peered out the window. "What do you suggest?"

"We could get a cleaner and split the cost."

He wanted to leap at the offer but negotiations weren't fully concluded. "I don't need to be threatened with eviction every time we disagree."

"You won't be."

"How do I know that?"

"I promise, you won't.

He picked up the chinos and put them back in the wardrobe.

Giving it a go

Every time the door opened, Danny looked over his shoulder to see who had entered the post office. His response was automatic. He no longer really expected to see the man who'd been on Piper's doorstep. There'd been no sighting since that night and the passage of time had diluted his anxiety. He'd even begun to think he had been a little paranoid, that the stranger hadn't really been the same man he'd seen at St Giles church. Coming from Northern Ireland and a Catholic, he'd been too sensitive, too fearful of authority and too suspicious that they were watching his every move like they did real IRA suspects.

Danny took the letter out of the envelope and started to reread it as he shuffled forward in the queue. Written in haste an hour ago, the walk had afforded time for doubt and now was his last chance to reconsider before he posted it.

42 Chumley St
London, W6

Dear Susan,

I hope this finds you well. While it would be preferable to speak in person, sending this letter is the next best thing as I can't come over to see you just now. As you know, I'm midway through the course and can't afford to miss even a single class.

It was quite a coincidence that you bumped into

Dad. How very odd.

I was happy to hear from you and at the same time very surprised. Before I continue, I want you to know I accept full responsibility for hurting you. I'm sorry and still feel terrible. I was in a very bad place then. It amazes me how a couple of months away from home has changed my life and made everything clearer.

I didn't ring back after receiving your message on the answering machine because I needed time to really think. Because you no longer wanted to see me again, I'd assumed our engagement was off. So I was astonished when you said you still want to marry me.

Susan, I'm not ready at this stage in my life. London has shown me this. I'm too young. I don't want the responsibility. It would be a great mistake for us to get married. I understand it makes financial sense to our fathers that we marry, but a loving relationship can't be premised on economies of scale. You are a very practical woman and I know you well enough to know you'll see I'm right about this.

It may be you're thinking you'll wait for my return, or that you'll give me more time (to come to my senses?). If this is the case, while I appreciate your generosity, I do not ask or want it. I can't guarantee I'd marry you at the end of the time.

Please know I've enjoyed the times we shared and hope you have, too. I want you to know I'll never discuss the circumstances of our breakup with anyone and would appreciate if you'd do likewise. Certainly, our fathers don't need to be involved in *our personal lives any further. We're adults now.*

However, should you decide it necessary to blame the breakup entirely on me, I won't contradict you in any way.

I know this letter isn't what you want but honesty is always the right way. I know this now.

Sincerely,
Danny

All his doubts were gone. He replaced the letter in the envelope, sealed it and waited to buy the stamp.

Julia and Clive were in the living room when he returned, Clive fashioning a joint from a mound of cigarette tobacco mixed with hashish. A lighter and Rizzo papers lay next to him, beside a small lump of hashish wrapped in cling film. They'd been smoking already. The air was unpleasantly acrid and a blue-grey smoke as thick as a summer mountain haze hung above the dining room table at the far end of the room.

"Hello there, handsome." Clive licked the edge of the joint.

Danny nodded.

"What have you been doing lately?" Clive laughed. "I mean who've you been doing?"

Julia's friend was bright but Danny disliked his juvenile need to play the clown. In his thirties, he was no longer exactly young.

"Would you like some vino, Danny?" Julia called from the kitchen, over the thump of the harsh house music she loved to play when she smoked hash.

"Yes, please."

"Coming right up."

Clive began to roll another joint. He noticed Danny watching. "Supplies for later." He removed the joint from the rollers, "You ought to come clubbing with me one night."

"Me?"

"Why not?"

"Isn't it obvious?"

Clive looked nonplussed for a moment. "Lots of straights go to gay clubs." He winked mischievously. "It's just a straight man's fantasy that gay men are always trying to get into their pants." Clive peered with mock salaciousness at Danny's crotch. "Absolute fantasy, mate."

Danny glanced toward the kitchen.

Clive held out the joint for Danny to take.

"Thanks, I don't partake."

"*Thanks, but I don't partake*." Clive's mouth hung open for a moment, and then he lolled back his head and guffawed. "You sound like a vicar's daughter who's just been asked for a shag." He lowered his head again and jiggled the joint to indicate Danny should take it.

"Give it a go, mate. People need to try everything once, if you get my drift."

"I don't think… "

"Come on. See what you've been missing."

Julia came in with a tray containing two glasses of wine and a plate of sliced cheddar and crackers. "Are you corrupting my flatmate?"

"So far, unsuccessfully."

Julia and Danny laughed. Clive took a deep pull of the joint and then held it out for Danny to take. He jiggled his fingers as if he were enticing a puppy with food.

An image of Danny's father sitting in his study with a tumbler of scotch came to mind as Danny regarded the joint. It was five years ago. His father was giving him a lecture before he left home for university. He warned him he'd encounter students who habitually took drugs and he was to stay away from them. Lest that warning wasn't sufficient, he finished by saying, 'I'll break your back if I ever hear you've been taking them.' Danny recalled what he'd said, how London was full of degenerates who took drugs, how it was a trap for naive young Irish people.

Danny took the joint and gingerly placed it between his lips. He was instantly repulsed by the tip's unexpected wetness. He willed himself to ignore the sensation, and closed his eyes as he carefully inhaled. The smoke hit hard against the back of his throat and he immediately expelled the rank tasting air.

He held it out for Clive to take back. "I don't feel a bit different."

"You need to take a few more hits."

A hollow thumping not in synchronisation with the loud beat of the music commenced.

"Oops, pissed off Mrs. Hartley again," Julia said.

"Take a few more puffs," Clive said to Danny.

He did as Clive suggested, happier now that the saliva on the remainder of the joint was his own. While Clive and Julia watched, he took deeper pulls, breathed in and held it for a moment before expunging the smoke.

"Excellent," Julia said, taking the joint from him.

It felt like he was back in school and had just been praised by a teacher for some extraordinary work he'd done. As he watched Julia tilt back her head and expel a funnel of smoke toward the ceiling, a sensation of warm serenity overtook Danny. His head felt very light. He blinked lazily as he watched her pass the joint to Clive.

An assembly line commenced, Danny taking the joint every time Clive finished his turn. Then he passed it on to Julia. The serenity intensified and his ears started to buzz.

"This is fantastic," Danny heard himself say. It sounded as if he were outside his body.

"What'd I tell you, mate?"

"Oh God, we've corrupted him," Julia said.

Someone knocked on the front door.

"Mrs. Hartley's persistent," Julia said.

As Danny watched Julia go into the kitchen, she seemed to glide in slow motion. It also seemed to take her forever to return. When she did, she had a can of air freshener. She spritzed the room liberally. The door was knocked again, more persistent this time.

"I'm coming." Julia went to the door. "Mrs. Hartley, I'm not playing... Katie?"

"Julia."

Danny pulled himself up on the sofa.

Clive pulled a mock-terrified face at Danny.

"You never return my calls," Katie said. "Can I come in?"

"Clive and Danny are here."

Another silence before Julia stepped aside allowing her to enter. She greeted the men with a nod.

"Sit," Julia said, and she walked over to where she'd been sitting on the sofa beside Clive.

Danny's buzz dissipated. The cozy atmosphere felt suddenly awkward. Clive tilted his head and pushed against the sofa back. Katie took a seat across from Danny.

"Smells interesting in here," Katie said.

"We're corrupting Danny," Julia said.

"You are?" Katie laughed, but it sounded anxious to Danny.

"He's a pro now," Clive said. He fished in the breast pocket of his shirt and retrieved a new joint. "Do you want a puff, Katie?"

She looked over at Julia as if needing permission, but Julia remained deadpan.

"Just a quick one, then," Katie said. "I mustn't take too much because I have to drive home." She glanced at Julia again.

The delicious buzz Danny had previously experienced returned. He adjusted the cushion and settled contentedly into the armchair. The music on the CD player changed to techno, its energetic tribal beat making him want to dance. He began to sway in time to the beat.

Clive watched him. "You go, girl."

"Why don't we all go dancing later?" said Julia.

"I can't." Katie crossed her feet. "Not tonight."

"Isn't Mrs. Ratcliffe looking after the children?"

"Harry is."

"Call and tell him you're coming out tonight." Julia took a long drag of the joint.

"You can stay here."

"It's not that simple, Julia. I was hoping we could talk."

Crystal clear, fully formed thoughts streamed through Danny's head as he swayed it back and forth. Soon Susan would receive the letter and the last bonds between them would be severed forever. His father's face loomed now. He was wrong about England. He knew nothing about London life. Danny should have lived here years ago. He should even have gone to university here. What had he been so afraid of? He knew the answer. His father had made him afraid. Fear was his father's weapon. The hash allowed him to see very clearly. He should have smoked it in Belfast.

"Don't you think she should call her husband, Clive?" Julia's voice seemed to arrive from Mars.

"You should, Katie."

Clive was a nice guy but totally obsessed with his sex life. That thought made Danny realise he wanted sex, too. Badly. He hadn't had it for ages. He felt suddenly horny. Finty's pert breasts and gorgeously firm arse sprang into Danny's mind. He wanted to fuck her. His testicles crawled. He grew erect. But it wouldn't happen. She was uninterested. She was far more interested in her puppy, wanted him only as a friend to study vocabulary with. His hard-on began to subside. His thoughts segued to Katie.

"What do you think, Danny?" Julia asked.

Katie shouldn't be here is what Danny thought. She was selfish. She had responsibilities at home.

"*Danny?*"

He opened his eyes and saw everyone was staring at him.

"Miss Ireland's out of her bloody tree," said Clive.

Julia and Clive began to laugh.

He blinked fast. "I don't appreciate you addressing me like I'm female, Clive."

Their laughter grew until tears began to stream from their eyes.

Danny and Katie looked at each other in astonishment and then turned in unison to regard Clive and Julia. He watched until they managed to rein themselves in, both wiping away their tears with their fingers.

"Don't you think Katie should ring her husband and tell him she's staying over with me tonight."

He was smart enough not to get embroiled in a nasty argument. "Well, I can see your point about that... and then again, I can see Katie's, too."

"Very decisive, that is," Clive said.

"Katie's got kids," Danny said. "Not everybody can be free and easy like you, Clive."

Katie took a tissue from the pocket of her jeans. "Julia, I came here to talk but I see you're enjoying making me feel bad. Rupert told Harry he saw us kissing at the river. I've only yesterday managed to convince my husband our son was mistaken. I can't stand it that you don't return my calls. I've *tried* to make things work as best I can so nobody gets hurt. I'd even decided I'm prepared to leave my husband one day." She rose and went quickly to the front door. "It's clear now you don't give a damn about me." Pulling the door open, she ran out to the street.

Julia went after her.

Making plans

She regarded Todd's profile as he slept, bathed in the orangey glow of the streetlight filtering through the window. His breathing was barely audible, his chest glistened with sweat. When she touched his cheek, he stopped breathing for a long moment before settling back into a peaceful rhythm.

It had been bad again. No, bad wasn't the right word. That was too final, a pronouncement, a judgment, something that could never change, would never change. Why could she not get into what was happening when they had sex? She was twenty-three. She'd been with eight men in her life up to now. All the Americans except the two Hispanics were within five years of her age, the rest older up to forty-five. Piper drew the line at forty-five no matter how athletic the guy's body. There'd been one professor, a Broadway singer, one muscled NYC sanitary worker, two African and one Asian-American NYU students. Three had had varying shades of blonde to red hair including Todd, one was silver-grey and another had even been bald. The variety was deliberate. Piper felt she should have been turned on by at least one man by now.

She realised she couldn't blame the hang-up on anything physical, certainly not penises. That body bit induced neither curiosity nor repulsion. Piper didn't especially desire or loathe touching them during foreplay, whether flaccid or rigid. Nor could she blame her inability with Todd on the pressures of taking final examinations. They were over and all that remained was her dissertation *Ireland at another Crossroads...* which she'd already provisionally outlined.

Todd was a great guy, intellectual without being boring, funny and he had a nice body. He didn't snore. Her father would approve of him. She passed her index finger over his cheek. To her surprise, he responded, touching her thigh.

"I didn't mean to wake you."

He yawned. "How long have I been sleeping?"

"Half-an-hour."

"What's up, hon?"

"I'm thinking of when I go back home... seeing my dad again and stuff."

"When *we* go back, you mean?"

"That's what I meant."

He turned on his side and kissed the top of her shoulder. It was a gentle kiss. Without expectation. A car drove by on the street below, followed moments later by another. The silence closed in again. She listened to the tick of the clock on the bedside table.

"Can I ask you something?" she said.

"Sure."

She closed her eyes and parted her lips to speak but then clamped them shut again.

"I'm waiting."

"When we... when we make love... how do you feel?"

He reflected a moment. "Are you serious?"

"I wanna know."

"I feel good."

"Why?"

"Because I enjoy it." He kissed her shoulder again.

"Is it enjoyable every time?"

"Why are you askin'?"

Her skin felt cold on the place where his mouth had kissed her shoulder. "No reason." She faked a yawn.

"Hey listen... " He reached out and put his hand on her

cheek, turning her face gently toward him so she could see his. "No complaints here."

She turned away and stared blankly at the window. The bed felt suddenly vast. The clock's tick irritated her.

"You awake still?" he asked.

"No."

"What's the matter?"

"Sleep tight."

Two weeks after her final exam, a group of them including Todd, met at the library to do research for their dissertations. Afterwards they'd gone out to the Three Tuns because the booze at the student pub was cheaper and then to a club. He'd insisted on spending the night at her place. But rather than go directly to bed, he'd wanted to drink coffee and talk. The subject of her future plans came round. She'd known it would, just hadn't expected it that night. While Todd knew she intended to return to London after her visit home, (they planned to travel together to New York where he'd stay for a few days before continuing on to his folks in San Francisco) he needed to know if her plans included him, and whether they were officially 'an item'. If they were, he told her he'd also return to England (a month or so after her) because he'd found out it wasn't in any way detrimental to start his career in Mergers and Acquisitions with a US subsidiary in London, as opposed to the main New York or San Francisco office.

As she'd listened, Piper wondered how he could be so certain about them. Had her mother been as certain when she got involved with her father? She also wished she could be as sure as he about what she wanted to do with her life. Soon, she'd graduate from the LSE and yet was still as uncertain as she'd been at NYU about a career. A cornucopia of possibilities daily ran through her mind: work at a bank just like Todd, analyst with a brokerage house or one of the start-ups on the web, some kind of political research, a position with the European Commission given her dual citizenship. All these possibilities were open. And then there were the alternatives, enticingly offbeat, even ironic alternatives like writing the great American novel while living in London or the biographies of famous American politicians she admired. She could become a reporter for a serious magazine or national newspaper. Maybe even try her hand at acting while she was young enough. A Masters in History of International Relations mattered little with these options and every time she considered them, the realisation she'd have to find a good paying job with flexibility and minimum stress to pay the bills and loans became more pressing.

A growing draw toward the offbeat choices was fuelled in part by the high she'd experienced during her unsuccessful attempt to interview Paisley at Westminster and partly by irritation arising out of the content of her mother's email. Especially its opening paragraph, where she'd asked what Piper intended to do after she graduated, and then answered it by expressing a hope it'd be something 'useful connected to her diploma.'

Piper knew decisions had to be made now. It was only fair to Todd. She feigned tiredness to spurn his advances when he awoke next morning. After he left, she called her next-door neighbour Sonia Berg at the hospital and they arranged to meet when the doctor was next free.

Womb sack therapy

When Sonia Berg answered the door she was dressed in a cream-coloured dressing gown which had 'SB' monogrammed in royal blue and an embroidered sunflower on each sleeve. There was also a palpable stink in the house that grew more intense as Piper drew near the staircase, parma violet or lavender combined with something clinical.

"What's that smell?"

"My birth oil." Sonia's eyebrows lifted in positive anticipation. "You like?"

"What did you say?"

"I am a Leo and this is the essential oil of my birth. Whenever I have a crazy day, I put it in my bath water because it soothes."

"That's why you're in your robe. Would you rather I come back another time?"

"Now is fine."

After offering Piper a choice of German wheat beer or wine, the doctor told her where she'd find the red bottle, asked her to pour a glass for her too and went upstairs to change. While she waited in the living room, Piper leafed through a copy of *Stern* magazine.

Sonia returned dressed in jeans, short-sleeved cotton top that ended mid-thigh and sporting a necklace of large multi-coloured wooden beads. After lighting a thick candle perched on a brass stand, she put on the CD player and strains of Enya's ethereal music began to languidly unfurl and co-mingle with the molecules of floating birth oil. As she watched Sonia assume the lotus position on a corduroy beanbag-cum-sofa across from hers, Piper considered whether she should launch immediately into the problem or engage in small talk first.

As if reading her mind, Doctor Berg said, "What is the little problem you wish to discuss?"

"I'm feeling stressed out."

"Is it worries about your examination performances?"

Piper regarded the ceiling as she tried to formulate the right words. "Remember the night Todd cooked for all of us?"

"The delicious sour bread from San Francisco."

"Sourdough bread," said Piper. "Danny was talking about Julia and you said something that night about how you've helped women back in Germany with certain intimacy problems."

"Ah, it is an intimacy problem." Sonia eased forward in the beanbag sofa. "A sexual problem can be mental or physical and is something I work with, *ja*."

"When Todd and I are making out, I just can't get into it much. That's my problem. It bothers me."

"How much is this not much?"

"I've always found sex, um, not that interesting."

"You have never enjoyed love-making?"

"I haven't, no."

"I must ask these next personal questions because it is necessary for me to narrow things."

Piper sat up.

"Does it cause you pain?"

"For sure."

"Then something may be deficient with your anatomy. This is physiological and I am not… "

"There's nothing wrong with my vagina. It's not that kinda pain. I just can't get into the mindset is what I meant."

"There is no physical problem?"

"No pain."

Sonia sat back and picked up her wine glass. "Tell me how you feel when you make sex."

After Piper finished, Sonia didn't speak. The song *Book of Days* wafted from the CD player. Until this moment, Piper hadn't realised how artificially perfect, how manipulated, how laughably sentimental New Age music was. She hoped Sonia was silent because she was considering an appropriate medication. Or did her quiet stare mean she regarded Piper as a failure in this part of her life. A freak? Incurable?

"What's your diagnosis?"

"There is no great anxiety and you are able to function normal in the other parts of your life. This is good."

"Is there a pill?"

"This is always the American way." Sonia's smiled indulgently. "You do not need medications. There is a blockage and this is more a question for therapy. I believe I am the right person to help."

"I'll pay, of course."

"This is also wery American," said Sonia. "We can talk about the payments another time. For now, I have some additional questions. Do you have a better relationship with your father or mother?"

"Dad, definitely."

Sonia's brow creased and she looked disappointed. "What is your relationship with your mother like now?"

"Almost non-existent."

"And when you were a child?"

"It was pretty normal. She loved me. I loved her. She liked to bake cookies. I liked to eat 'em. We argued. We made up. We weren't a touchy-feely family. Then she had my brother... " Piper's gaze fell to the floor and she stopped talking for a moment. "I morphed into the angry teenager and became a real bitch. I smoked dope and did ecstasy. You know how it goes. It's the same in Germany, right?"

"Did your mother punish you often as a child?"

"I was sometimes smacked with a paddle, but mostly I was grounded."

"What is this 'grounded'?"

"I was sent to my bedroom and forbidden to come out. She'd even lock me inside if I refused to stay there."

"These are wery important things you are telling me, Piper. Continue, please."

"There's not a lot more to tell."

"Did you often feel unloved by your mother?"

"All kids think their parents are mean sometimes. Teenagers do all the time. I hated Mom and Dad a lot, but I got over it."

"Do you know if your mother experienced large difficulties when you were being borned?"

"I was a big baby." Piper chuckled. "I remember her telling me she thought I'd never come out. She said it was like I didn't want to be born."

"This is most interesting." Sonia rose, fetched a notebook and pen from a drawer in the coffee table and began to write prodigiously. "Was your brother borned with such difficulties also?"

"Nah. He just about slipped out."

"Did she treat him the same as you when he was a child?"

The corners of Piper's mouth trembled. "Rory was only ever a child."

"I am sorry. I forgot this."

"Mom always wanted a boy so she fussed over him a lot. Hey, so did I."

"Did it make you jealous to watch this behaviour by your mother?"

"I had my friends and school stuff by then."

"And you loved your brother?"

"I still do."

The questions continued, questions about her family circumstances and her parent's separation, questions delving into Piper's relationship with her father in the past and today, about her past friendships with both females and males, questions about sexual experiences at high school and university.

"Have you ever been abused sexually by any persons?" Sonia asked.

"God, no."

Sonia raised her hand. "Take your time to think."

Piper tilted her head back and regarded the ceiling. "Some boys touched me when I was about nine. Maybe ten. I can't remember."

"*Ach so.*"

"But it wasn't abuse," said Piper. "It was more kind of, 'you show me yours and I'll show you mine' kinda stuff."

"No male or female adults touched you?"

"Zilch."

Sonia consulted her notes for a minute. "You do not need my services as a psychiatrist. But I can help you in my role as a psychotherapist. For many peoples, I believe a lot of pain begins during the birthing. They can be starved of oxygen for a time and this causes trauma. Other sources of pain feeds silently off this primal pain. For example, if we feel rejected or unloved by our parents. These traumas can become neuroses and result in many dysfunctions including sexual."

Piper leaned toward the doctor. "You think my not getting turned on comes from feelings I had as a kid?"

"Possible. Here is my plan, which has two prongs. First, you will have a rebirth."

"A what?"

"I have my patients experience a rebirth during which they confront the primal pain. Once this basic pain has been acknowledged, the patient can begin to move on. It is a simple process. You are wrapped so you experience being again in the womb. But I do not practice it in the way many therapists do. These therapists keep the person bound in this womb for many hours and have many sessions of confronting this pain. That is not my method." She shook her head as if she were indignant.

"For me, the objective is to get rid of the primal pain in the birthing and move quickly to the counseling prong in order to confront the other psychological pain that is giving rise to the problems. All goes in order." She looked at Piper. "You understand, *ja*?"

"Yeah."

"As we move deeper into your adult blockage, Todd would have to be present for some sessions."

"Not happening, Sonia."

The doctor looked nonplussed. "This is wery important."

"Not happening."

"The two of you must do exercises together as part of the therapy."

"What *kind* of exercises?"

"First would be simple kissing. The next is hugging. Then intimate touching without sexual intercourse so you do not feel any pressure. There would be no complete sex until I tell you that you are ready."

As she listened to Sonia explain her plan, Piper subconsciously placed two fingers on her front teeth and began to tap.

The doctor stopped talking and asked, "You are worried?"

"We're going to have to do this without Todd. I've told him our sex is great. It's my hang up, not his."

The upstairs room Sonia used for therapy sessions had a wooden floor as shellacked as a gym floor and walls painted primrose. Framed abstract art posters in a Jackson Pollack style, African tribal masks and Sonia's medical diploma adorned the walls. In the lower portion of the room was a lavender and white striped two-seater couch and matching armchair. A smoked glass coffee table lay between them. Sonia opened the door of a built-in closet and took out a fuchsia blanket that she spread in the middle of the room. Next she took out a six-foot poinsettia red sack with a drawstring at one end. She placed the sack at one end of the blanket.

After informing Piper she'd be 'immersed' in the womb sack and wrapped in the blanket, she retrieved a bunch of short fat candles from the closet, placed them in a circle around the blanket and lit them. She drew the curtains shut and dimmed the overhead lights so the room took on the appearance of an ancient pagan initiation site.

Sonia switched on the CD player and stepped inside the illuminated circle. Piano music riffs began to trickle from the stereo. "Take off your clothes and climb inside the womb sack, please."

"All my clothes?"

"You may keep the underpants."

Piper hesitated, and then began to undress. "Is that *Yanni* playing?"

"It is a German composer who is a friend," said Sonia. "He created it for this purpose."

A faint beating or tapping sound became audible.

"*Schnell*," Sonia said. "Quickly. The heart begins to beat."

Piper stepped inside the circle and looked at the candles. "I don't think I can do this, Sonia."

"Why?"

The heartbeats grew louder. "I don't like the candles so close. And can you turn the lights up a bit?"

Sonia's face, now rendered chiascuro in the flickering light, was a study of incredulity. The heartbeats began to overtake the tinkling piano.

"I don't like so many flames this close around me. Sorry."

"If I make the circle bigger?" Sonia asked.

"What have candles got to do with rebirth anyway?"

"It is my way."

"Um, make the circle bigger… and brighten the lights."

After doing so, the CD was started again. Piper climbed into the scarlet sack and Sonia tied it, instructing her to lie down. She proceeded to roll her body in the blanket until it became almost dark. A moment later, something pressed against Piper's bottom. "What's happening, Sonia?"

"I'm putting some pillows around your body so you will feel surrounded by your mother's fet stomach. You will begin now to breathe in and out continuously."

It began to feel warm and the constriction, while not freaking her out, was unnerving. The heartbeats grew louder.

"You are breathing in and out like I have ordered?" Sonia asked.

"Yeah."

"No further talking." There was a smack on the pillow against her backside and another on her back. Her head was smacked next, first at the back then the front, then her thigh, calf, and her backside again.

"What are you doing?"

"Do not talk. It is a simulation. Breathe in and out wery fast like I told you."

The sporadic hitting interspersed with Sonia's pushing down on her shoulders lasted for ten minutes. Piper's body was bathed in sweat. She felt lightheaded from breathing rapidly. The sound of the beating heart grew louder. Sonia began to occasionally groan.

"Are you still breathing the way I wish?" Sonia asked.

"Yes." She hoped the ritual would soon end.

"One continuous rhythm in and out. Soon comes the birth."

The loud heartbeats ended abruptly. The music changed to what sounded like trickling water amid a melody of soothing electronic music.

"Keep breathing in and out, in and out."

The water trickle changed to a gush and Sonia began wailing. It was very hot inside the sack now. A trickle of sweat entered Piper's eye and stung.

"Sonia, what is going on?"

"Do you want to be borned now, Piper?"

"Yes."

"Do you?"

"I want out."

Piper felt hands on her body, and then she was rolling as Sonia shrieked and moaned as if in the midst of a terrible labour. She saw the gold-yellow flicker of the candles through the fabric of the sack. Fingers fumbled on top of her head. The sack then opened and was pulled down over her head and shoulders.

"Come out, Piper. You are borned again. Come out to your new, beautiful life." She helped Piper stand and then peeled the sack down to her feet. Sonia opened her arms wide and embraced her. "It is over. It is all over. You have dominated the primal pain. It is gone forever." She led Piper to the chairs and fetched a towel so she could wipe her face.

"You may dress now," she said, after Piper handed her the towel.

Piper struggled to put on her blouse. She really did feel like a helpless newborn. Her limbs and fingers shook from the rebirth experience. She could not make them obey.

"How do you feel?" Sonia said, after Piper sat across from her on the armchair.

"Weird." Piper looked down at the rumpled sack that resembled a placenta now. "What am I supposed to feel?

"We can start the second prong tomorrow."

"I'm gonna take a raincheck."

"I do not understand this raincheck."

She looked at the doctor. "This will sound crazy but maybe I'm just not really into sex. It's that simple."

"It is difficult to have a relationship with someone without the sex. Especially in the beginning years."

"I really like being in a relationship with Todd so that is a problem." Piper sighed. "Sex is important to him. I'll have to try harder, that's all."

"What will you do?"

"Keep trying till it comes right."

"My door will always be open." Sonia's professional concern was apparent despite the warm smile. "Counseling can often help in situations that seem impossible." Sonia rose. "And now I prescribe some wine for us, *ja*?"

Helping out

A strong wind had kicked up while Agnes had been inside visiting Martha. The branches of the sycamore tree cracked like pistol fire each time they struck one another. Pages of a discarded newspaper were wedged against the kerb and the right rear wheel of her car. Agnes disliked being out late. She wouldn't have been out had it not been for her friend's recent accident. Martha had fallen and sprained her ankle and cut her face, a fall resulting in her having had to spend five days in the hospital because she'd no family members at home to care for her and had refused to have a stranger from Social Services in her flat.

The roads were empty except for occasional taxis taking late night revelers home, delivery vans and trucks. When she saw the massive piers of Hammersmith Bridge, Agnes knew she was just five minutes from home. She relaxed her grip on the steering wheel, even indulged herself by turning up the volume on the radio to hear the early morning news. She entered the deck of the bridge. In the mid-distance, over the top of the bridge's outer banister, the canopies of oaks and elms alongside the towpath swayed in the wind. The river's inky black water gleamed in the pale moonlight. Light manufacturing establishments hugging the Thames were bathed in the sterile neon glow of security lights. A solitary pedestrian crossing the bridge turned his head against the wind to look at her as she passed by.

Halfway across, the car lifted off the surface for an instant. A huge flash of orange flame filled the rearview mirror. Her vehicle struck against something unyielding and hard. Agnes shrieked, quickly realised she'd crossed a traffic lane and the car's front wheel had struck a portion of the bridge's steel barrier. The engine died. The bridge emitted a low metallic growl as if it were in terrible pain. Looking over her shoulder, she saw the right side of the bridge was burning as brightly as the Iraq oil wells she'd seen bombed on television. A pillar of thick smoke rose into the night sky. Terrified the structure would collapse, she tried to restart the car but couldn't. Her hands and legs shook uncontrollably. She gripped the wheel, willed herself not to panic and tried the engine again. It started and she began to move forward, initially in tiny leaps because her right foot feeding fuel to the engine would not fully comply.

When Agnes pulled into the parking spot across from her house and turned off the engine, her body began to tremble. She sat for five minutes trying to recall the journey from the bridge but couldn't remember anything, not a street name or single turn she'd made. The devouring shrieks of fire engines consumed the city's tranquility when she opened the car door.

Inside, the shock she'd felt weakened. She sat on her rocking chair in the living room unable to expunge the image of the pedestrian crossing the bridge. A cup of very sweet tea calmed her and she switched on the television. A journalist reported a body had been found and there'd been a warning, a coded warning similar to the one given by the Real IRA when they'd bombed the bridge the previous year as policemen, clad in flak jackets and carrying stubby black rifles, stood on the bridge's piers.

Reconnecting

The possibility that Katie might decide to leave her husband and move into Chumley Street with her children now that Julia and she had reconciled worried Danny. Worried him that is until, asking matter-of-factly if she ever wanted to have children, Julia informed him 'absolutely not' because they'd destroy her lifestyle.

"Danny, what's the plural for *Pferd*?" Finty called into the kitchen.

"I think it's *Pferde*."

"German sounds very harsh or is it just me?" Julia said. "How can you make that '*Pf*' sound without spitting on someone's face?"

"Easy," said Finty. "Don't talk with saliva in your mouth."

The screams of a police siren penetrated the front window. The wail grew louder until it seemed the windowpane would shatter into a thousand shards. Every time he heard police sirens, Danny was automatically hurled back to Northern Ireland, to a past era of daily bombings and tit-for-tat murders. Even a car backfiring had once caused him to duck to the ground much to Finty's surprise.

"Bloody hell, what's happened?" Julia said. She swung her feet off the sofa and switched on the television. "Don't tell me another bomb's gone off somewhere." She watched the screen for a moment. "Nothing on the news."

Danny came back from the kitchen carrying two very full

cups of tea and set one carefully before Finty who was seated at the dining room table. He took the other to Julia on the sofa.

"How do you know it's not *Pferden*," said Finty. "I'm hopeless."

"Don't put yourself down like that." Danny sat at the table beside her.

Now they were two-thirds of the way through the German course, there were an increasing number of work assignments and ever more complex vocabulary lists to be absorbed and Finty was now a weekly visitor at his home as a result. Brought up to view reciprocal invites as expressions of interest, it disappointed Danny that he still hadn't been invited to study at her flat. He found her circumspect about her private life, rarely talking about her domestic circumstances other than to tell him how the puppy was faring or complain about her part-time job.

He sipped his tea and watched Finty discretely as she leaned over the table. He loved entertaining her at any time, but today was particularly special. They never met at the weekends, and were doing so only because Herr Fehler had arranged for the class and any of their family and friends to attend a mid-July picnic concert at Hampstead Heath. He'd invited Piper and Julia, who couldn't attend due to a prior engagement. The concert was to feature works by Pachelbel and Brahms and Danny had suggested to Finty she come over beforehand under the pretext they could study for a while.

They worked quietly until Danny announced it was time to leave for the picnic. While Finty went upstairs to freshen up, he removed the bottles of white wine she'd brought from the fridge and packed them together with salads he'd prepared into two backpacks.

The phone rang. Julia answered it.

"It's for you," Julia called into the kitchen. "Your father."

They hadn't spoken since he'd come to London. A multitude of bad scenarios raced through Danny's mind.

"Everything okay at home, Dad?"

"Aye. I just thought I'd give you a ring. How's London?"

"I'm enjoying myself."

"Grafting hard, I hope."

"Yep."

"Almost finished the course, eh?"

Upstairs, he could hear Finty as she moved about the bathroom. "Almost," he said. Danny braced himself for the order to come home.

"Do you know who I happened to bump into the other day?"

"Who?"

"Susan." His father laughed his insincere laugh. "I met her completely out of the blue. That's why I decided to give you a ring."

Since sending the letter to Susan, Danny hadn't heard from her. For two weeks after he calculated she'd have received his letter, he'd expected an irate call at any time, at the very least a note from her pleading with him to reconsider. There'd been only silence. But a month had since passed and he concluded she'd accepted his decision and their engagement was now a part of his past.

"I thought there might be a reason for your call, Dad."

"The girl's not looking so well, son. You probably know her father's not in great shape."

"She mentioned that."

"He's had his heart surgery."

Danny didn't comment.

"The doctor's warned him he has to cut down on his work or it'll kill him." His father sighed ponderously. "The man's going to need help or he'll have to sell up. That's a hell of a business he's built. Lot o' money there. Sure his wife knows nothing about running a farm. And Susan's not up to it. It's too much for a slip of a girl."

"Tell her father I wish him well."

"Remember what I said to you a while back about his business?"

Danny took a slow, deep breath. "Things have changed between Susan and me."

"Aye Susan mentioned you two had a difference of opinion. But that's between the two of you to sort out as far as I'm concerned."

"It is sorted."

There was a silence. His father didn't get it or refused to understand Danny was his own man now. He wondered what it would take to ram the message home.

"I'm worried about that wee lass, son."

Danny didn't speak.

"So I says to her 'Why don't you take a wee holiday to yourself?' Sure a couple of days away would do her the power of good.' Don't you think I said the right thing?"

He could hear Finty's footfalls as she started along the landing.

"Sorry to have to cut you short but I'm going out, Dad. Some friends are waiting for me."

"That's okay, son. Anyway, I just wanted to fill you in on what's happening to the wee lass. Enjoy yourself now. Sure I'll call again some other time."

The vehicle of life

Danny knocked on Piper's front door a third time. Still no-one answered. He peeked through the letterbox. Newspapers and leaflets lay strewn over the floor. Four pages of handwritten notes were on the bottom three stairs. Near the kitchen threshold, the ponytail palm he'd repotted into a glazed blue and yellow striped ceramic pot and given to her for her birthday lay at a forty-five degree angle against the wall of the hallway.

"Maybe she left already," said Finty. "We need to go or we'll be late."

A dense crowd of people, many with blankets and picnic hampers, milled around the terrace of Kenwood House when Danny and Finty arrived. They waited for ten minutes to see if Piper would show up but she didn't. Reluctantly, Danny followed the other concertgoers toward the park. Not a leaf stirred within the limbs of the mature beeches and oaks as they made their way along the winding pathway. Even the white and lemon butterflies were languid, fluttering in the sultry air that reeked of damp earth. A film of sweat developed on Danny's arms and forehead, the latter swelling into a trickle that wended its way toward his nose where it formed crystal droplets that he wiped away with the back of his hand.

They tendered the tickets to the attendant and strolled over the lush, ankle deep grass until they came to the brow of a gently sloped hill. Along the breath of the slope, hundreds of people reclined on deckchairs or lay supine on the grass.

Beneath them, the parabolic concert hall nestled by the curved bank of a freshwater pond whose size he couldn't determine because one side was cut off by a twin-arched bridge. Danny scanned the crowd for Herr Fehler but Finty spotted Hilary's lurid violet hair first. They wended over to the group. About forty people including the two Chinese students, their wives and children were already there, far too many to greet personally.

"You must try Fredi's German potato salad," Hilary said, as Finty poured them glasses of chilled wine. "It's awfully good."

Finty pulled a faux-surprised look when Danny's eyes locked in hers. Hilary, who was receiving extra tuition from their teacher, was letting them know that he was no longer Alfred but rather Fredi now.

The food had been placed within the circle the group had formed. It was a massive feast: plates of cold chicken breasts and drumsticks, potato salad, rice and Waldorf salads, pots of store and homemade hummus, tzatziki, French bread, sandwiches, beef satay, and the standard array of prepackaged supermarket quiche, cold meats and pork pies.

"My salad is not so terrible, if I may say so," Herr Fehler said. He was sitting nearby talking to a woman Danny didn't recognise.

"I'd love to try some of Fredi, I mean Alfred's, salad in a minute," Finty said to Hilary. Again, she gave Danny a faux-surprised look. He loved this small, exclusive connection to her even if it was only to poke fun at Hilary.

They lay down side by side, he resting on his elbows as he gazed out over the pond, she nibbling on the bunch of black grapes he'd brought.

"What else is there to eat?" Finty asked.

Aware she was vegetarian, he'd prepared a mescaline salad, cold pasta salad with olives, sliced hardboiled eggs and an assortment of roasted vegetables drizzled in a sweet chili oil. She placed a portion of mescaline salad on her plate, poured oil and vinegar over it and then heaped some of the roasted vegetables alongside it.

"The pasta salad's tasty, too," Danny said, as he spooned some of it on his plate.

"No, thanks."

Hilary held out a plate of thinly sliced French bread smeared with a pinkish substance. "This tzatziki's delicious."

"No thanks," said Finty.

"It's homemade," Hilary said.

"It is delicious," Danny added. "Try one."

"I don't eat any eggs."

"Why ever not?" Hilary asked.

"Religious grounds."

Hilary shrugged and offered a slice to one of the Chinese men.

"Eggs are vegetarian," Danny said.

"They're not, actually."

"I've never heard of any religion banning eggs."

"I really didn't want to get into this, Danny." Finty sighed. "You'll think I'm crazy. That's what many people think."

"No, I won't." He reached out impulsively and put his hand on top of hers. "I'm really interested."

"Well, eggs come from animals so they can't be vegetarian, can they?"

"So does milk and cheese."

"Exactly."

He recalled the occasions they'd been in cafés and how he'd never seen her put milk in her coffee, drink cappuccinos or eat cream cakes. She always ordered garden salads or vegetarian chilies without sour cream, foods he considered boring. "What is your religion?"

"I'm a Satsangi. It's actually more a philosophy than a religion."

He didn't articulate his next thought, that its very name implied some kind of weird cult.

"It's a science of the soul. Our body's a cage and the soul is

181

the bird inside longing to fly toward the truth."

Finty rummaged in the pocket of her shorts and took out a packet of cigarettes. As he watched her light up, Danny couldn't help thinking it a bit incongruous.

"I'm not as good a Satsangi as I'd like to be," she said, as if she'd read Danny's mind. "I have my vices. But under *no* circumstances will I break the rule against eating eggs. They're extremely powerful."

"Fish roe is powerful?" He regarded it on his half eaten slice of French bread.

"All eggs are powerful," She scoured his face. "They're the vehicle of life. Eating them would have a negative influence on my meditation."

The orchestra began to assemble on stage. Suddenly remembering Piper, he looked back up the hill to see if she might have arrived and was now searching for him. Only a middle-aged man and woman stood at the apex.

The musicians began to tune their instruments. A minute later, the first violinist gave the bowings. The conductor announced the first half of the programme and began the concert. Danny was amazed at the precipitous cessation of chatter among the group as soon as the first notes of the *Canon in D* drifted out over the pond. He peered down over the quilt of heads. Everyone was rapt, some with their eyes closed and faces uplifted to the sinking sun, some watching as they nibbled food, others gently swaying with their hands clasped around their knees.

The tangy scent of crushed grass floated up to mingle with the swirling, invisible notes. Everything was perfect. He closed his eyes to allow the music to transport him. Finty's arm brushed against his. Moments later, it happened again. His penis began to harden. He couldn't stop it. It grew and grew until it began to protest the confines of his underpants. He shifted position and tried desperately to will it into quick subsidence.

"Isn't this lovely?" Finty said. She sat up, took off her floppy sunhat and shook out her hair.

"Shush," Hilary said.

Danny regarded Hilary, the Dame Edna lookalike seated now on a rug with Herr Fehler. Her eyes were closed and she swayed her head slowly from side to side. The strategy worked. A moment later, he was able to lie on his back again. Propping himself up on his elbow, he leaned over and whispered "Fredi, oh my little Fredi" in Finty's ear. Her torso began to shake. She pressed the palm of her hand on her chest to stop herself laughing.

"Stop," she said wordlessly.

She took her hand off her chest and gripped his thigh. Immediately, the stirring inside his trousers commenced again.

When Danny reached Chumley Street just after eleven-thirty, he stopped at Piper's house and rang the doorbell. Still no-one answered. He peered through the letterbox. Although nearly dark inside, he could see the dull glow of the handwritten pages of notes on the stairs. He checked the answering machine when he got home but she'd left no messages.

On Sunday, he stopped at her house every time he passed by on his way to and from the shops. She was never home. Although surprised she hadn't come to the concert, Danny wasn't unduly concerned: people often changed their minds last minute and they both led busy lives, days sometimes even an entire week passing without their contacting one another. Only when Todd arrived at his home that evening saying Piper and he were scheduled to leave on Wednesday for the States and he hadn't heard from her did Danny start to worry. They went to her next-door neighbour Sonia Berg who said she'd seen her on Friday evening because Piper wanted to discuss a private matter with her.

"Before Piper left me she said she was wery behind in her thesis," the doctor said, "and was going to hide herself away until she made progress."

"Yeah, she is way behind schedule on some reading lists," said Todd.

"Maybe she's just not answering the door?" Danny asked.

"I think she'd answer if she knows it's me," Todd said.

"I've shut myself away from friends when I've had a deadline," Danny said.

When Todd suggested they file a missing persons report with the police, Sonia disagreed.

"She is a grown independent woman with no record of mental illness," she said. "The police will not take this seriously until sufficient time passes."

The doctor's logic made sense and they agreed to wait until the following day.

Early morning visitor

Danny looked at the alarm clock on the bedside table. It was six a.m. The rapid knocking on the front door continued as he put on his dressing gown.

"Who the hell can it be?" Julia stood on the landing battling with the belt of her robe. Behind her, he could see Katie sitting up on the bed rubbing her eyes.

"I'll get it," he said.

Piper stood at the door, her hair utterly unkempt, the skin on her face waxy and upper lip so dry it had split in two places. Her blouse and jeans were heavily wrinkled.

"Who is it, Danny?" Julia called, her voice still hoarse from too much marijuana and wine the previous night.

"It's Piper." Danny pulled her gently inside and closed the door.

"Is she all right?" He could tell Julia was at the head of the stairs now.

Piper nodded languidly to indicate she was fine.

"No need to come down."

The floorboards creaked and then he heard Julia's bedroom door shut.

"Todd's worried sick."

"I got arrested."

Danny was amazed the police had worked out she was the one who'd been to Westminster.

"How'd they find out it was you at Paisley's office?"

"Wasn't for that. They accused me of having an IRA arms dump on my property."

Danny's heart leapt. The hair on his scalp and nape crawled.

"Pat's in the Real IRA. They're saying his cell planted the bomb that killed the guy on Hammersmith Bridge. Anne Marie wasn't his girlfriend, either. She and another woman are part of the cell, too." Piper bit on her cracked upper lip. He winced. She ran her fingers over her spiked hair. "They're still searching for Pat. It makes sense now why he didn't stay at my house so much." She paused. "In a way, I kinda suspected him of something when you showed me those shots of the two bridges. Boy, I'm sure glad I tossed 'em into the garbage."

Danny recalled the man he'd seen outside her home, the man in the denim shirt whom he'd feared was following him. It was Pat and Piper they'd been watching. He felt relieved and then instantly guilty.

"It was true what you told me. Someone was on my tail." She laughed. They screwed up and didn't get Pat though."

He wondered how she could laugh after her ordeal.

"Jeez, this country really is a police state," she continued, "what with goddamned surveillance cameras everywhere. It'll soon be you can't wipe your ass in private. Folks have to wake up here and put a stop to this bull. We wouldn't put up with that kinda crap back home."

"Did they have a warrant?"

"Yeah. They found that bunch of notes I'd made of an interview I'd done with an IRA volunteer when I was in Ireland."

"Shit."

"And they found tilt switches and Semtex and a bunch of stuff they wouldn't disclose." Her puffy eyes widened. "How the hell would I know what fricken Semtex looks like even if I'd come across it in my shed?" The phone started to ring. She stopped talking and looked over at the dining table. Danny rose to answer it. "Anyway, the guy comes running into the house with this stuff that looked like tan-colored putty. He was all excited to show it to his boss."

No-one spoke when Danny picked up the receiver. All he heard were two rapid batches of clicks, as if someone were punching out Morse code followed by static.

"Hello," he said.

Still no-one spoke. He had a sense someone was on the line. There was a click and then the dial tone came on.

"Probably a wrong number," he said.

"Maybe Special Branch's still on my tail."

"But they released you."

"Only because they couldn't find anything to charge me with when they didn't find my fingerprints on the Semtex and whatever else they found in the shed. They tried to pin something on me because of the interview notes. Can you fucking believe it?"

Danny didn't reply.

I said the notes are mine, so of course my prints are on them. I was real pissed. I demanded they allow me to contact the US Embassy. They stormed into the house when I was still in my robe and didn't even want to give me time to clean up before dragging me off to the precinct. But I told them I had the right to get properly dressed."

"We do?"

"I've been researching the IRA long enough. Those guys know the law." She paused. "I also told the cops about Dad and demanded they contact him at work and he'd verify I'm a legit' student." When she rose, he could see she was in pain.

"They talked to one of my professors at the LSE. He gave them a brilliant reference, or so one of the nicer cops told me. The embassy was cool, too. I was real surprised how helpful they were. They gave me the name of an attorney who represents Americans over here and he came to the station and gave 'em hell. Told them my notes weren't subversive and they had to let me go." She laughed but it sounded hollow. "Just as well they didn't check I don't vote Republican in presidential elections."

Despite the attempt at humour, he saw deep vulnerability in her eyes. "It's over now."

"I've got to go back and sort out the place."

"Do you want me to come with you?"

"Todd's on his way over but I don't feel like being alone there." She smiled. "I'm really glad we've become friends, Danny. I sensed on the ferry we'd things in common."

Back in the Big Apple

The waiting on the tarmac always rattled Piper because it gave her too much time to imagine the horrible possibilities. Wandering around duty free had relaxed her because the takeoff, with its attendant dash down the runway and disconcerting fuselage shudders as the jet became airborne, was not yet impending enough to whip up her primal terrors. Now they were raging. It made things easier to have Todd sitting next to her. Piper was staying with her old NYU roommate in the West Village and she was glad Todd was spending two nights with her before flying off to visit his parents in San Francisco.

There was a sudden jolt. She leaned over Todd and peered out the window and saw the plane was reversing from the gate. Ten minutes later, the pilot announced in a British accent, the type of calm British accent that always reassured her everything would go smoothly, that they were next in line for takeoff. He ordered the cabin crew to take their seats. Immediately, she picked up the in-flight magazine on her lap and tried to busy herself with an article she'd already begun. This was a departure trick she'd learned from experience. She had to begin an article while on the ground, just a paragraph or two to get her interested, and then pick up where she left off as the plane did its final turn and the engines hurtled to maximum speed. If the article was begun while barreling down the runway, her effort was doomed to failure.

"We're officially outta here, hon," Todd said.

She already knew that because she'd heard the wheels fold into the undercarriage.

"Wow. Catch a look at the number of planes on the ground."

"Busy reading here," she said.

He laughed. "Sorry."

Half-an-hour later, following an announcement from the cockpit that the weather was cooperating and the flight to Newark would be calm and on schedule, and with a glass of Bordeaux now on the pullout tray (another small bottle stuffed into the seat pocket thanks to the generosity of the friendly cabin steward), Piper returned to her old self. She gave Todd a kiss before starting to peruse the in-flight magazine again.

After landing, they took a taxi to her friend's townhouse, one they shared for the last two years she was at NYU. Situated in a quiet street near the 1 and 9 subways, the three-story rental was one of a group of four townhouses with a brick façade painted burgundy. White shutters framed the windows, five of which hung lopsided from broken hinges. Nestled between two older single-family houses, entry to the complex's brick paved front garden was through a heavy wrought iron gate containing a weathered sign 'Private Court'. Two towering buttonwood trees whose trunks and gnarled limbs were sheathed in ivy rose above the roofline. As she crossed the yard to the door, Piper saw Vanessa seated at the table by the ground floor window, her dark hair turned coppery from the glow of an overhead lamp.

As svelte as Piper though two inches taller and slightly broader, they kissed one another excitedly and danced around the room holding hands like they were back in kindergarten. Todd watched them amused. Piper realised how much she'd missed her friend, though their friendship was the sort that lasted a lifetime. It didn't matter how long they spent apart. They simply picked up where they left off.

When Vanessa left to fetch champagne, Piper looked around the old apartment, unchanged except for a buttery leather sofa, two matching armchair recliners and a wall to ceiling bookcase made of solid mahogany. A tacky rhinestone framed mirror bought on a whim one afternoon still hung on the wall and an old bearskin they'd found among the rubbish outside the apartment still covered the deep scratches on the wood floor.

A twinge of jealously caught Piper by surprise when the three of them clinked their champagne flutes together. In two years Vanessa would be a successful senior editor at a publishing house, living on the Upper West or East side in a gorgeous apartment, attending the hottest Manhattan parties while Piper still didn't know what she'd be doing.

Despite Vanessa having to leave for work at seven the next morning, she fetched beers after the champagne was finished and they began to catch up on mutual friends now scattered throughout the country. An hour later, Todd said he was tired and went to bed. The friends chatted until one-thirty before retiring. Not even the rattle of an ancient air-conditioning unit wedged into the bedroom window stopped Piper from falling quickly asleep.

She awoke to the morning sun streaming through the grimy bedroom window.

"Hey, honey bun. How's your head?"

"We didn't get rat-assed if that's what you're thinking."

He leaned over and kissed her on the mouth. The kiss grew more passionate and he put his hand on her right breast.

"Not now."

"Aw, come on. It's my first time in Manhattan with you." He pouted. "We have to."

She looked at him with mock sternness. "You don't have protection."

He fished under his pillow and held up a condom.

"Got it all planned out, huh?"

"Like I said, first time in Manhattan."

"I need to brush my teeth first." She climbed out of bed. "You do, too."

Whether because Sonia's unorthodox therapy session had

inadvertently untangled something within Piper's subconscious or due to the novelty it was indeed the first time with Todd in her home city, their lovemaking flowed spontaneously. For the first time, Piper experienced tiny flashes of desire within her body. She enjoyed the firm touch of his pressed lips against hers, his warm palms cupping her breasts. Her skin tingled as he began to gently explore the curves of her torso and hips. Things did fall apart toward the end as once more, finding climax unobtainable and anxious she was taking far too long, she reverted to faking it. But she'd wanted him physically and that was progress. Sustainable progress.

She propped herself up on the bed using her elbow as support and watched until he turned his face to look at her.

"Todd, if we're going to live together, I need to tell you something."

"Sure."

"This is hard to say."

"There's nothing we can't say to each other."

"Okay." She hesitated. "I'm not into sex so much."

"What do you mean?" His eyes narrowed.

"Don't think it's to do with you or anything."

"What am I supposed to think?"

"The reason I'm telling you this is I want to get it right with you. I want us to be happy and that includes sex because I know it's important to you."

She could see his confusion. He turned away and stared at the wall.

"Truth is I've never wanted to have sex much and did it only because I figure everybody's doing it so it must be normal."

He turned back to her. "I never would have guessed."

"Don't get all facetious on me."

"I meant that you've felt this way all along."

Piper sighed. "I spoke to Sonia Berg about it."

"So that's the private matter you guys discussed."

Piper stiffened. "What did she tell you?"

"Nothin'. He cocked his head. "So what'd she say?"

"The therapy session was a bit unorthodox but it helped me realise I'm maybe one of those people who just doesn't care about sex."

"Asexual, you mean?"

His eyes darted toward the door and she wondered if he was mentally opening it.

"Where does that leave me?" he continued.

"I wanted you just now," she said. "It's the first time I've ever wanted anybody. That's a good sign."

His head whipped back to her. "That means you can't be asexual."

She placed her hand lightly on his chest. "You want us to get close, right?"

"I thought we were."

"Closer, then?"

"Sure."

"I promise it'll be fine, Todd." She hesitated. "Down the road it might mean you and me talking to Sonia as a couple. We might also have to take supervised instruction from her."

"Supervised instruction? Sounds kinky."

"It's not, and only if I need more therapy."

He pulled himself up on the bed. "Whatever it takes to get you right."

"So you're swearing on your Grampa's grave you haven't gotten yourself in trouble with the authorities over there?" her father said.

He was relentless. His gaze was unblinking and penetrating, just like she remembered on the day he'd come into her bedroom years ago. He'd come in to grill her about smoking pot when her mother had come upon her stash and told him to deal with it because she was done with Piper's lies.

She matched his stare. "I fricken swear, Dad."

They were in an Irish restaurant-cum-bar on Forty-Sixth

Street and Sixth Avenue. Downstairs, signed photographs of New York Yankee and Mets ballplayers and mugshots of a young Cassius Clay adorned the walls, but, as Piper had made her way up to the second floor bar, the ambience had grown increasingly native. Posters of their national sports heroes including the famous showjumper Paul Darragh and framed Gaelic football jerseys representing a bunch of Irish counties ran along the wall of the barroom toward the open French doors of the street-facing balcony. The draft beers were imported because many of the patrons had accents as velvety thick as the Guinness she was drinking. Through the French doors, Piper could see the sagging defined head and upper chest of Christ as he hung from his huge concrete crucifix attached to the façade of the Episcopal Church across the street.

"You know her name's not Piper, right?" Her father picked up his glass of soda.

"Dad, enough already."

Her father's eyes cut from her to Todd. Despite his sunny grin, she saw him look Todd over in that cold, measured New York cop way that was enough to make innocent people squirm or plead guilty just to get away. At forty-four, in his navy cargos and shirt that had his surname spelled on the front pocket, NYPD patches and sergeant stripes on its sleeves (short sleeves because of the ferocious August humidity inhabiting the city's canyons and streets), her father still cut an impressive figure. People noticed him, certainly some of the barflies who turned on their high backed wooden stools to peer discretely (or so they thought) at him through gaps in the lunchtime office crowd. Even the dour barmaid kept coming over to the nearside corner of the bar on the pretext of wiping down the counter to land an eyeful.

Piper was secretly thrilled Todd didn't flinch, instead tossed him a casual shrug to convey he wasn't bothered.

"Did you hear what I just said, Todd?" her father continued.

"She's Piper to me, sir. She's been working real hard at school, too."

The 'sir' and allusion to her hard work did the trick. She'd known it would. Her father gulped down the last of his soda and asked if they wanted another beer.

"Wow, he sure is one tough cookie," Todd said.

Piper didn't reply as she watched her father ordering from the barmaid who'd a grin on her face like a performing seal.

"I don't know him so good, but from what I've seen, there's a lot of him in his daughter."

"What's that supposed to mean?"

Todd's eyebrows raised. "He's direct. I like that."

"Haven't seen her round here before," Piper said, nodding vaguely in the direction of the barmaid as her father approached. "She just off the boat?"

"She's been here a while." Her father slid their drinks across the table. "Don't mind telling you I nearly fainted when that Special Branch cop came on the line to ask about you."

"Aw Dad, no more of the cop stuff, please. Pat's in jail now. It's over."

"Fair enough." Her father turned to him. "You're from free-rollin' California, huh? Growing up there must have been a lotta fun. Tell me some about your life there."

Making a move

It was one of those summer days that made Danny feel especially happy to be in London. The underbelly of a passing jet gleamed white as a fish's in the unblemished blue sky, the warm breeze carried the heavy scent of the late summer roses growing at the back of the garden. He'd been working for an hour weeding the flower border and around the shrubs.

From inside the house, Katie called out someone was at the door and then warned Julia to hurry or they'd be late for a lunch appointment. Moments later, he looked toward the French doors and saw Finty watching him.

"You're early," he said.

"I still have to be home by six."

He peeled off the rubber gloves, immediately feeling the coolness as the sweat evaporated off the back of his hand.

"Doing something fun this evening, eh?"

"You're doing a great job here." Finty swept her eyes over the overgrown garden and scrawny lawn grass.

This was one thing Danny noticed about her. Though he'd give her opportunities to discuss what was going on in her private life, she never availed of them. Of course he realised he had no right to expect her to, but it niggled him nevertheless.

"Why don't we sit out here and study today?" she said.

Danny regarded the fan-backed wicker chairs and tall root bound rubber plants flanking them. He'd also promised Julia he'd repot them but hadn't had the time. Or more truthfully, he'd been too lazy. She'd bought beautiful new pots a month ago and asked a week ago if he still planned to transplant them for her. He felt guilty.

"Let's do that," he said.

Excusing himself, he left to freshen up. The phone rang when he arrived downstairs again.

"Hello," Julia said. "Hello. Who is this? Answer me."

She put the mouthpiece back on its cradle. It was the eighth anonymous call they'd had in a week. Each time they happened, Danny thought about what Piper said the morning she'd arrived at his house following her release from jail, about how she thought the police weren't finished with her yet. Maybe it really was the Special Branch. Maybe they'd followed Piper to his home and had now bugged his phone to eavesdrop or find out some things about him.

"It's definitely some prank or school kids playing tricks," Julia said. "They'll get bored. This happened to me a couple of years ago at my old flat."

"This isn't all that unusual, then?" Danny said.

"They'll knock it off soon. Mine did. Just like that." Julia snapped her fingers to emphasise her point. "I never heard from them again."

"*Kann ich Dich eine Frage stellen?*" he asked Finty. He sat back on the fan-backed chair and smiled.

"That's really good, Danny. Okay, my turn now."

"Seriously," he said. "I want to ask you something."

She looked at him nonplussed.

"I'll say this in English because it's far more complicated." He smiled again to reassure her it wasn't an interrogation. "We're almost finished the course and I don't know much about you. I know you're a strict vegetarian. I know your puppy... whom I haven't seen in a while and would love to, by the way." He pulled a sad look. "You live in South London and have a part-time job you never really talk about."

"What else do you need to know?"

"That sounds a wee bit harsh, Finty."

"It does?"

"Yeah, you said 'need to know' like I'm being nosy."

"Aren't you?" She immediately put up her hand, palm out. "That was rude. I'm sorry." She went over to him and planted a kiss of apology on his cheek.

"I like you Finty and I'd like to know you better." His face flushed. He felt exposed. He looked away toward Mrs. Hartley's garden where a magpie, perched in the shade of her chestnut tree, was watching him. Superstitious, Danny scoured the tree and beyond, needing urgently to see a second one. There wasn't any.

"Okay," she said. "What can I tell you?"

He turned back to her. "Start with your work." He held out the wine bottle and she brought her glass up to its opening so he could refill it.

"Psychological assistant sounds very grand but it's really just a fancy name for doing anything I'm told to do."

As she described working with young offenders in the Probation Service, some of whom were very troubled, he watched spellbound. The sun played with her dark hair, making its natural red and copper highlights glint and sparkle. He imagined its softness between his fingers. Her full mouth and parting lips as she spoke sent shivers through his body.

"Talk about pent-up rage," she said. "Poor kid sat opposite me at a table for nearly an hour and didn't speak, just stared at his hands or looked past me to the wall."

"Why was he locked up?"

He wanted badly to lean over and kiss her, to run the tip of his tongue along her slender neck. He wanted to put his hand inside her T-shirt and cup her breasts.

"Slashed his sister's face with a knife when she caught him taking money from her room."

The words cut into his thoughts. He nearly dropped his wine

glass on the flagstone platform.

"I didn't know your job was so dangerous."

"I bet you're sorry you asked about it now?"

"No. It's just… "

"I love my job and hope it'll become full-time at some point. These kids have very little going for them."

Her flashing eyes were now wide open windows. Danny saw the intense conviction she felt. It was a side of her character he'd suspected she had and he loved her now it was revealed. He rose off his chair and moved toward her before the logical side of his brain could order him to stop. Stooping, he put his hands against the sides of her face and kissed her on the mouth. As soon as his lips pressed against hers, the spell broke. He opened his eyes and wondered what the hell he'd done. Still, he wasn't sorry. Her lips were as lush as he imagined. No, far more than he imagined. She made no effort to rebuff him. Her hands hung in the air for a moment and then she put them around the back of his head. Emboldened, he slipped his tongue into her parted lips. Again, she reciprocated. He eased her gently to her feet, their kiss still unbroken. But the process of activating body muscles required superimposing thoughts and, a moment later, she pulled away.

"What's the matter?"

"I have to leave."

"It's only five."

"I… I have a boyfriend." She gathered her notes hastily and stuffed them into her bag. "I shouldn't have let this happen. Please don't think badly of me."

"Is it serious?"

"We live together."

The muscle cords in Danny's neck tightened.

"I'm sorry. I didn't mean for… " She started toward the French doors. "I'll see you in class next week."

"Finty, wait a minute." He ran after her.

She'd already crossed the living room and was opening the

front door when he got inside.

"Finty!"

She stopped and looked over her shoulder. Her eyes glittered with tears.

"I shouldn't have kissed you like that." His words sounded as hollow as he felt. "Can we stay friends?"

"I'd like that, Danny. A lot."

He watched her walk away. He watched until she turned into King Street. Still, he stood rooted, staring now at the vacant air she'd just occupied. Inside, he threw himself on the sofa just as the phone rang. He rushed to it. No-one spoke.

"You fucking weirdo, stop calling here."

He listened again and thought he heard people talking or perhaps it was a radio or television in the background. He slammed the receiver down.

Lunch with Mom

Several things struck Piper like she was now a tourist in her own city. They were things she would never have thought about had she not lived for the past year overseas. She kept forgetting the subway was air-conditioned and was always delighted by the refreshing cold air smacking into her sweating face every time the doors opened and she stepped into a carriage from the stifling platform. She also persistently forgot the map of the subway grid was adjacent to the train's doors and not above the window as on a London tube, and kept checking there first to see which station the train was next approaching. Another thing was the raw energy on the Manhattan streets, so different in character to London's well-mannered busyness, an energy intensified by the brash presence of colossal skyscrapers, wide avenues and jets of pristine white steam curling from manholes in the streets. And there was also the energy from the traffic. Nowhere did drivers honk more than in New York City. The final thing was the food served in the restaurants and delis: bagels containing a quarter pound or more of cream cheese, challenging sandwiches piled so high with sliced meats and cheeses they were lopsided, and colossal burgers served alongside a mountain of fries, or plates of steaming pasta, and steaks so enormous they were obscene. It was little wonder so many of her countrymen and women were obese, or dying of heart disease and diabetes related illnesses.

After exiting the train at Chambers Street, she made her way up to street level. A wall of searing heat slapped her face. The sun's glare forced her to narrow her eyes as she looked up to take in the view of the twin towers in the near distance. That was actually another thing: she'd forgotten how brutally hot Manhattan was in the summer. London never got this kind of energy draining humidity. When she arrived five minutes later at the law office, she felt she'd been exercising in a dry sauna because her face, cleavage and arms glistened with perspiration. The firm was situated on the fourth floor of a pre-war office block. Its reception was panelled floor to ceiling in English library style dark wood. A corridor nearby the reception desk ran to the attorneys' offices within the heart of the floor. Behind her, a client reading the *Wall Street Journal* occupied the nearest of two sumptuous maroon leather couches separated by an over-sized solid oak table. Invited by the friendly receptionist to take a seat, she sat on the other couch, took out a portion of her dissertation and began to proofread.

Five minutes later, her mother came out. "Hey, Phila." She opened her long arms in preparation to embrace as she approached.

Piper was shocked by her mother's youthfulness. She'd expected her to be on the plumpish side still, but her body was taut and defined. Tanned thighs disappeared above a fashion-ably cut summer dress. Gone was the bluntly cut dark hair well threaded with grey, replaced by a lopsided bob that made her look not unlike Linda Evangilista. Only faint lines around her eyes and a softening of the cheeks and chin belied she was forty-six years of age.

"What's happened to you, Mom?"

Her mother laughed.

"You've been working out."

"Not too shabby, huh. What can I say? Gotta keep myself healthy."

Her mother ran her hand up and down her left arm. "I thought we'd eat at an Italian restaurant I know two blocks from here.

They make a killer chicken parm and serve whole wheat pasta."

The restaurant was already packed with bankers and lawyers from the World Trade Center, many wearing de-rigueur light-weight summer suits and chatting animatedly into cell phones. She took her mother's recommendation and ordered the chicken parmesan but had a glass of white wine in addition to the large bottle of sparkling water her mother selected.

"You've been here three days already, huh?" her mother said, as she returned the menu card to the waiter.

"I know what you're thinking and you're wrong. It's just... "

"What am I thinking?" Her mother broke a piece of bread and dipped it in the plate of golden olive oil.

"That I didn't get in touch sooner. I've got this dissertation and I'm researching like crazy."

"You don't have to apologise."

"I'm not."

They fell silent. Her mother chewed bread as she looked about. Piper watched a dust strewn construction worker whose upper body and arms bounced as he drilled into the pavement with a jackhammer.

"By the way, I meant to say you're looking good as well," her mother said. "You've dropped round your face and it suits you."

"Thanks."

"Phila, you should think about growing your hair again. It's kinda severe so short. I always liked it shoulder-length. Remember how you wore it in the eleventh grade?"

"Call me Piper like I asked? Yesterday, I started the process to get it changed."

"That's the kind of research you've been doing."

"*Mom*, please."

"What's wrong with Philomena anyway?"

"I don't like it."

"It's my name."

Another silence occurred that was broken by the waiter's arrival with their house salads. Pointing a huge pepper mill, he asked Piper if she wanted some. She nodded.

"How much pepper you wanting, Phi… Piper?" her mother asked, staring wide-eyed at the bowl.

Piper nodded at the waiter. She stuck the fork into the greens and began to toy with them. "Why do we always end up doing this, Mom?"

"Doing what?"

"We're together half-an-hour and already arguing."

"We're not arguing. It's only because we're alike." She popped a cherry tomato in her mouth. "You were always your own person. Look how you went off to England. Not every girl would do that."

"Is that a compliment?"

"It is." Her mother took a sip of water. "How's your father?"

"As well as to be expected."

"Which means what, exactly?"

"He's renting an apartment on the Lower East Side now, Mom. It's tiny. His rent's sky-high because the area's gentrifying."

"And that's my fault, how exactly?"

"You made him sell our home."

"Half that house was mine. I needed the cash to put myself through law school." She picked up her fork. "He should buy if it's gentrifying. He'll make a bundle in a couple of years."

"I thought the law firm's paying."

"Only after I graduate. Until then, I'm on my own." Her mother pushed her plate aside. "Anyway, that wasn't a home. You're smart. You know that."

"Hmm."

"There's still time to change your mind about being a bridesmaid." Her mother leaned away slightly to allow the waiter space to place the bowl of bowtie pasta with pesto in front of her.

"I'm still going to pass."

"Fair enough. You're still up for meeting Juan, aren't you?"

"Aha."

"You'll like him."

"I will?"

While the food was delicious, Piper didn't feel hungry anymore. Her mother inquired about the state of her finances and plans for the future, questions Piper responded to with concise vagueness.

"Let me see if I've got this straight." Her mother's fork was poised halfway between her plate and mouth. "You're about to get a Masters diploma and still don't know what you want to do."

"That's it."

"You're unbelievable." She shook her head. "Do you know how many women would love to be in your position?"

"How many, Mom?"

"If you come back to New York, you'd find a job with an investment bank starting at... " The wrinkles around her mother's eyes deepened as her face puckered in concentration. "Oh, I'd say over a 100k, easy."

"I've just turned twenty-four, Mom. I've got time."

"Time goes fast, Piper. I was twenty-three when I had you. You need to start building up a solid work history. It ain't so easy. You'll find out."

"You're starting over and it seems to be working fine."

Her mother regarded her for a moment before stirring her fork around the pasta. "You seeing anyone?"

She told her about Todd, his family in California and their plans to live together when he returned to London.

"Sounds like I'll have to meet him. By the way, you been out to see Rory yet?"

So abrupt was the transition, Piper dropped her fork. It hit the plate with a loud rattle before sliding onto the table. She'd known the conversation would turn to her brother, just hadn't expected it at that moment. Her mother's eyes zeroed in on the splotch of tomato sauce beside Piper's plate, as if she were scouring for evidence of guilt.

"Changing a name sure takes a lot of time," said her mother.

She decided to ignore the barb. "Tell me all about you going back to school again, Mom. You excited?"

The remainder of their lunch was spent talking about her mother's career plans and upcoming wedding. On the way back to the office, her mother accompanied Piper to the Chambers Street subway where they briefly embraced at the entrance. After they parted, Piper didn't go downstairs immediately. She lingered, watching her mother merge into the city throng, lifting her manicured hand and running her fingers ever so carefree through her hair.

Striking a deal

Someone grabbed hold of the car door and she couldn't shut it. Julia peered up through the triangle of shadowed space to see Katie's husband, his shoulder length salt-and-pepper hair tied back in a ponytail.

"What are you doing here?" she asked.

"I need to speak to you."

"About?"

"There's three in my marriage and it's feeling a bit crowded."

She almost burst out laughing. "Your marriage is between you and Katie."

"Please, I really need to talk to you."

Out of the corner of her eye, Julia spotted movement. Mrs. Hartley emerged from her house with a broom.

"It'll have to be quick because I'm running late."

"It'll only take a few minutes."

"Let's go into my house."

They crossed the street in silence. Though she heard the rustle of the broom on the concrete pavement. Julia felt Mrs. Hartley's eyes bore into the back of her head as she turned the key in the door.

Over six-foot, Harry made the living room seem suddenly very small. She was glad to see Danny was in the kitchen.

"This is Katie's husband," she said.

As he came up from the kitchen to greet him, she noticed his shock despite the wide smile.

"Have a seat," Julia said, and pointed to an armchair while she sat on the sofa.

"What exactly do you want to talk about?"

He looked at Danny, then back at her, as if he expected her to ask him to leave.

"Danny knows about Katie."

"Does he know she's the mother of two young children?"

"I'll give you some privacy to talk." Danny started hurriedly toward the stairs.

"You don't have to leave," Julia said. She nodded furtively when she caught Danny's eye. He returned to the kitchen.

"I know my wife's been staying here a lot lately."

"How do you know?"

"I know."

"Has Katie told you?"

"I know."

"Katie's talked to you while she's been here?"

"No."

"I'm not with you then."

"I've followed her… and I've rang here because I knew she's been with you."

She looked toward the Danny. "Have you spoken to Harry on the phone?"

"Actually, I didn't speak to anybody," Harry said, as he started to massage his forehead. "I wanted to speak to her and tell her to come home, but I couldn't do it. I knew in my heart if I asked to speak to her while she was here, it'd be the end of my marriage."

There was a sudden clatter as cutlery hit the base of the sink. She looked over at Danny. It all made sense now. Every time the prank calls occurred, Katie'd been here.

"That's called stalking, Harry."

"I apologise."

Julia was silent for a moment. "Katie comes here of her own free will. I don't beg her."

"That's why I've come to see you." He pinched his Adam's apple and then bent forward in his chair. "I love my wife. She's a very good mother. We've been very happy." He stood and began to massage his forehead again, then sat and leaned toward Julia. His face was now scarlet. "You seem like a reasonable woman. I'm not a fool. I know Katie has needs I can't satisfy. But the children need her."

"I'm sure Katie knows what she's doing and won't hurt them."

"Aren't they already hurting?"

Julia stood. "This is really between you and Katie. Besides, it doesn't feel right discussing this without her being here."

"I doubt she discusses me or my children when she's here screwing you." He cupped his chin in his large right hand and shook his head. "I didn't mean that. I'm sorry."

"I really can't help you. You should leave."

"Julia, let him speak," Danny said. He approached with a handful of knives and forks in his hand. "What he's saying's true. They have children who need both their… "

"This isn't any of your business."

"I know you now, Julia. You wouldn't want the children to get hurt. You need to work out something with Harry and Katie."

She stared at Danny without speaking.

"Anyway, I've said my piece." He set the cutlery on the coffee table and went up the stairs.

She turned back to Harry. "What do you suggest?"

"I'm not asking you to stop seeing my wife. I know that won't happen. Even if it did, she'll meet another woman at some point."

"You're right."

"I'm a pragmatic chap," he said, and smiled wanly. "I'm prepared to accept an arrangement between the three of us for the sake of the children… and because I love my wife. All I ask in return is you don't pressure her to leave us."

Julia went over to him and laid a hand on his shoulder, but then retracted it quickly. It felt too weird. It felt like she was giving some kind of benediction.

"I'm fond of Katie," she said, "and I'd never ask her to do anything like that. Anyway, I'm not ready to go there."

"Thank you." He rose as if to hug her.

"Please understand Harry, I can't guarantee she won't divorce you. That's not in my power."

"Has she talked about that?"

"I suspect she's going to want her freedom. We're living in a different world now. You need to be aware of that."

"I'm a film director. Don't you think I know?

"So long as you do."

"Until that time comes, I'll take my chances."

As soon as Harry left, Danny's bedroom door opened and his heavy footsteps came down the stairs. He took a seat across from her.

"I was out of line." He began to pick up the cutlery off the table. "It's just, I had to speak my mind. It's been bugging me ever since I knew Katie was a mother."

"I'm glad you said it. I wasn't sure how to deal with this."

He rose, but made no attempt to leave. "Hey, isn't it great we know now who's been making those damned calls?"

"I told you it was a prank."

Arranging closure

Her father held up two brown bags and cans of diet coke to Piper. "I was in the area and figured you'd be here."

The sumptuous majesty of the Rose Reading Room at the New York Public Library with its spectacular ceiling murals of vibrant skies and sunlit clouds had always been a productive place for her to study during her NYU years, especially when she'd had to write essays or cram but had cabin fever and needed to get out of her apartment. They sat by Prudence, the south-facing lion. He'd bought her a BLT on wholemeal with extra mayo and a layer of 'bread and butter' pickle chips, a favourite sandwich from her childhood she rarely ate now because it was so unhealthy. Near where they sat, a young, immaculately dressed woman stood before a middle-aged man. He'd set his briefcase between his legs and was clutching a slim rust-coloured folder, the sort litigation attorneys carry to court. As Piper listened, the woman responded to his rapid-fire questions. It was a job interview for an associate position at the man's law firm.

"Only in Manhattan do they hold interviews on the street," Piper said. "What a rat race."

Her father broke off a piece of rye bread and tossed it viciously into the street. Three pigeons immediately scrambled to reach it first.

"I didn't make detective."

"Jeez Dad, I'm sorry."

"My life's going south with no stops in between."

"Don't say that."

"Some guy five years younger got the job." He sighed as he looked out to the street. "Really thought I'd get it too. My buddy's a first grader and he told me the crime and narco work I've done would be recognised as investigative by the department. Go figure."

"Next time."

A pause ensued. "If there is a next time."

"What's that supposed to mean?"

"Nothin'. That's what it means."

"What's bugging you?"

"It's not as if people are depending on me anymore, is it? Your Mom's gone. You're grown up and making it on your own now. Rory's... well, that's all I'm tryin' to say."

Her father was a fighter, it wasn't like him to talk like that. "I depend on you."

"I love you too, hon. You're all I have left."

"You're young, Dad. Apply again next year."

He looked across the street for a moment. "I want you to think about something." He paused. "When you decide to get married someday, would you maybe think about not switching our last name... and give the kids the name, too."

Piper watched the people walking up and down the library steps.

"I know, I know. I'm the traditionalist and this is kinda unusual. It's just when I pass, our name dies." He slapped his hands on his thighs. "This probably sounds dumb, huh?" He smiled. "You don't have to give me your answer now."

Piper gripped his forearm. "You can still meet someone, settle down and start another family. People do that all... "

"Your mother's the only woman for me."

"She's moving on and you should too. "

"How come you've never said what you think of this guy she's seeing?"

"I... you never asked."

"Come on now. This is your old man you're talking too."

Piper squeezed the remains of the sandwich into the grease-proof sheet of paper and put it into the bag. The truth was, the evening she'd gone to dinner at the Bronx apartment Juan and her mother shared had been full of surprises, the first of which had been Juan. He was six inches shorter than her mother, as well as eight years younger. Surprise number two had been the revelation her mother had taken up swimming because Juan was a member of a snorkeling club. Her mother had always been terrified of water. The final surprise had been the amount of fawning, her mother's Irish reserve about displaying affection clearly tossed out with her marriage. She'd tousled Juan's hair, giggled and stroked his biceps at the table like a mob boss' moll.

"You want the truth?" she said to her father. "He's a nice guy who makes great fried plantains."

Her father didn't smile.

"I think you and Juan would get on if circumstances were different."

The blare of emergency vehicles racing down Fifth Avenue grew louder and louder until it drowned out the natural city din. When the vehicles reached the intersection, the traffic lights were still on red. A fire engine crossed, then another, their occupants seated in the cabs staring out impassively at the rubbernecking pedestrians. Instinctively, Piper covered her ears with her hands and stared at her knees until the sound receded.

"I've been thinking about something for a while." Her father stared deep into Piper's eyes. "I'd love if we could all go to Rory's grave together."

"No problem."

"Ask your mother when she can make it?"

"Mom, too?"

"Sure. Things'll be changed forever after she marries that

guy. Let's be a family one last time. It's not too much to ask. All of us together with Rory one last time."

"Mom, all I'm saying's, I don't see what the problem is," Piper said.

"It's dysfunctional. That's my problem." Her mother did another half-turn in front of the dressing mirror, smoothed the dress around her waist and hips and checked her profile again. "I do like this, you know."

"It's too short, and this country's full of dysfunctional families. Dysfunctional's the new normal."

"My legs look good in it, no?"

"It's appropriate for someone in her twenties, Mom."

"Appropriate. I hate that word. It's... it's so... "

"Appropriate?"

"Judgmental." Her mother put her face closer to the mirror and checked her face, pulling back the skin around the corners of her eyes so the shallow crow's feet disappeared. "And no offence, but you've never been interested in clothes so your opinion doesn't amount to a hill of beans."

"None taken."

They were in the ladies department at Bloomingdales to purchase Piper's dress for the wedding, which she'd decided upon after trying on just three. Unfortunately, her mother spotted dresses she liked as well, but was annoyingly indecisive. As a teenager, Piper stopped going shopping with her for this reason.

"I suppose you're right," her mother said. She returned to the changing room and Piper began to type at her laptop again.

"The other thing is, I like to go to see Rory alone," her mother said. *"That's* a problem." She came out. "Let's get outta here."

Piper saved her document and stuffed the laptop into her satchel.

"I think we should go to the cemetery," she said, in a last ditch effort while they were on their way to the café on the sixth floor. "Think about it. All of us together with Rory one last time. You owe Dad that."

"I owe him *nada*."

"Learning Spanish, are we?" Her mother didn't speak. "Rory, then. You owe it to him."

Her mother glared at her. "Don't say that to me *ever* again. A long life was what Rory was owed and he never got it."

Her remark was so bitterly loud, two women ahead of them on the escalator turned to stare.

"I'm sorry," Piper said.

They travelled the remainder of the journey in awkward silence. When they arrived on the sixth floor, her mother said, "Look, I'll come to the cemetery… " She started toward the down escalator. "Right now, I really need to leave."

Tea and rancor

"You had a visitor this afternoon," Julia said to Danny as he came into the garden.

Wearing a canary yellow, orange and blue tie-dyed sarong, she was sitting on a fan-backed wicker chair reading a romance novel. Julia's gaze darted beyond him to Finty emerging from the French doors, and then lowered to take in the sight of her ungainly puppy loping toward her. It had been weeks since Danny had seen the puppy and, after remarking on it at the *Institut* that morning, she'd asked him to wait in a pub and then surprised him by driving back to her flat and fetching him. A small gesture, but one that pleased Danny enormously.

For a while after Danny declared his feelings for Finty, he'd felt excruciatingly awkward in her presence. They still sat together in class and chatted, but never about what had occurred that afternoon. They also went for coffee, or to the park, or quiet pubs where they wrote their assignments side-by-side, but it was now always uppermost in his mind she had a boyfriend. But inevitably, as time passed, their awkwardness diminished and the friendship resumed its earlier pattern.

"Your puppy's a cracker," Julia said. She put down her book and hugged him as he joyfully licked her cheek with his very pink tongue. "I wish my hair was that soft."

"It's the poodle in him," said Finty, as pleased as a new mother. "They have hair not fur."

"He's utterly adorable."

Adorable was what Danny had once thought when the puppy was a small cute ball of fur. Now it was in the gangly stage of early adolescence, with long awkward legs and a snout too long for his head.

"Who was my visitor?" Danny said.

"Your ex-fiancée."

"That's not funny, Julia."

"I'm serious. I asked if she wanted to come in and wait, but she said she'd try again in a couple of hours." Julia ceased patting the dog and looked at her watch. "Round about now, actually."

His heart pounded. Why was she visiting him? Hadn't his letter been enough?

"You never said you were engaged," Finty said.

There was a curious expression on her face, a sort of hybrid between astonishment and disappointment. Despite his predicament, Danny liked her response.

"'Were' being the operative word," he said.

"I should leave," Finty said.

Their end-of-course examination was imminent and they had a lot of grammar and vocabulary to revise.

"You don't need to leave."

"*I* have to, though," said Julia. "Time I got ready for work." She patted the dog's head one last time before leaving.

"You *are* a dark horse," Finty said.

"Well, you are, too."

Susan's jeans were designer and so tight they looked uncomfortable. It didn't help she'd put on eighteen pounds since he'd last seen her, especially on her tummy and backside. Finty's dog sprinted to the front door, leapt up and placed his front paws on her.

"Get this brute away from me." She arched her back and held out her hands.

"He's harmless," said Danny

"You've bought a *dog*?"

"He belongs to a friend of mine. Come and meet her."

"A woman?"

After introducing them, Danny invited Susan to sit on his chair and left to fetch another one from the dining room. Finty was explaining how they'd become friends when he returned.

"How's your Dad doing?" Danny said to Susan.

"It's a slow recovery. So much has been going on at home, you can't believe."

"I'm sorry to hear your father's been ill," Finty said.

Susan nodded and turned back to Danny. "You wouldn't recognise him. He's skin and bone. We might have to sell the business." She wiped the corners of her eyes. "This has been so hard on me, your father suggested I take a holiday. But I wouldn't until now. I mean, how could I leave Mother to cope all alone? It wouldn't have been responsible." She paused and looked at him.

"I'm just going to go upstairs a minute, Danny," Finty said.

"Gosh," Susan said, "I hope we're not boring you with our troubles."

"So sorry again," Finty said. She started hastily toward the house.

Susan watched until Finty and her dog disappeared inside. "She's pretty, isn't she?"

"Yes."

"And not a pick of fat on her. I'm sure I must look as big as a bus in comparison, eh?"

Danny shifted in his chair. "Did Dad suggest you come to London?"

She continued to look toward the French doors. "That dog certainly makes itself pretty free around this house."

He didn't speak.

"Aye, not many visitors feel free to go upstairs in people's homes?"

"It was a polite way of saying she needed to use the loo."

"Didn't I see a toilet at the far side of the kitchen when I came through just now?"

"Was it my father's idea you visit me?"

She picked up Finty's dictionary and began to leaf through it. "You have to learn all these words?"

Finty came outside. "I'm leaving now."

Susan held out the dictionary for her to take.

"We'll revise another time." Finty gathered the rest of her books and clipped the puppy's lead onto his collar.

He escorted her to the door. Susan was poking about the kitchen when he returned. While he made tea, Susan talked about her flight, the hotel she was staying at and updated him on what was happening to people they both knew back home.

"What do you plan to do while you're here?" Danny asked, as they walked into the living room.

"I thought you might show me round a bit."

"Unfortunately not. My final exams are coming up and I've got stuff to do."

"It's great the course is over soon."

He sipped his tea.

"Will you get a certificate at the end?"

How like his father she was, Danny thought. "Probably."

"Your father's looking forward to you coming home." She smiled coyly. "Me, too." Another smile. "Do you know when that will be?" Her eyebrow lifted slightly as she awaited his answer.

He set his mug down so hard on the coffee table the tea splashed over the rim and pooled at the base.

"We need to talk."

"I wondered how long it would take until you brought the subject of us up. I said to myself, 'He'll wait until tomorrow. He'll wait until I'm feeling comfortable.'" She sighed. "It's not to be."

"There is no *us* anymore. You know that, Susan."

"I don't know anything of the sort." She looked at him

without blinking for a few moments. "What I do know is you're taking advantage of my situation. Instead of supporting me when I'm suffering under a terrible strain, you decided to stick the knife in."

She turned away and began sobbing. The sight of a woman crying always unsettled him. He went into the kitchen and fetched some kitchen roll.

"Please don't cry."

"How can I not?" She took the paper sheets and dabbed her eyes. "No-one knows what I've had to endure except your father. He knows how to keep promises. He knows the meaning of the word 'responsibility'. I wish you did."

He didn't immediately respond. His gaze focused on the lime-green and scarlet lights moving up and down like dancing bar graphs on the CD player's front panel as the music played. He'd never understood why they surged and ebbed with equal fervour. It didn't matter whether the music played loudly or softly.

"I admit I said I was postponing our marriage when I told you I was moving to London. But I didn't lie. That's what I believed."

"Like hell you did."

"I have the right to change my mind. And I took responsibility when I told you I had."

"It's not that simple. There are other considerations in play now, Danny."

His eyes narrowed but he didn't speak.

"What if I were to tell you you're going to be a daddy?"

An enormous quake erupted inside Danny's chest. His brain ran frantic, trying to recall when they'd last had sex. "We used condoms."

"Which aren't foolproof."

He remembered the morning Julia burst into the house in a panic looking for the telephone number of the family planning clinic. Was this why Susan had put on so much weight?

"You'd have told me before now."

"Two can play the surprise game." Susan flicked a piece of lint off her jeans. "So what are we going to do about it?"

His mouth felt dry, as if he'd eaten a ball of cotton wool. He took a large sip of tea. "If you're pregnant, I'll help raise the baby."

"I'm glad to hear it."

"But I'm not going to marry you."

"I'd have your baby and you won't marry me?"

"That's right."

"Do you know what people will say about me? They'll say I'm a whore. They'll say I'm immoral. They'll talk about me and my family behind our backs." She picked up her mug and threw the tea over his face. Its contents were lukewarm. She smacked him across the face, the whack so hard it reverberated around the room. "Fuck you, you spineless cur." Making a fist, she hit him on the mouth and began pummeling his chest.

He seized her wrists and held them. "Calm down."

"You bastard. I came all this way for nothing."

"I said, calm down."

"LET GO OF ME."

He thought she would attack him again when he released her wrists and Danny prepared himself, but instead she pushed away and strode into the middle of the room. Danny tasted blood. He wiped his mouth with the back of his hand.

"Whatever you need me to do for you during your pregnancy, I'll do." He licked his swelling lower lip, feeling the loose tag of skin where it had split. "If you need me to come home for a while, I will."

"Go to hell."

"Do you need money?"

"To think your father thought it'd be a good idea for me to come over and talk to you. Just shows he doesn't know you at all. He doesn't know what a callous bastard he has for a son. But I'll be sure to tell him. That's one responsibility *I'll* take."

"Name calling isn't going to get us anywhere. We need to decide what to do... "

"There is no baby, you... you brute."

His brain spun as if in rinse cycle.

"Me have a child by you?" She laughed shrilly. "I'd rather have the devil's any day." She went over to the front door and pulled it open so forcefully it banged against the inner wall.

His father called the following afternoon while he was on the platform at Hammersmith waiting to take the tube into town. He knew who was ringing even before he took the mobile out of his pocket.

"I'm very disappointed," his father said.

Danny moved further along the platform for privacy.

"That was no way to treat a woman. You weren't brought up that way."

"There's two sides to every story, Dad."

"You've disgraced this family. You've disgraced me."

He pressed the phone tight to his ear. "How, Dad?"

"Don't you bloody-well give me any of your lip."

"You shouldn't have got involved." The train rounded the bend and advanced toward the station. "It's none of your business."

"Who do you think you are? Listen, I want you back here as soon as that damned course ends."

Danny struggled to keep his voice calm. "I'll decide that."

"Home. Two weeks."

On the overhead speaker, a voice announced the train. He sensed his father was no longer there, checked the LED screen and saw the call had been terminated.

Sixth time, a charm

Mrs. Hartley ripped the page from the pad, scrunched it until it formed a tight ball and tossed it into the unlit hearth where it landed beside four others. All evening she'd struggled. Her reply would always begin promisingly. But every time she arrived at the bottom of the page and reread what she'd written, her penmanship looked suddenly childish or the sentences weren't as articulate as she wished, or worse, the content appeared deficient.

Since the recent arrival of the reply from Her Majesty in which she'd thanked Agnes for her letter and expressed a hope she was well, writing back to thank her had become both a joyful necessity and horrid predicament. Such was the blessed curse of receiving a communication from the Queen Mother, a woman who wasn't at all well.

She began the sixth attempt:

40 Chumley Street
London, W6

Dear Queen Mother,
  I just wanted to write and thank you for your recent letter.
  Last Saturday, I went up to Clarence House. The crowds were something terrible but I got a glimpse of you in that gorgeous pale blue

dress as you drove by in your little buggy with the balloons floating up from its roof. It made my heart happy to join in with the crowds and sing Happy Birthday to you. One hundred-and-one-years old, Ma'am! What a milestone.

I've had my ups and downs since I last wrote, though I'm glad to report my health is steady. It was my late husband's first anniversary a few weeks ago. I went to his grave and planted his favourite flowers. I know it's late in the season for planting, but I'm sure they'll do nicely next year.

Finding herself stuck again, Agnes got frustrated but didn't toss it into the fire this time. Instead, she went out and did some food shopping for Martha who was feeling ill again so she had kept her company until late that night.

On her return home, just as she was about to exit her car, the Irishman drove up. He parked in a spot one car ahead of hers, got out and checked up and down the street before walking over to his house. He opened the front door but surprised her by returning to his vehicle again. Intrigued and fearing the overhead streetlight would expose her if he looked her way, Agnes slid down in the seat and watched.

He opened his car boot, leaned inside and removed with difficulty a large plastic bag that glinted in the light. Clutching it with both hands, he closed the lid of the boot with his forehead. Once again he checked up and down the street before walking across to the house. The bag's heft made him bend over slightly as he walked and he stopped after he reached the pavement to readjust his grip.

As soon as he disappeared inside, Agnes climbed out and walked up to his car where she discovered the boot wasn't properly shut. With eyes riveted on his front door, she eased the deck lid open and peeked inside. More bags were inside, but her angle of vision and the gloomy interior prevented her from seeing what it was. Her eyes instantly smarted when she lowered her head into the boot's cavity. The uppermost bag had a tear and she knew instantly what its contents were.

"Hey there, what are you doing?"

Agnes straightened up so fast a spasm of pain passed through her lower back. Her head hit the edge of the boot's lid.

"Oh, it's you, Mrs. Hartley." Danny said as he approached.

"Your boot was open and… and I was just about to close it for you."

As she rubbed her head, he regarded her with concern.

"Did you hurt yourself?"

"Didn't half give me a fright, you did."

"Here, let me help you to your house."

"No."

He made no attempt to remove another bag from the boot, just stood waiting for her to leave.

After she got inside her house, Agnes ran to the front window and watched him take out three more bags. An opportunity had just presented itself. A brilliant opportunity to remove Julia Ralston and the Irishman from the house and get her son back home. Brimming with excitement, Agnes sat and began to complete her letter:

I'm almost recovered now from the terrible fright I got when that bomb went off on Hammersmith Bridge. I was there that night Ma'am and reported what I saw to the police.

Now I find out there's another of these IRA terrorists living next door. I never trusted that Irishman from the minute I set eyes on him. Ever so dodgy, he looks. When I saw him carrying bags of fertiliser into the house he's sharing with Julia Ralston, you could have struck me down with a feather. I'm so frightened he's making bombs there, Ma'am. I shouldn't have to put up with neighbours like her at my age. But what can I do? Nobody cares or listens to old people anymore.

Well, I'll sign off for now but will write again.

With loyalty and affection, I remain yours,
Agnes Hartley

Family time

Piper started around the park a second time. She watched three old men playing bocce, lingered in the shade of the hangman's elm and finally stopped to admire the intricate carving on the Washington Memorial that reminded her now of Marble Arch. As she reached the weathered picnic bench again, the one where her friends and she had sat at when she was a student, she pondered again if it was a good sign Todd was now an hour late.

Three days ago, he'd called to say he was returning to New York for a short visit because a Wall Street investment bank wanted to interview him immediately. Although they chatted regularly on the phone, Piper'd been so busy with her research she hadn't realised until he arrived how much she'd actually missed him. They'd gone to an off-off Broadway show the previous evening, a monologue written and directed by an old NYU friend, and afterwards met up with Vanessa for drinks but stayed only half-an-hour because Todd wanted a good night's rest.

The angry honks of a car horn drowned out the shrieks of toddlers playing at a nearby jungle gym. Piper glanced over the low hedge toward the street. A pedestrian had stepped off the pavement and almost gotten knocked over. She scanned the onlooker's faces watching the scene but Todd wasn't among them. Famished, she took out the sandwiches she'd bought for their lunches and began to eat while typing into her laptop. She spotted him five minutes later walking past the Arts and Science

Center across the street. He looked handsome in a black pinstriped suit though she still much preferred him in jeans. She stood and waved until he saw her.

"This place's a lot shabbier than I thought it'd be," he said. His gaze travelled diagonally to a homeless man stretched out on a park bench.

"San Francisco has homeless people, doesn't it?"

"A lot."

"None in Nob Hill, I'd imagine."

"True." He wiped the bench seat before sitting beside her. "My folks want to meet you."

"I'm too scared of the Big One happening."

"Oh stop. I want you to meet them, Piper."

"All in good time."

"Hey, working together on our relationship's going to be a two-way street, you know?"

She scratched the surface of the picnic bench with her nails for a moment. "Okay, the suspense is killing me. What happened?"

"Job's mine if I want it."

"Oh my God." She handed him the lunch bag. "You're officially a suit."

"If I take the job." He opened the bag. "I'd be required to spend four months here first before transferring to London for a year."

"Just for a year?"

"That's what they said. But things can change." He looked inside the bag. "What'd you get me?"

"Ham and Swiss on rye. Will you take the job?"

"Well first, I'm going to interview with that bank in San Francisco next week. Better to have two or three places wanting me. That way I can up my starting salary." He laughed. "You know what they wanted me to do as part of the training when I get here?"

"Learn some kind of in-house research programme."

Damian McNicholl

"Take etiquette classes."

"Get outta here."

"The guy said there's a lot of kids coming out of the ivy leagues who can't use a knife and fork." He regarded his sandwich. "At first I thought he was kidding until their personnel director told me that kids today have the smarts to get into the right colleges and close multi-million dollar mergers, but they don't have a clue about entertaining clients and stuff."

As she watched him eat his sandwich, Piper realised he was right. It took two to work on a relationship and he was prepared to do it. He didn't need to return to London to work, in fact his career path would be far better served if he moved to New York permanently.

"Hey," she said, and lightly touched his arm. "Next time we're over I'll come with you to meet your parents."

As she walked along the narrow path with its neatly trimmed verges, the sun kept disappearing behind the low scudding clouds. It was like the constant switching on and off of a light bulb. Cloud shadows flitted over the obelisks and headstones on either side of her. The breeze became a moderate wind as she advanced, making the limbs of the elms restless and exposing the paler undersides of their leaves.

All the network meteorologists had predicted thunder and downpours but, as the morning slid into early afternoon and the pale blue sky remained unchanged, Piper figured it was just one of those oddball summer days that fooled everyone and didn't bring a jacket or umbrella. After the mile walk from the train station, she realised her mistake and hoped her father would travel back directly to the city so she could ride back with him. He'd called and offered to give her a ride to the cemetery that morning, but then called before she left to say something urgent had come up and he had to go to Garden City.

As she rounded the copse of fir trees separating this part of the cemetery from the older section, she saw her father, dressed in a denim jacket, standing with his head bent in prayer. His right hand rested on the horizontal of the cross forming part of Rory's black granite headstone.

"I thought you said you were coming with your mother. Where is she?"

"She said she'd be here round quarter to four. You know, we could have come here earlier like she suggested."

"It's more peaceful near closing time."

She regarded the oval photograph of her brother's impish face positioned just above his name, birth and death dates etched in gold lettering. As Piper knelt on the marble coping and blessed herself, her father checked his watch. She leaned over and placed the small bunch of roses she'd brought on the bed of dazzling white marble chippings, right beside a potted geranium with two broken flower heads. When she visited Rory alone, she'd talk to him rather than pray because it felt more natural. But her father's presence returned her now to the solemnity of the funeral and saying a prayer seemed more appropriate today. She looked at her grandparents' adjacent plot, their twin hearts headstone made of polished red granite. A weathered Irish tricolour and American flag stood inside a vase.

The sharp edge of the coping began to bite into the soft flesh beneath her knee.

"I miss him," he said.

"Rory's always with us."

"It's not the same."

She looked down trying to imagine exactly where her brother lay asleep just a short distance away, the silence between them broken only by the rumble of distant thunder. A couple walked by on their way to the exit. Further along the main pathway was the only other remaining visitor, an old woman with a grizzled Labrador on a lead standing beside a grave blanketed with fresh wreathes.

"Your old man loves you, Philomena. You know that, right?"

She moved closer and put her hand around his thick wrist and squeezed. It was an old signal between them, a sign she needed him to put his arm around her, one she hadn't used since puberty when she'd stopped wanting him to do it anymore. He remembered. As he turned and began to raise his arm, the front of his jacket opened slightly and she saw the black grip of a handgun.

"What the heck's keepin' your mother?"

His arm felt heavy on her shoulders.

"She'll be here." She waited a moment before speaking again. "Were you on police work earlier?"

"No." He squeezed her left shoulder and then took his arm away.

Two large crows rose noisily into the darkening sky. She looked over just as her mother came hastily round the copse of trees. She waved as she approached.

"I forgot just how crazy the L.I.E gets on Friday afternoons." Her mother blessed herself, touching her forehead and shoulders lightly with her orange painted nails. She placed a bunch of scarlet roses and a chocolate bar on top of the white chippings. Tears welled in Piper's eyes. Her throat constricted.

"I always bring him his favourite chocolate though I'm sure the birds eat it as soon as I leave."

Piper wiped her eyes.

"But it makes me feel good. Crazy, huh?"

"It's not crazy, Mom."

Her mother looked about the cemetery. "Twice this summer, I've brought a book and just sat here for hours. I just feel so close to him when I sit here."

"Sometimes I think we'll see each other here, Philomena," her father said.

Her mother didn't answer, just watched the old woman and her arthritic dog pass by.

"I was beginning to think you weren't coming," her father said.

Piper detected a tremor in his voice, peered over and saw him regarding her mother with a strange look in his eye.

"I thought it was a crazy idea when Piper told me," her mother said. "I nearly didn't come after I thought about it some more."

"What changed your mind?"

"Juan said it was a good idea."

"What matters is we're all here," said Piper.

A finger of lightning darted across the distant horizon and was chased twelve seconds later by a peal of thunder.

"Piper tells me you're living in the city now. You liking it?"

"Manhattan's for young people."

"Age is just a state of mind," her mother said. "Forty-five's the new twenty-two."

"That why you're dressed like one of those young pharmaceutical reps?"

The skirt of her mother's business suit was very short. "*Dad*, we're with Rory."

"You think he's looking down on us right now?" her father said.

"You bet he is," said her mother. "One thing about Rory, he was always a curious kid." She laughed sharply. The wind swallowed it instantly.

"I've got an umbrella in the car, Piper." Her father held out the keys.

"I'm okay, Dad."

"I meant for your mother."

"I'm good." Her mother looked at the sky. "We should get outta here or we'll get soaked before we make it back to the parking lot."

"I'd like to talk to your Mom alone."

"What do you need to talk to me about, Kevin?"

"It's between us."

"We've nothing to say to each other that can't be said in front of her."

"Philomena, let's just you and I talk for a minute."

His voice was high-pitched now.

"I'm not going anywhere, Dad."

"Leave us."

"No."

"I'm outta here." Her mother turned to leave.

Her father reached quickly inside his jacket and pulled out the gun. "Don't move, Philomena."

"Who do you think… "

"I didn't want it this way." Her father pointed the revolver at her mother. "Not in front of our daughter."

"Dad!" Piper moved toward him but he stepped back. "What are you doing?"

Everything was surreal. She saw the gun but couldn't believe it was there. She blinked slowly. It was still there, still in her father's shaking hand, still pointed at her mother's chest.

"Dad, you're the cop."

"Kevin, think of your daughter," her mother said, her voice unsteady now.

"You've ruined my life, Philomena. There's nothing left."

She'd never seen her father's eyes so dead. Their dark blue cores were black and had no light.

"Kevin… listen to me." Her mother swallowed hard. "Think before you pull… "

"'For better, for worse. Till death do us part.' Remember that promise?"

Everything unfurled in slow motion as her father's hand began to move. The revolver turned inward and then its muzzle was pressed against his right temple. A surge of raw energy passed through Piper's body. His finger flexed. For an instant she was at once captivated and horrified.

"NO. Dad, no. What Mom's done to you is wrong. She's treated you badly. But why kill yourself because of her?" Piper's mind whipped through other convincing things to say. She could not fail. "It's a sin what you're gonna do. A big sin. There's no grey here." The revolver stayed pointed. "Dad, I won't change my name when I marry. I'll do that for you. I promise. I need you. But you have to promise you'll stay for me. That's what *I* need. Rory's watching, Dad. He wouldn't want this."

His hand began to shake. Piper moved toward him slowly. Reaching up, she gripped the icy snout of the gun. His grip slackened. He released it and began to sob. Huge, strangled sobs. She tossed the gun onto the grass and embraced him tightly.

"Mom, go now."

Her mother's stricken expression looked pathetic. Piper was glad when she turned away. When she reached the path, her mother stopped and looked back.

Piper stroked the back of her father's head. "Not a word to anyone about this, Mom."

A very long day

At first he thought he'd awoken from a nightmare. The knocking continued. Still groggy, he wondered if it was Julia and she'd forgotten her keys. Danny slipped on his dressing gown and went downstairs.

When he opened the door, six men forced their way inside, two with handguns drawn.

"Special Branch," one of the men brandishing a gun said. He held up a Metropolitan police badge. "What's your name?"

Blood rushed from Danny's head. He felt very lightheaded but managed to raise his hands.

"What's your name?" The man had close-set, steely eyes and a Roman nose that was off kilter.

"Danny Connolly."

"Anyone else here?"

Danny shook his head as the second detective and a colleague went upstairs. Their footsteps so heavy he thought the staircase would collapse. The others began ransacking the living room, pulling books from the bookcase and searching drawers. Cutlery dropped on the kitchen's tiled floor. Upstairs, heavy furniture shrieked and the ceiling shook. A toilet was flushed, followed immediately by the sound of glass shattering.

An officer with a snow-white scar on his chin tumbled the fichus plant by the French doors. He rolled it with his foot and went outside. Another detective followed him. Policemen shouted from every corner. Minutes later, the officer with the scar came running in from the garden.

"We've found it."

"Found what?" Danny asked.

"We're detaining you under Section 41 of the Terrorism Act," said the detective with the gun who'd been guarding him. "Hands behind your back."

"I'm not a bloody terrorist," Danny said. "What am I accused of doing?"

The detective ordered his colleague to handcuff him, then said, "You don't have to say anything, but it can harm your defense if you do not mention when asked something which you later rely on in court. Anything you do say may be given in evidence."

"Let's go," the detective said.

Danny remembered what Piper had once told him. "I'm not going anywhere till I've showered and am properly dressed. It's my legal right."

The muscles in the detective's face twitched. "Uncuff 'im," he said. "You've got two minutes."

He escorted Danny to his bedroom where he discovered the carpeting had been ripped up in two corners. The wardrobe and chest of drawers had been pulled away from the wall. The contents of the bin were dumped on top of the chest of drawers, beside his German dictionary and textbooks. Crumpled pages of sentences he'd composed and tossed into the basket two days prior lay smoothed out on the disheveled bed.

As he made his way to the bathroom, a detective was searching in the tiny spare room. Another was in Julia's room. A lime-caked rinsing glass lay broken inside the sink, together with his and Julia's tubes of toothpaste and brushes. The hot water was running. He closed the bathroom door, but privacy was obviously not a legal right because the detective pushed it open. Danny lathered his face and began to slowly shave.

"You haven't got all fucking day."

Danny didn't reply. He opened the shower door and turned on

the tap to allow the water to run until it became hot, then returned to the sink and resumed shaving.

As he showered, the detective continued to demand he hurry. Danny didn't change his pace, though also knew he had to be very precise about his acts of passive aggression. His secret insubordination imparted a sense of tiny control in the massively uncontrollable situation. That Piper had survived a similar invasion also calmed him. When he was finished shaving, he climbed into the shower and slung the bath towel over the clear glass door so it acted as a curtain. Senses extremely alert, he noticed things he hadn't before: how slick his skin became when he ran his fingers over his soaped arms and chest as if it was actually melting beneath his fingers; that fragrance-free soap actually had a smell.

"Nothing up here," said a detective. He peered from the loft as Danny was escorted along the landing back to his bedroom.

"Go downstairs and help Mike finish out back, then."

As he put on his shirt he looked out his bedroom window and saw the detective with the scar searching within the rosebushes at the back of the garden. Danny's fingers, plump and wrinkled by the hot water, felt clumsy. He struggled to push the buttons of the shirt through the eyeholes.

"Stop gawking and get a move on," said the detective.

Ten minutes later, after dressing in a pair of chinos and putting on a silk tie, he was ordered downstairs where he walked over to the phone on the dining room table.

"That's not on," said the detective.

"It's my right to make a call."

"Not under the Terrorism Act, it's not. We decide when and who you ring. Put your hands behind your back."

Danny didn't argue. A car was parked in the middle of the street outside his door with its engine already running. Mrs. Hartley's light was on and her front door ajar, but he couldn't see her. Two men on their way to work stopped to watch. Sonia Berg was unlocking her car door further along the street.

"Sonia," he called.

She turned around.

"I've been arrested. Tell Julia."

Gripping the back of Danny's neck, the detective pushed down his head and forced him inside the vehicle. The others climbed inside. Squashed tightly inside the vehicle, Danny's arms and legs pressed against his incarcerators' limbs. He hated the feeling. He could also hardly breathe. The serrated edge of the handcuffs bit into his wrists. Before the back door was properly shut, the driver sped away.

As no uniformed police officers were present, he assumed the building was some kind of special detention centre used by the Special Branch. Upon arrival, they'd confiscated his watch, credit card, mobile phone and cash and stuffed them into a clear plastic bag before escorting him to a room where a female officer brusquely informed him she needed to take his fingerprints. When he demanded to see a lawyer, she added the police had the right to prevent him from access for forty-eight hours (longer if they decided to get a court order) and the prints could be taken by force if he didn't cooperate. The woman's cold professionalism as she pressed his fingers one by one into the film of black ink and then turned them left to right on the glass surface of a scanner device heightened Danny's humiliation. Something essential, something intimate, was being stolen from him and put into a database without his consent.

He was now sitting on a flimsy chair inside a small windowless cell that's walls and ceiling were a dingy off-white colour, the sort of colour brilliant white became after years of exposure to cigarette tar. Across from him a three-foot wide ledge contained a shallow flimsy mattress, drab blue and white striped pillow and thin dirty blanket that smelled of old sweat. A toilet missing its plastic seat and adjacent washbasin with a large rust mark running from the faucet to the drain was attached to the wall on his right.

The lack of sound was unsettling, which hadn't bothered him at first. He couldn't even hear the drone of the buses or taxis he knew were passing by on the street, or the detectives' footsteps as they came to spy on him through the peephole in the metal door. For a third time in the four or so hours he figured he'd now been in their custody, a knife of panic pierced his chest at the realisation he was cut off from the world. He was at the mercy of the shadowy secret police. He'd watched movies and read newspaper articles about people harassed and injured while in police custody. They could even make him disappear permanently if they wanted. His chest broke out in a cold sweat. He began to pace the cell. A minute later, he went to the door and put his palms and forehead against it, instantly feeling the coldness of the unyielding steel despite its layers of thick paint.

How could the authorities have made such a terrible mistake? Surely they'd done their homework and discovered he was a university graduate, that he was law-abiding and never been actively involved in politics or the Troubles; that he shared a house with a respectable immigration officer, someone as crucial as them within the British law enforcement machine. He wondered what they'd found in the garden. Had they planted something sinister to frame him? Danny banged the door with his fist four times. He put his ear to it and listened. Not a sound. He banged again, harder this time until his fist hurt. The noise felt good. He listened again. Nothing. He began to pace.

The hours passed by and he had no idea now whether it was day or night. No-one came with food or water. He was parched. Though repulsed, he turned on the tap, put his mouth near it and drank. The water was overly chlorinated, tepid and foul. He lay on the bed, supine, not permitting any part of his face to make contact with the disgusting pillow. As he stared alternately at the walls and naked overhead light, he imagined Julia calling police stations all over London looking for him. He thought about his parents and his former life in Northern Ireland, how he'd never truly been inconvenienced by the conflict or endured intense bigotry like so many Catholics had in the towns and cities. All he'd had was a car search one night. No relatives of his had joined the IRA. No-one close to him had been a victim of the violence. He'd been oblivious and ignorant and this ignorance had caught up with him and he didn't know what would be the result.

To distract himself, he looked about the room and said aloud the German name for each object he could see. It took only a minute. He composed ever more complex German sentences. The grammar and word placement was wrong but he didn't care. Despite his best efforts, his mind kept returning to his predicament and he'd panic and torment himself with a jumble of both sane and crazy doubts: whether his father had been right when he'd said he should never come to London; whether the police would unlock his cell door if a fire suddenly broke out in the building; whether they'd beat him up, or serve him with an exclusion order banning him from England if he was ever set free.

The grinding of the metal door as it opened awoke him with a start. Danny stared up at the ceiling not knowing where he was until his brain snapped into gear and it all flooded back. He peered down the length of his body, saw he was covered by the thin, filthy blanket spotted with dried blood in places, but couldn't remember pulling it up. A young, well-built detective with a pale English tan and strong jaw line entered carrying a tray.

"Rise and shine," he said. "Hope you like porridge."

His accent was Northern, from Manchester or Liverpool, Danny wasn't certain.

"What time is it?" Danny pulled the blanket down and swung his feet to the floor.

"Not sure. I'll find out for you."

He decided to take advantage of the stranger's friendliness. "Where am I?"

The officer set the tray on the bed beside him. "Eat up, mate."

Danny examined the tray's contents, a bowl of lukewarm porridge with a film of bluish milk floating around the rim and centre, a mug of weak tea, two slices of pale toast scantily smeared with butter. He avoided the porridge fearing it was laced with some kind of truth drug. He'd read they did that. As he swigged the last of his tea, the door opened and another detective entered.

"Let's go," he said.

Danny stood and began to adjust his clothing.

"*Now*," said the detective.

He was escorted down the corridor and entered a large room with metal filing cabinets lining its two walls. A dying spider plant on top of one cabinet reminded him of his mother's plants and he wondered what she was doing at this very moment. Pinned on a cork notice board on the wall were Metropolitan Police mugshots of wanted terrorists and a child's finger-painting of a bright sun and stickman and stickwoman holding hands. Detectives, including the brusque woman who'd taken his fingerprints, sat at fourteen desks running up both sides of the room. On the desktops were phones, computer monitors, keyboards and stacks of cream-coloured folders.

Along the back wall were three doors. The detective gripped his upper arm, led him up to the middle door and pushed him into a small, brightly lit room containing a metal desk upon which was a tape recorder. Three chairs were positioned around the desk. He was ordered to sit and the detective left the room. Directly opposite from where he sat was a large oblong mirror. His hair looked unkempt and he began to smooth it until he remembered this was probably a one-way mirror and the police were observing him. He sat rigid with his eyes fixed on the door. Like back in his cell, he could hear no noise.

Presently, the door opened and the fierce detective who'd read him his rights came in clutching a file. A second man followed him. Tall with a thick neck and wide shoulders, he looked familiar but Danny couldn't place him. The detectives were immaculately dressed in pressed shirts and ties in contrast to Danny whose clothes were very wrinkled. He felt dirty inside and out.

"Hello, Danny," said the new detective. "I'm Detective Ian Tompkins and this is Detective Moore. We need to ask you some questions. Before we begin, do you need anything?"

"A glass of water, please."

"Bill, fetch him water."

"He needs to answer a couple of questions to earn that privilege."

"Get the lad some water."

As Moore was leaving, Detective Tompkins took a cassette out of his shirt pocket and jammed it into the recorder. "Bill's got a bit of a temper," he said, and he switched on the machine. "Testing one, two, three." He rewound the tape. "Don't worry though. I'm here."

After the detective was satisfied the recorder was functioning, he leaned toward Danny. "Let's get this over with as quickly as we can, eh? I'm going to ask you questions and, if you answer them truthfully, we'll be done before you can say 'Bob's your Uncle.'" Long front teeth and incisors appeared when he smiled. "That sound fair, lad?"

"Yes."

"What say we begin before Bill gets back?"

"Fine."

After he switched on the tape recorder, he gave Danny the same caution Moore had given him the previous day.

"What's your full name?"

"Danny Francis Connolly."

"Where do you live?"

"42 Chumley Street, W6."

"How old are you?"

"Twenty-one."

A barrage of questions about his family and upbringing in

Northern Ireland ensued, which Danny answered without hesitation. After twenty minutes, Danny asked about the whereabouts of the water and the detective explained his colleague had probably got waylaid but was sure he'd return shortly with it. The recorder switched off and the detective inserted the other side.

"When did you come to London?" he asked.

"In May."

"Why?"

After he explained, the detective opened the file, read for a minute and then stared at Danny. "What part did you play in the bombing on Hammersmith Bridge?"

A shock wave ripped through Danny's chest. "*I* wasn't involved in that."

"We agreed we'd get this business over with quickly, Danny. What part'd you play?"

"I know nothing about a bomb."

It was suddenly surreal. The word 'bomb' had been used in conjunction with his name.

"Where were you that night?" the detective asked.

Danny thought for a moment. "I think I was home." He pondered again. "Yes, I definitely was."

"Anyone with you?"

"No."

"So no-one can vouch for your whereabouts?"

Danny leaned slightly across the table toward him. "You must believe me. I had nothing to do with that bombing."

"So you've had something to do with *a* bombing, then? Which one?"

"I haven't bombed anything."

"An innocent man was murdered on the bridge by the IRA," Detective Tompkins said. "He'd just got engaged three weeks before."

"Why are you telling me this?"

"His fiancée will never get the chance to be his wife. Can you imagine how that poor woman feels?"

Danny met his gaze and didn't immediately reply. "I'm sorry for her loss."

"Prove it. Tell me what part you played."

"No part. I'm innocent."

The door opened and Moore entered with a yellow envelope in his hands. He tossed it on top of the table and then sat with his eyes riveted on Danny for a minute though it seemed much longer.

"You've made a mistake," Danny said, to end the horrible silence.

"No more bullshit," said Moore. "What's your job in the cell?"

"What cell?"

"You their bomb maker?"

"This is crazy." Danny began to rub and squeeze his forehead. He pulled his hand away abruptly. "I wouldn't know *how* to make a bomb."

"Don't fucking-well lie to us," said Moore. He pounded the table with the side of his fist. "Were you planning to make mix?"

"What's mix?"

Moore leapt up, planted his hands on the surface of the table and leaned over toward Danny, a feline snarl on his face now. The action was so unexpected, Danny instinctively reared back raising his hands.

"Steady on, Bill," Tompkins said. "There's no need to scare the lad. He's going to tell us everything."

"He's a murdering Irish bastard."

"Easy, Bill." Detective Tompkins turned back to Danny. "Tell us about the fertiliser we found."

That's what had made the detective so excited at his home. It made sense now. Danny couldn't understand how they'd found out he'd bought it in the first place. Had his Irish accent alerted the cashier and he'd called Special Branch? Did MI5 monitor all sales of fertiliser?

"This is all a big mistake, I bought a few bags a couple of weeks ago. I was going to do the lawn and repot some plants."

"It's late summer," Tompkins said. "People do that in spring."

"I promised my flatmate I'd do it when I moved in and just never got round to it. You can ask Julia. She owns the house and she'll verify this. Honest."

"Where's the rest of it?"

"There isn't anymore."

The detectives exchanged a hasty glance.

"You use the rest to make the mix they bombed the bridge with?"

"I don't know anything about what happened on the bridge. Please believe me."

"How do you know Patrick Scully?" Detective Tompkins asked.

"Who?"

"Patrick Scully."

Danny paused. "I don't know anyone by that name."

"I told you he'd lie," Moore said. "First he lies about the fertiliser and now he's letting on he doesn't know Scully." He glared at Danny. "Listen Paddy, you must think we're bloody idiots."

Moore rose and began to pace, smacking a fist hard into the palm of his hand every time he reached each end of the interrogation room. The door opened and a female detective put her head inside.

"Ian, you're wanted on the phone."

"I'll be back in a minute," Tompkins said, and switched off the tape as he rose.

At the door, the detective turned his head and regarded Danny before he left. A bolt of shock made his heart race. It was verified now. The stranger wearing the handsome denim shirt the day Danny stood with Piper outside the house where

Benjamin Franklin had lived, the same man who'd been lurking near her home was a British detective.

Back pressed against the wall, Moore stared at Danny. Trickles of sweat ran from Danny's underarm. His scalp felt suddenly itchy. He wanted to scratch it, but something warned him not to raise his hand.

"Are you going to tell me now how you know Paddy Scully?" Moore said finally.

"I don't know him and I want to see a lawyer."

"Let's see if I can jog your memory."

Moore sat again. He opened the envelope. He took out a wad of photographs and set one in front of Danny. It was a mugshot of Pat. He set down another of Pat in the company of two men Danny didn't recognise. Then one of Pat and Piper together. Another photograph of Piper and Danny walking along Hammersmith Broadway followed, then one of Finty and he sitting at a café on Chiswick High Street just the previous week. Finally he laid down a shot of Finty and him lying on the grass at Saint James' Park, on the day Finty's puppy had chased one of the ducks. Danny was shaken.

"Do you remember him now?"

"I know him as Pat. I never knew his last name."

"Don't mess with me."

"It's the truth. He rented a room from her." Danny pointed to Piper's photograph. "I didn't know him very well. I only met him a few times. Even Piper didn't see a lot of him. Just because we're both from Northern Ireland doesn't mean we all know each other, you know? I swear I really don't know him."

Mounting panic and Danny's lack of control were making him talk too much. Instinct warned him not to show any fear. He wanted a lawyer, yet to demand one again risked being inflammatory.

"The Civil Administration Team trained you well," Moore said.

"I don't know what you're talking about."

Leaning forward, the detective eye's narrowed. "I'm a lot tougher and nastier than the IRA bastards who've trained you not to answer questions." He paused and stared. "I'm going to give you one last chance. Who's in your cell?"

While it was excruciating, Danny kept his eyes locked on the detective's. To look anywhere else would be construed as guilt, evasion at the weakest.

"I'm not in any IRA cell."

"You're part of Scully's. Admit it."

"I swear to you, I'm not."

Moore rose and came swiftly round to the other side of the desk. He grabbed Danny by the hair and pulled him out of his chair.

"AHHHH. Stop. AHHHHHH." Danny raised his hands, put them on top of Moore's and tried to pry them off. He couldn't. It seemed all the hair was being ripped out his scalp in a single piece.

The detective dragged Danny across the room and slammed him against the wall, kicked his legs apart and pushed his right knee hard into his groin. His pubic bone throbbed sharply. Tears smarted in his eyes.

"Tell me what I need to know, you stupid Mick." He jerked his head toward Danny as if he intended to give him a headbutt, but instead slapped the side of his face hard with his open palm. "You're in the IRA. You had an arms dump at your house. Admit it."

"I can't admit what isn't… "

Wrapping his huge hands around Danny's neck, the detective began to squeeze. "Confess."

"I'm not in any cell."

"Confess, *now*."

Danny couldn't speak. The detective's thick fingers tightened until Danny was certain his Adam's apple would be pushed out the back of his neck. He had an urge to cough violently, but couldn't. More tears streamed from his eyes. Moore's furious expression began to soften, then blur. Danny's heart drummed in his ears. Tighter and tighter the detective squeezed. The walls and ceiling grew indistinguishable. Just as he was about to pass out, Moore released his grip. He dragged him back by his hair to the desk and swung him into the seat.

Danny laid his forehead on the desk's surface and struggled to breathe. His body trembled. He felt he was going mad. He wanted to beg for his release, wanted to howl with anger, wanted to kill the detective. Desperate to exert a fragment of control over his predicament, he searched for something only he could do to himself, something that did not originate from this man's absolute power over him. Something only he would know. He bit into the lining of his inner lip. It hurt, yet the pain was hugely empowering. He could be as strong and resilient as the detective. He bit harder until he tasted blood.

The door to the interrogation room opened. As he pushed up with his hands, Danny braced to meet Moore's evil gaze. He wasn't there. The photographs, envelope and file were gone also. He turned his head slowly toward the door as the detective with the snow-white scar entered carrying the file and photographs. He came up to the desk and started the recorder. Leaning toward it, he said the date and time.

"What's your name," he said to Danny as he leaned back in his chair.

"I gave it already. It's on the tape."

"What's your name?"

"Danny Connolly."

"Your full name?"

"Danny Francis Connolly."

"Where do you live?"

"I demand to see a lawyer right now."

"What's your address?"

Carrot and Stick

He no longer knew exactly how long he'd been in detention, though it was definitely longer than forty-eight hours. He knew that because one of the friendlier detectives informed him on his way back to the cell after one interrogation that they'd obtained a court order allowing him to be held for another five days. How many interrogations had there been? He'd lost count. It was now just a stream of constant comings and goings between the cell and interrogation room. Often, it was just one detective present during a session, sometimes two. Sometimes it was a 'good cop, bad cop' routine. It took Danny a while before he'd latched onto that tactic.

Detective Moore had assaulted him three times now. He'd made him stand spread-eagled leaning into the wall supported only by his fingertips for an hour at a stretch. He'd also hit Danny on the sides of his face with his open palm and twisted his arms, though he'd been careful not to leave any permanent marks. Danny demanded to have a doctor examine him after the last attack. Although his demand had been ignored, it resulted in his being permitted to shower and shave. Food had also been provided a few times. Gruel-like soups, unappetising watery potatoes, liverish textured beef, too dry chicken, corky parsnips and French beans so overcooked the beans had fled their pods. Despite its putridity, he'd eaten it all. Under his arms, his shirt had begun to stink. His shirt and trousers were grimy and disheveled but he no longer cared.

Danny fully understood now what innocent young men had endured back in Northern Ireland when they'd been taken in for questioning by the British army. His father had also often been on his mind. He'd always thought him the most unreasonable, the most pig-headed, controlling man he'd ever known, but he was a lamb in comparison to these wolves. Danny was too stressed and frightened to appreciate the irony of this. Irony was intellectual. Irony had its place in normal life only.

As the cell door opened, Danny rose from the narrow bed. He swung his feet slowly to the floor and obediently walked out into the corridor. A minute later, he entered the familiar detectives general office with its dying spider plant and rows of desks. A woman laughed loudly. He raised his head toward the sound. Seated at a desk almost twenty feet away, was Finty with her back to him smoking a cigarette. She was chatting to the female detective whose laugh had prompted him to look over in the first place. The detective met Danny's glance and then turned back and laughed at something Finty said, at the same time pushing what looked like a large scrapbook across the desk toward her.

His legs began to tremble violently. He felt himself fall toward the floor. The detective escorting him seized his right arm, pulled him up and pushed him into the interrogation room before he shut the door

"Are you okay?" Detective Tompkins asked, the sleeves of his denim shirt rolled up to his elbows. "You look like you've seen a ghost. Sit down, mate." He nodded at the detective who'd escorted Danny into the room. "I'll call if I need you." Turning back to Danny, he said, "You recognise someone on your way here, maybe?"

"I'm entitled to a lawyer. You've now held me longer than forty-eight hours."

"We've got someone coming in to see you."

The image of Finty sitting so casually at the desk would not leave Danny's mind. Was she being questioned about her association with him? It hadn't looked like a formal interview. She'd been smoking and laughing. Was she in the Special Branch? Had they planted her at the *Institut*? The strain of detention was making him paranoid. Danny didn't know what was real anymore.

A three-inch thick cardboard box lay beside the tape recorder on the table. Tompkins drew it toward him. After opening it, he pushed it halfway across the desk. "Have you ever seen these?"

The tip of Danny's tongue was already pushed against the roof of his mouth in preparation to deny he had. When he looked inside the box, his tongue retracted and came to its natural resting place against the back of his lower teeth again. The walls of the room started to close in.

"Well, have you?"

The handgun was easy to deny. He'd never seen that before. The compulsion to also deny he'd ever seen the sawn off shotgun was very strong, but the analytical side of his brain won out.

"I think I recognise the shotgun."

"Oh, I'd say. Your prints are all over it."

"I can explain that."

"I'm all ears." The detective sat back in the chair. He placed his hands behind his head as if he were about to be entertained.

"It was in the wardrobe of the room I stayed in when I first came to London. When I first saw it, I thought it was a toy and took it out to look at it. That's why my fingerprints are on it. But then whoever owned it took it away and I never saw it again."

"You sound nervous."

"It's the truth. I swear."

The detective unclasped his hands, put them on the desk and began to interrogate Danny, asking the same questions repeatedly, demanding to know everything about the period he'd lived at Piper's, about Pat and Danny's part in the bombing of Hammersmith Bridge and how he'd come across the shotgun. It was as if he were looking for the slightest inconsistency with which to pounce and shred apart the truth. Without warning, he'd change the subject and pepper Danny with questions about his current residence, the fertiliser and the whereabouts of the main arms dump. Every time the detective nodded or agreed with something Danny said and he believed he was getting somewhere, Tompkins would switch the subject back to Pat, the fertiliser or shotgun and ask about his fingerprints being found on it.

"This isn't good," Detective Tompkins said. He'd been staring at him silently for a minute now. "You could be in serious trouble. You're looking at five to six years for the arm's dump. Another five for possession of a sawn off shotgun."

"You didn't find that thing at *my* house."

"Who says we didn't? You?"

"You can't prove it's mine." Danny rubbed the heavy stubble on his chin.

"Look at the facts. You lived in a house with a guy who's a known IRA terrorist. We've got proof he was involved in the Hammersmith bombing, as well as the shooting of a police officer two months ago. We've found bags of fertiliser in your home. You've got a dump somewhere. And mix was used to make the Hammersmith Bridge bomb. We've got your prints on a shotgun. You're going down, mate."

A flash of hot sweat soaked Danny's chest and back.

"I want a lawyer *now*."

"I'll arrange it."

The detective rose, picked up the box of evidence and left the room. He realised the detective was right. Danny had no idea how he could prove his innocence. It was his word against the police and his Irish nationality and accent would count against him in an English court. Danny sat rigid and stared at the two-way mirror across from him. No longer did he believe the detective was arranging for a lawyer, but rather was on the other side of the mirror with a group of other policemen scrutinising his reactions. He summoned every remaining ounce of self-possession and stared into the mirror to show he was neither afraid nor intimidated.

"A solicitor's on his way," Tompkins said, as he came in and took a seat. Danny turned away and focused on a part of the wall where the paint bubbled just beneath the ceiling. "I can't see how a lawyer's going to be able to help you. Can you?"

"I'm not talking anymore until a lawyer comes."

"Here's the thing, Danny," the detective said. He intertwined his thick fingers and leaned across toward him. "All my colleagues think you're guilty. But I don't. My gut feeling is you're innocent." He fell silent until Danny looked at him. "You want to know why I think that?"

Danny shook his head.

"Because the IRA never cooperate. From the moment they enter an interview room, they say nothing even though the Terrorism Act doesn't give them a right to silence."

"Why can't I leave then?"

"I'm working on it."

"What's to work out?"

Tompkins smiled in the same patronising way his father sometimes did. "Here's what I think we can do to sort this mess out for you."

Danny said nothing.

"You're Irish and still fairly new to London and you've already… " He laughed, but it sounded fake, "Let's put it this way, you've had the misfortune of falling in with an IRA man. The way I see it, this IRA breakaway faction's stepping up its campaign over here and we need eyes and ears on the ground." He paused. "You hear what I'm trying to say, Danny?"

"No."

"You're smart."

"I don't."

"You could go into pubs where IRA sympathisers and volunteers socialise and behave like you're a patriotic Irishman who hates the English. After a while, these blokes would trust you and you could do a bit of sniffing around for us. You know, things like where new cells are being organised and who at the telephone companies and driving license departments is providing them with intelligence on the whereabouts of potential targets."

"Be an informer?"

"A British agent."

"Informers get a bullet in the head."

"This is London, not Belfast. You'd be working with handlers whose job is to protect you. We'd never put you in danger."

"I've never been interested in politics. They'd spot me as a fraud a mile away."

"You're a resourceful bloke. We'll even pay you."

"I'm not interested."

"A lot of our best agents said that when we first talked to them. That's why I'm not looking for an answer right now."

"I mean it.'"

"I'm going to give you time to think about it. But while you're thinking, it'd be smart to keep in mind what we've got on you." He stopped talking and moments later began to drum his fingers on the surface of the desk. "On the other hand, I can make this all go away, Danny. Everything." The detective nodded toward the two-way mirror. "I can let you walk out of here today without them arresting you."

"I *am* under arrest."

"This is detention, Danny. You haven't been brought before a custody sergeant at a police station yet. Let me tell you, some of the blokes in there don't want me to give you this chance. They're angry about what happened at Hammersmith and want you charged right away." He shook his head and drove air trapped inside his mouth through the wide gaps in his teeth. "Even when you make bail as often happens when the lawyers get involved, things can still be very difficult for you."

"What do you mean?"

"You'd better make sure your car's always in good nick for

starters. The traffic police might stop you every time you drive around London. And we mustn't forget the parking and speeding tickets. I heard they had one bloke running to court every week they gave him so many tickets. The amount of fines he had to pay." He tutted. "Then there's the regular coppers you meet on the street. You could find yourself stopped and searched so often, you might lose your temper and get booked for public order offenses. I'm not saying these things *will* happen. But they could."

His threats infuriated Danny. "Where's the lawyer?"

"I don't think you need him now."

"I want to make a personal call."

"Who do you want to ring?"

"My flatmate, Julia Ralston."

"Give me her number. I'll arrange it."

"You've already got the number."

"She got a mobile number in case she's not at home?"

After he'd given it to him, the detective rose as if to leave but then sat again. "Do we have a deal?"

"You said I've time to think about it and I intend to do just that."

The detective's face tightened, "Fair enough. I'm going to talk to my boss right now. I'm going to stick my neck out for you and tell him we have to let you go because you're not involved in anything. It won't be easy. He's going to say we can keep you for another three days as well as sit in when you talk to your lawyer. That's our right." His eyes widened. "But I'm going to look out for you. Okay, Danny?"

He knew it was just another attempt to soften him up. "Fine."

"If this works, and it's a big if, I'll need to know if you'll work with us in return. What do you say?"

"I'll think it over."

The detective didn't speak for a long moment. "You've got a week."

Was the end of the nightmare to be concluded so simply, so

informally? Could it really be almost over? He could scarcely bring himself to believe this was possible. He'd expected to be returned to his cell until he was ready to give Tompkins the answer he wanted. But he didn't care because all he wanted right now was his freedom. His mind was already running ahead. He was already visualising the sun or rain against his skin. He didn't care which it was, just wanted to feel something natural.

"I want to speak to Julia now."

"Absolutely." The detective rose and walked to the door. "But let's not get ahead of ourselves, eh? First, let me see if I can get you out of here without them arresting you."

He hadn't expected to feel such disconnectedness. Danny was ecstatic to be free but felt like he were an extra in a movie watching the principal actors execute their roles, the skinny, long-haired youth running across the street to meet a smiling young woman outside the supermarket, a middle-eastern man exiting a fast food takeaway that smelled of roast lamb and aromatic spices, an old woman standing by the open doors of a bus asking the driver a question before she boarded. Even the ride home on the tube was otherworldly: the way the train rocked and leaned inward as it turned corners, its brakes shrilly menacing as it decelerated pulling into the stations and sudden emergence of hate-filled graffiti and rude drawings etched into the windows every time the train plunged into the dark tunnels.

Julia and Katie were in the living room when he got home. Julia embraced him tightly but Katie remained on the sofa, shocked by his unshaven face, body odour and utter dishevelment. When he'd called Julia to tell her he was being set free, she'd offered to drive up to Paddington but he'd declined the offer. He'd needed time alone to steel himself back to real life. The living room was restored to its natural untidiness; stacks of CDs lay scattered on the carpet beside the player, magazines and newspapers were splayed open on the tables. Even her knickers were drying on the backs of the dining room chairs. When he sat, the armchair felt so soft he thought he'd drop right through the seat to the carpet beneath.

"What about some tea?" said Julia.

The ingenious English remedy for all happenings, good and terrible. He understood it now. "Make it strong."

"Would you make it?" Julia asked Katie. She rose, came over to where he was sitting and gave him a hug.

Over tea and cake he told them everything, including the bizarre offer securing his release.

"Sounds like they know they haven't a strong case if they press charges and took a chance they'd be able to recruit you as an agent," Julia said.

"I hope so."

"You'll need a good lawyer. I'll ask my boss' boss if he knows anyone."

"I'd appreciate that."

"You really need to get some sleep," said Katie.

"I look *that* terrible, do I?"

"You look bloody awful," Julia said. "Give your father a ring first, though."

"He called?"

"Twice since yesterday morning." She laughed. "Boy, I see now what you mean about how forceful he is. The last time, he demanded to know where you were and why your mobile was switched off. I had to come up with something fast. He'd make a bloody good immigration officer, you know?"

"What'd you say?"

"That you were arrested yesterday due to some mix up about your car insurance because the policy was issued in Northern Ireland. I think he bought it because he told me to call this afternoon with an update."

"If you hadn't got out today, I'd have had to tell him the truth because I was getting worried. I've been ringing every police station I could think of including Scotland Yard and nobody had a record of your arrest. It was getting scary, actually."

"I owe you, Julia."

Au revoir

Not wishing to cause unnecessary distress to his parents, Danny confirmed Julia's lie when he rang. His father was nonplussed, especially since an English company underwrote his company's fleet policy and one of his employees had been involved in a car accident in Manchester seven weeks ago and there'd been no problems then. He also told Danny that his office manager was looking into the matter and refused to listen when Danny said it was resolved and thus unnecessary.

"You now have a police record," his father said. "You'll have to disclose you've been arrested when you fill out certain kinds of official forms and some countries you want to travel to might not let you in."

"It was a detention not an arrest, Dad."

"If the police lock you up even for a couple of minutes, it's an arrest plain and simple." His sigh was audible. "Did they take your fingerprints?"

"I had no choice."

"Those'll be on file as well. They'll be checking your prints every time a crime's committed in London now. Rape. Murder. Burglary. What a bloody mess."

Danny hadn't considered that aspect. Could the authorities enter fingerprints into their central database even if the person wasn't convicted of a crime? He didn't think so. It seemed too draconian. Did the Terrorism Act give the government a new legal authority to do it?

"What should I do?" he asked his father.

"Come home after that course ends like I told you."

Even if he did want to return to Northern Ireland, he couldn't. The police had him under surveillance. "I'll ask the lawyer to get my record expunged."

When he went to his bedroom after the call, he discovered Julia had tidied it while he'd been away. After a long, hot shower, he climbed into bed. It seemed larger and so much softer than he remembered. He stretched out his legs and arms and luxuriated in the crisp feel of the sheets against his naked body. He fell asleep quickly but kept waking up through the night thinking he was back in the cell.

Though his incarceration had seemed endless, he'd missed only two days of German and knew he could catch up before his exam in four days. During the drive to the *Kant-Institut* the next morning, he frequently checked in the rearview mirror when slowly approaching or stopped at the traffic lights. He didn't see anyone suspicious but could not shake off the unsettling feeling he was.

Finty's desk was empty when he got to class. When she hadn't arrived by the end of the first class, Danny knew she wasn't coming. Nor did she come the next afternoon, which was the last day of formal instruction before the exam. After classes ended, he went directly to the administration office to inquire about her but no-one had any information. He began to rehash every detail of their friendship: her initial evasiveness to talk about her background; the failure to invite him to her home; how gullible he'd thought her behaviour in smuggling letters out for an IRA prisoner. Her gullibility seemed unbelievable now. Perhaps she'd been appointed to develop a friendship with him and the story was a ruse to make him feel comfortable and confide in her. Or maybe she'd been a principal actor in securing the IRA man's imprisonment. Perhaps the man was innocent like him, had found himself in the exact position

Danny found himself in now and refused to become an informer.

Tempering his rush to convict her was the knowledge that deep anxiety and a lack of control over one's circumstances could spawn irrational conclusions. It was he who'd first made contact with her after all, and he who suggested where and when they study together. There was also the comical absurdity of a hardnosed Special Branch detective making her puppy a vegetarian, or not eating eggs because she followed a strange philosophy.

On the morning of the exam, as Danny was leaving the house, Mrs. Hartley was crossing the street from her car carrying a shopping bag. When she looked up and saw him, the bag slipped from her grasp, its contents including tins of cat food and a jar of strawberry preserves falling onto the road. The jar smashed and the preserves pooled around her left foot. As he rushed to assist her, she emitted a high-pitched shriek. He picked up the bag and put everything but the broken jar inside. Her face looked dangerously pale.

"Are you okay?"

Gently, he gripped her arm but she pulled it away, her power surprising him. The blood returned to her cheeks and she snatched her shopping bag away. Without thanking him, she marched to her house and went inside, slamming the door behind her.

Finty bustled into the classroom five minutes after the exam began. She apologised to Herr Fehler who permitted her to take her place beside Danny.

The exam lasted two hours and, though very demanding, Danny felt confident he'd done well.

"That wasn't as bad as I thought it would be," Finty said after Herr Fehler had collected their papers. "I didn't get as much time to cram as I'd have liked."

" How come?"

She avoided his gaze. "I've been ill."

"That's why you missed the last classes," he said, as he watched the Chinese men approach and bow as they said goodbye to the teacher.

"Let's say goodbye to Herr Fehler."

Determined to find the truth, he walked to the tube with her after they chatted briefly to their teacher.

"I guess it's all over apart from getting the results," she said as they arrived at the tube station entrance. She moved aside to allow a woman carrying two heavy bags to exit the stairs onto the street. "I take it you'll stay on in London."

"Why would you assume that?"

She didn't look at him, instead hung her head slightly.

"Why would you think I'm not leaving?"

"You're so good at German. Why would you not stay and do the advanced course?"

"I have my reasons."

"So you're leaving?"

He said nothing.

"When?"

"Can we walk for a minute?"

She looked at her watch. They walked in silence for a bit.

"I'm amazed you haven't asked why I missed class last week."

"I did wonder, actually."

"Have you been spying on me, Finty?"

Her face turned scarlet. Her mouth opened and closed twice. "Why would you even ask that?"

"I saw you talking to a female detective at the place where *I* was interrogated."

"*You* were there, too?"

"The two of you were very chummy." He stopped walking and stared into her eyes. She didn't look away. "I didn't know what the hell to think."

"We weren't friends. She… "

"You were smoking and laughing together."

"I'm not a friend of that woman. I had no choice. I was told to come with the detectives." She swallowed hard. "You know my feelings about the police."

He kept his eyes riveted on hers.

"When I came out of my… " she stopped talking as a stocky, middle-aged man passed by within earshot. "As I was on my way to the tube, a car drew up alongside me and a man opened the passenger door. He said he needed to speak to me urgently. He didn't even ask my name. He flashed a Metropolitan Special Branch badge, held up a photo of you and I lying on the grass in Saint James' Park. He said he needed me to come with him to their office to answer questions. I said you were a friend from class and I didn't have time to go with him, but he mentioned my past run-in with them in connection with the IRA chap and said it'd be in my best interests to cooperate." She touched his wrist lightly. "They didn't tell me you were there. You've got to believe me, Danny."

He scoured her face, scouring for the tiniest twitch of insincerity. She made no attempt to divert her gaze.

"Something weird happened when I was with her, I'd been sitting sideways at the desk and her phone rang. After she came off the phone, she told me to quickly turn my chair round and face her. Then she lit a fag, offered me one and told me to relax because I wasn't under suspicion. All they needed was my assistance for a couple of minutes, but she didn't explain how I could help them. I was baffled." Finty paused and her eyes creased as if she were recalling the meeting again. "The only thing she did was push an album across the desk and ask if I recognised anyone in it. When I came to your photo, I said I knew you and then she said I'd been really helpful and was free to leave. I was blown away. Before I left, she warned I was not to tell anyone I'd been helping them. It was crazy. I don't know how I helped because they already knew I was friends with you." She fell silent for a moment. "You're not in trouble, are you?"

It was obvious the police had intended him to see Finty with the detective, though for what reason Danny couldn't tell. Was it to create doubt and suspicion about who his friends were, or was it to make him paranoid that they were watching every aspect of his life?

"The bastards accused me of being in the IRA and want me to turn informer in exchange for their not pressing charges."

"Fuckers."

"They're playing mind games."

"Special Branch does that."

He looked toward the station. "We should go back now."

After passing through the turnstile, they stopped to take their leave as Danny had to take the Piccadilly line west and she the Northern.

"So this is it," she said, and laid her hand on his.

The coldness of her hand instantly penetrated his own. He'd forgotten how cold her touch was. He wanted all coldness gone between them. He pulled her to him and kissed her. He could hear people pass silently on the street. She stayed there for what seemed a long time but was actually just seconds.

"I'd like to keep in touch with you."

"I'd like that, too." She smiled. "He'd miss not seeing his Irish uncle."

"How do I do that? You don't have a mobile."

"No."

"Give me your home number."

"I'd rather not."

"Ah yes, your boyfriend."

She looked down the street a moment and then reached into her bag, pulled out a pad and tore off a sheet of paper. She scribbled something and handed it to him.

As he looked at it, she said, "It's my current work number."

Labour day

Her mother's wedding was in two days and she wanted, no needed, her father to be on a structured recovery path before she left three days later for London. She met her mother after 'the incident' (as her mother referred to it on the phone) for lunch in a section of the Dag Hammarskjold Plaza on Forty-seventh Street and Second Avenue. Piper couldn't figure out why her mother suggested meeting there until she informed her when they met that she couldn't stay long because she had a final dress fitting with a seamstress who lived in a highrise one block from the plaza.

"I didn't mention the incident to anybody, not even Juan. Just like you wanted. But he frightened me. All that rage. I'm still shaken."

"I understand, Mom."

"Do you, Phila?" She sighed. "I should be thinking of my wedding, not this bullshit."

"He feels bad."

"If I did tell Juan, he'd have to report it to the NYPD. And you know what that means?"

Across from them, on a bench near the fountain that resembled a huge chalice, an old woman sat filing her nails while her heavily panting dog watched intently, as if willing her to finish up so he could get out of the midday sun.

Her mother put her sandwich on her lap and turned round fully on the bench toward Piper. "What if there's another incident? What if he goes crazy and kills Juan and I after you leave?"

"He won't."

"You're an expert, are you?"

"You can't ruin Dad's career. You were married to him for nearly twenty-five years. Cut him some slack, for Christ's sake."

Her mother didn't reply, instead brushed crumbs off her lap. She looked at her watch. Her mother's selfish indifference to her father's pain signaled how far she really had moved away from him.

"You need to know I've been pissed at... " Her mother stopped when the old woman looked over. "Oh, never mind." Her mother sighed. "You wanna come see the dress?"

"I'm meeting Dad." Piper rose.

"'Course, you are."

It'll be more of a surprise when I see it on Monday."

"Your hair needs cutting before then."

Piper wiped her fringe from her left eye. "I'm not part of the bridal set-up."

"Yeah, but the photos... please."

"Will do, but only if you give Dad a chance. I'm working to get him help."

Her mother regarded her for a moment. "Has he agreed?"

"He will."

"If he starts therapy, I'll agree."

Piper spent the rest of the week alternately talking, threatening and pleading with her father, even shared the fact she'd had some therapy in London and would be having more so they could compare experiences if he wanted. When he asked about hers, she glossed over the reasons. As she pleaded with him, it felt on occasions as if she were the demanding parent and he the stubborn child. When the breakthrough came, she leapt into action and contacted anyone she could think of in the city who would be able to suggest names of psychiatrists or psychologists. After she and her father settled on a doctor, she made an appointment and insisted on accompanying him for good measure.

The initial portion of the appointment comprised of a negotiating session about cost that began on hard chairs positioned before the taciturn administrator's desk but quickly advanced to the buttery leather armchairs of the psychiatrist's office commanding a view of the sparkling East River and cable car crossing to Roosevelt Island. Though fully insured, her father refused to file a claim because bills would be forwarded to his NYPD medical insurance carrier and he feared some anonymous insurance bureaucrat would pass on information he had an emotional problem to his precinct superiors. This fear, Piper took as an encouraging sign of his willingness to continue living.

Labour Day morning was sunny with only wisps of cloud in the sky as she hurriedly entered the North Garden at Central Park's Conservatory Garden. A refreshing breeze played with the leaves of the rosebushes climbing the nearest of the four archways to the Three Dancing Maidens fountain within the heart of the garden. Jets of water rose like a whale's blow above the heads of the copper maidens before tumbling in bursts of coruscating droplets into the shallow basin below. In front of the mouth of the southerly arch, her mother stood with the wedding party that included Juan's mother, his teenage daughter and a boyish-faced judge in a black robe who looked no older than twenty-five yet was a childhood friend of Juan's.

"You've come," her mother said.

That her mother articulated her fear Piper would be a no show was touching. The wedding dress was simple, elegant and snug, its snugness amplifying the curves of her mother's hips and breasts. Her hair was tethered into a perfect bun and she wore a gold necklace Piper had never seen before. A small oval silver frame containing a photograph of her brother Rory was pinned just above her left breast.

After requesting the photographer take photos of the two of them by the fountain, her mother said she wanted them to take a short stroll.

"Don't be long," Juan called. He pointed to the judge. "He's got another wedding before he can come to our party."

"Okay *Papi*," her mother said, and blew him two kisses.

It felt strange for Piper to see her mother so beautifully dressed for her marriage to another man, especially when her father was at this very moment at work in a shabby precinct twenty blocks away. She couldn't shake the feeling she was being disloyal to him just by being here, even though she was attending with his blessing. The harsh hiss of water from the fountain softened as they strolled further from the garden's centre.

"I wanted to say something," her mother said.

"He's started therapy."

"It's about you and me."

A bumble bee started dancing around the head of a large pink rose whose inner petals were brown and withered.

"Today's a new beginning and I want to have good luck from the get-go. I wanted to tell you that day in the plaza but I chickened out."

"What is it, Mom?"

"I've been real pissed at you Phila but I'm working on letting it all go."

Piper took a step back. "For what?"

The corners of her mother's glossy lips quivered before she spoke. "For one, you said at Rory's grave that I'm the one in the wrong. You're blaming me for ending the marriage."

"I'm going to get the 'two to tango' argument, am I?"

"Even the way you say that Phil... Piper."

"And what way's that?"

"Real mean."

Juan called out to them to come back. Her mother gathered the skirt of her dress in preparation to leave.

"What's the other thing?"

"I made a mistake. Now's not the right time."

"Come on, Mom."

Her mother paused. "My future's happening right now and that's what today is all about." She touched Piper's arm. It felt like a bolt of electricity travelled through her body rendering her immobile. "I know we haven't been all that close but I need you to know right now I'm trying to forgive you."

Piper snatched her arm away. "What the hell am I missing here?"

"Philomena, come on," Juan called. "You wanna get married today or not?"

Her mother quickly walked away.

The ceremony unfolded in the garden as if Piper were watching it through a pair of photochromic glasses after they've been transitioning from sun to shade and vice-versa for three or four months: the colours of her mother's white and scarlet roses were no longer as vibrant, the grass and leaves of the shrubs were still green but not as fresh as viewed with the naked eye, the sky blue but no longer azure. Her mother's words 'real pissed' and 'trying to forgive' circled her brain.

After boarding a limo outside the Vanderbilt Gate with five of Juan's relatives including his mother and her new minted half-sister, Piper immediately popped open the bottle of free champagne. Four of them were teetotalers and Juan's mother, a diminutive, elegant woman, watched disapprovingly as the car made its way uptown.

At the party held in the lush quadrangle of a brownstone on the Upper East Side belonging to Juan's sister who'd married up. Piper quickly drank two more flutes of champagne and a glass of Sauvignon Blanc, nibbling on hot fried plantains and assorted canapés to keep the effects of the alcohol in check.

Communication with her mother throughout the afternoon was confined to exchanges of glances, nods and smiles when they found themselves near one another on the dance floor. Cool embraces also occurred when they were asked to pose for guest photographs. Towards the end of the evening, her mother left to change as Juan and she were catching a flight from JFK to St. Barts for their honeymoon.

Ten minutes later, Piper went looking for her. She found her in the bathroom of the master bedroom. She'd already changed and was applying lipstick.

"I'll be in London when you get home." Piper stepped into the bathroom. "I need to know."

"I'll call when I get back to the office." Her mother licked her lips. "I promise. Hey, we'll come over for your graduation. The dollar's doing good now." She examined her reflection in the mirror and then tugged her dress to smooth out a nonexistent wrinkle. "Would you fix my hair at the back? The limo's gonna be here soon."

The walls of the spacious bathroom were sheathed in over-sized dove-grey, black and dusty pink marble tiles and accented by a heavy wall-to-ceiling guilt mirror that permitted the confident to admire their body profiles even while sitting on the john. It smelled of French lavender, though whether from the mound of enticingly shaped soaps or votive candle burning on a glass shelf, Piper wasn't sure.

"Mom, please tell… "

"Not now."

Piper stopped brushing her mother's hair. "*Now*."

"Are you drunk?"

"No."

"You smoked weed then? Your Dad's to blame. It's not just me, you know? He had an affair with a woman at his precinct when you were a kid." She pulled away unexpectedly from Piper's reach, leaving her holding the brush in mid-air. "I stood by him."

"Is this true, Mom or... ?"

"Yeah, your father. The religious man who doesn't believe in divorce but does in suicide. Him. He screwed around on me."

Piper stared at her mother for a moment. She needed to know and yet understood it wasn't relevant to the conversation. "Did you enjoy the sex, Mom?"

"Jesus, what's that got to do with what I'm telling you? He screwed around and I took him back when the affair ended. I did, because you needed bringing up in a normal home. But something inside me was changed. When you fall out of love, it's forever. You can't ever get it back. So Rory... " Her eyes instantly filled with tears. "Your brother was made without a scrap of love or respect for your father."

Piper wasn't sure what was worse, not wanting sex or having it without any emotion. She took a gulp of wine.

"The other thing, Mom. You said there were two reasons you're pissed at me."

"I'm definitely not going there today."

Her mother started to leave the bathroom. Piper quickly crossed to the door, slammed it shut and stood with her back to it.

"Let me out."

"Not until you tell me."

As she tugged the door handle, the wine glass dropped out of her mother's hand and smashed on the tiles. Piper looked at it but didn't move. "You're not leaving till you tell me."

Her mother's head slowly lifted from looking at the broken glass. "I blame you," she said. "I blame you for Rory dying. *You* let him die."

Her mother's face blurred. Piper's ears began to ring. It sounded as if a tuning fork was vibrating inside her head. She felt she was going to pass out. She inhaled slowly and willed herself to clarity as her mother continued to assail her.

"How could you let your brother burn to death? He loved you. Do you know how scared he must have been?" Her

271

mother's hand raised to cover her mouth as if she were reliving the terror her brother must have experienced. "The… "

Fully sober now, Piper's mind's eye returned to the terrible summer evening. She was back inside the house again, felt the fierce wall of heat scorch her arms and face. She heard the splintering glass. "I couldn't do anything. I couldn't get up the stairs." Was this true? Could she really not have done anything? She'd replayed the scenario in her mind so often since it happened, she wasn't sure what was real and what wasn't.

"I asked you this before and this time I want the truth." Her mother's lips formed a perfect straight line. "Had you smoked pot in your bedroom that night?"

Piper didn't speak.

"Did you?"

"I'd smoked earlier with friends. But I wasn't high when I got home. I fell asleep on the couch. He was playing upstairs." She tried to keep her mother's face in focus, but even rapid blinking didn't help. "Mom, I wasn't high when he… "

"You're lying again."

"Honest to God. I wouldn't lie about that."

"Then you didn't try hard enough to save him. You *didn't*. You saved your goddamned cat instead." Her mother's hands rose and she covered her face. Her shoulders began to heave. She whipped her hands away and regarded Piper with pure venom. "A cat! How could you pick the cat over your baby brother?"

"I couldn't get upstairs, Mom. The banister was in flames. I was running out of the house when I saw her and just scooped her up." Tears streamed down Piper's face. "I was only sixteen."

"You were selfish. You did everything to provoke me. Well, I did my duty by you."

"I was working through stuff, Mom. I still am. But please… please, I would never have left Rory there to die." She felt her body move as her legs buckled. Her back slid down the door. "I loved him so much."

Someone knocked on the door. "Everything okay in there, Philomena?" Juan's sister asked.

Her mother went to the mirror and began to rub her eyes. "I'm fine, Salina."

"Limo's outside."

"Be right there."

Piper stood. "Mom."

"I didn't want to talk about this, Phila. You shouldn't have made me. Not today."

She went over, pressed herself against her mother's back and wrapped her arms around her neck. Her mother's arms didn't rise, not even to seize her wrists. "Please hug me, Mom." Still her mother's arms did not move. "Mom, hug me back. Please."

"I'm trying to work though this, Phila." Her mother stared at her in the mirror. "I'll get there with time." Her arms rose and her warm soft hands began to loosen Piper's grip. "I need to leave."

Her mother stooped and began to pick up the pieces of broken glass.

"Go. I'll clean up."

Her mother cracked the door open. "One last thing."

"Yes."

"That name you go by now. Did you stop wanting to be Philomena because you hate it or because it's also my name?"

"I don't know. I… yes."

"I thought that might be the case." Her mother came over and her eyes roamed Piper's face. "Look, maybe it's good we've talked now. It'll take me time but I will get to where I need to be and then we can go on." She laid her hands on Piper's shoulders and squeezed gently. "I'll come see you in London."

The rapid click of her pumps grew fainter and fainter as she passed down the hallway. The front door opened and the quiet roar of passing traffic rushed inside. Whistling and cheering followed swiftly in its wake as the guests moved down the staircase to the street.

Hawks and Sparrows

He'd been detained now along the hard shoulder of the A4 for forty minutes. If the flight from New York was on schedule, Piper would have collected her luggage and already be waiting in the terminal building. The traffic was loud, moved very fast and he could feel his car shake as if wanting to lift into the air every time a large lorry passed. First, the traffic officer accused him of exceeding the speed limit, which he had but only by three miles per hour, something everybody did. Then the officer walked leisurely around the car three times, checking each tyre at a snail's pace, asking him to switch on in turn the brake lights, headlights in low and high beams, the indicator lights and parking and emergency light. Finding everything in order, he'd demanded he open the bonnet and boot. Danny didn't have to consent to any such search, but it wasn't worth protesting because refusal provided grounds to accuse him of a public order offence, which meant court appearances and fines.

He was being harassed again. Since his release, he'd been stopped by a policeman on his way to the shops on King Street and asked for his name and address. Very politely, of course. "Be seeing you around I'm sure, sir," the bobby said, and strolled away with his hands linked behind his back. He'd also been pulled in by a traffic officer on a motorbike while driving from the *Institut* after getting his examination results, which had crimped his happiness about his success. Again, the tyres and lights had been checked. He was now driving the safest vehicle in London.

The lawyer he'd appointed to represent him was an Englishman who'd served as an officer in British military intelligence before going to law school. He had experience defending people accused under the new 'mainland' terrorism legislation. At the initial interview, he'd sympathised with Danny and said there'd be harassment that might even escalate if he decided not to cooperate. "It's how they work when they feel they can get someone to turn," he'd said. "The army was against using blackmail to recruit agents this way. It leads to unpredictable results, but the police never seem to learn that lesson." He'd advised Danny he had a case, both with regard to the technicalities (they'd held him longer than the statutory forty-eight hours without allowing him access to a lawyer) and facts, but also admitted the Crown was tough, inflexible and dogged in these matters should they decide to prosecute vigorously. Curiously, rather than make him more afraid, his words firmed Danny's resolve to fight the injustice and clear his name.

The traffic officer handed Danny a fine that included three penalty points on his driving license and a summons to appear in court. When he got to the airport and explained to Piper the reason for the delay, she felt so guilty for asking him to pick her up she offered to pay the fine.

"I'm going to fight it."

"And so you bloody should."

"Hey, I had a good teacher," he said, and winked. "We can't let them take away our rights now, can we?"

His mobile rang as he was climbing out of his car.

"Your father's on his way to London," his mother said before he could speak. "I just dropped him off at the airport."

"He didn't ring to tell me."

"It was spur of the moment. He asked me to call and tell you he'll be at your house round twelve-thirty and you should be there."

Danny checked the time. A taxi took forty minutes from Heathrow so he figured he had about two hours. "Why all the secrecy, Mum?"

His mother didn't answer.

"Mum?"

"He thinks you're hiding something from him."

A rapid fluttering started in Danny's chest.

"The insurance agent got back and informed him that he doesn't have to cancel the fleet insurance policy. There aren't any problems with it. He was also told the police would never have arrested you for an insurance issue because the policy's valid in any part of Britain." She paused. "Are you in trouble, Danny?"

"No."

The phone went silent. "Have you been caught drinking and driving or run somebody over?"

"Bloody hell Mum, give me some credit."

After she'd hung up, he went into the house and began to quickly tidy the living room. By one o'clock, his father still hadn't arrived. He was eating the last of a sandwich when he heard a car door slam. He peeked out the window and saw his father settling the taxi fare.

Danny made him wait half-a-minute before opening the door. "Welcome, Dad," he said. "Come in."

Dressed in flannels with knife-edge creases, his father at forty-five cut a handsome figure. His eyes inspected the entire room, the staircase and beyond to the sunken kitchen within seconds.

"Are you hungry?" Danny asked.

He shook his head. "I'd kill for a cup of tea."

As Danny was in the kitchen, his father called out, "This place is a bit pokey."

"I love it."

"Not much in the way of a decent stick of furniture. What did you say your landlady does for a living?"

"Don't you find the sofa comfortable?"

His father tugged down the sleeves of his navy blazer. While Danny made the tea, his father inspected the artwork and then walked out into the garden.

"I couldn't live in a place like this," he said, when he came inside a minute later.

"It's the city, Dad." Danny handed him a mug of tea and they went into the living room.

"I've no doubt your mother's already clued you in on why I'm here."

"She did."

"My fleet insurance is A1." He held the mug in front of his mouth. "Why'd you lie to me?"

"I just didn't want to worry you and Mum."

"Too late for that." His father thrust out his jaw, half-closed his eyes and peered at him in the same way he did when an employee screwed up. "Spill the beans."

"There was no need for you to come over. I don't need... "

"Are you going to tell me or not?"

"The Special Branch think I'm in the IRA."

While resentful of his father's brusque manner, Danny took no pleasure in watching the blood drain from his face as he told him the entire story of his arrest.

"I hope you can see why I didn't tell you," Danny said, after he'd finished.

His father set his mug down on the coffee table. "Jesus, you're in some pickle. Didn't I warn you bad things would happen if you came to London?"

"I didn't become a drug addict or fall in with degenerates. My trouble stems from meeting an Irishman who's accused of terrorism." Danny paused. "Ironic, don't you think?"

"This is a catastrophe." His father looked at him. "Is this lawyer any good?"

"One of the best." Danny smiled. "He's giving me a break on his usual fee because he's interested in fighting this type of case. But, if the government decides to prosecute me, he said he'd need to brief a barrister. That could get pretty expensive."

"You need money?"

"I'm okay for now."

"A criminal record for terrorism would ruin your life. You can't lose if this goes to court." His father looked out the window. "If you do need money to fight this, you must let me know immediately."

"Thanks, Dad."

"Here's what's going to happen." Thrusting his hands into his trouser pockets, his father began to jingle the change as he stared out the window again. "Inform the solicitor you're coming home. He can handle everything on your behalf. There's nothing to be gained by your staying here."

"Are you crazy? They'll do me for absconding as well."

"Don't *you* be crazy." His father slammed his fist into his palm. "Once you're away from London, they'll drop the whole thing. They got nothing out of you when they interrogated you, so they know the chances are you know nothing and they'll not be able to get a conviction. All they found was your prints on a shotgun and a couple of bags of fertiliser. That means nothing. Any lawyer worth his salt can tear holes in that sort of charge."

"Maybe. Maybe not."

"It amazes me they let you out instead of pressing charges right away, I don't understand that one."

He could see the sparks firing all over his father's brain as he tried to make sense of his release. Danny didn't say anything, merely watched as his father moved to the sofa and sat again.

"The police never release a suspect if they have a case. Didn't your lawyer tell you that?"

"I think he said something about that."

"You must come home. Let the lawyer deal with them."

"No."

"Don't think for a minute that they're going to come over to Ireland after you. They've got better things to do with their time."

"The police over there'll do the work for them," said Danny. "They'd make my life hell."

"Not a chance."

"They will."

"We'll cross that bridge when we come to it. You've had your jaunt away. It's time to get your life back on track."

"I'm an adult now. Why can't you understand that?"

"You're young and far too inexperienced. Hasn't this trouble you're in shown you that?"

Their discussion was headed nowhere and Danny didn't answer, instead searched to find something his father could relate to. His father was good at stories, liked to pepper his lessons to employees with anecdotes from his childhood. "Hey Dad, that time you took me to the rope bridge near the Giant's Causeway when I was a boy."

His father thought a moment. "What about it?"

"Remember we spotted the sparrow chasing away a far bigger bird. We watched until it won."

"It was some kind of hawk. What's that got to do with… "

"The sparrow was determined to defend its territory and you were impressed because it won. You told me to always stand up for myself. I didn't do that, but now I am."

"You're not a sparrow."

"I can't fucking win." Danny started pacing, his hands up by the sides of his face and shaking rapidly to convey his frustration. "You need to completely control my life and… "

"You're acting crazy."

"You've got to give me my space. You've got to let me sort this out my way."

"Very rich, given what's to be sorted."

Danny stopped pacing and stared out the French windows. "Dad, I've turned out pretty good. I've listened to you in the big things in my life. I've always done as you asked because you said you knew what was best. I graduated from a course you decided I should do. I almost married a woman you picked."

"I know what's best… "

"I'm grateful for everything you've done. But from here on in, *I'm* going to make my own decisions. Some of them will be good. Some bad. But they'll be *my* decisions. I'll bear the responsibility for them. That doesn't mean I don't love or respect you."

"I'd have loved it if you'd married Susan. But I accept you don't want her. I won't bring it up again." He sat on the sofa and regarded Danny. "But you have to come home. It's where you belong. England's not your home, son."

"I feel at home."

"The English don't respect the Irish."

"Do we respect them?"

"I *want* you home." He rose, walked over to the dining room table and stared at the phone. "I need you to help me."

Danny went over and laid his hand on his father's shoulder. "It means a lot to hear that."

"So come home."

Danny didn't speak.

"I need to fight this injustice. Why should I run away like I'm some criminal? You've always told me to stand up. It's hawks and sparrows, Dad."

His father buried his face in his hands for a long time. "Fair enough," he said. "I see you're not going to back down." He rose out of his seat. "A wise man knows when it's time to ask. So I want you to promise you'll ask for my help if you need it."

It had taken his leaving home for Danny to understand. He was like his father. No, he wasn't irascible or demanding like him, but still they were the same. Both loved and wanted to be loved. Both wanted respect and to be respected. The parent-child part of their relationship was over. Their locking of horns would now be replaced by something richer and far more beneficial for both of them.

"I promise, Dad."

Toast

Unable to sleep, he got up even though it was only quarter to five in the morning. He showered, dressed and went downstairs. He took his coffee out into the garden and sat on one of the ornate wicker chairs. Except for the occasional passing bus, the city was still asleep. Over the rooftops, a silvery sheen was in the eastern sky as dawn began to break. Perfume from the late summer roses enveloped him, so strong and thick it was almost tactile. He watched the sky lighten into a pale orange as the sun began to break the night's hold. Today would be gorgeous. No rain or wind in the forecast. He wondered where he would be at the end of it.

When he came inside again, he could hear Julia go into the bathroom. The familiar groan of the pipes inside the back kitchen wall commenced as she turned the shower on. Half-an-hour later, she came down with her hair still wet. She'd dressed in a sober business skirt, blouse and wore a single strand of pearls around her neck, fake pearls he knew because she'd told him.

Though he hadn't asked, he accepted her offer to swap shifts at work so she could accompany him to his meeting with the detective. This time, it was to take place at a regular police station, which made him feel safer. His lawyer was unable to accompany him due to a scheduling conflict requiring his appearance in court, but informed Danny if something went wrong, to immediately call him and stop all communication with the police until he arrived.

Danny's anxiety flourished the closer he got to the police station. Twice, he thought he was going to be sick. During the ride on the packed tube, Julia and he chatted at first and then she settled into reading while he stared out at the posters on the walls of the passing stations, each one drawing him closer and closer.

Inside, he spoke to the custody sergeant who informed him the detective had not yet arrived. At first the sergeant attempted to prevent Julia from accompanying Danny to the interview room, but her shiny pearls and weight of her status as an H.M.S Immigration officer came into play. Furnished with an ancient wooden desk that to Danny's surprise had graffiti on one side, the room was larger, more brightly lit and didn't have a two-way mirror.

"Maybe the detective's forgotten," Julia said, after five minutes passed.

"Maybe it's strategy."

A housefly walked across the floor in fits and starts. Phones rang intermittently and he heard footsteps as policemen passed up and down the corridor.

Fifteen minutes later, Detective Tompkins entered. After he sat, he turned to Julia.

"Are you his solicitor?"

"No."

"Who are you?"

"I'm sure your colleagues have already told you."

"You have to leave."

"I want her to stay," said Danny.

"This isn't a hospital bedside," the detective said. "No friends allowed. Not even pretty ones." He arched his eyebrows at Julia and then rose to signal he would evict her if necessary.

Julia rose and walked to the door, though stopped before opening it. "If he's not out of here shortly, I'll assume you've arrested him and will contact his lawyer who's on call. There'll be no repeat of the last fiasco."

The door closed. "Brought out the big guns, eh?"

Danny didn't answer.

The detective sat. "Let's cut to the chase. What'd you decide?" He splayed his elbows and rested his chin on top of his intertwined hands.

"I won't be an informer. I'm innocent. I know nothing about the IRA and have no interest skulking around Irish pubs in London on the British government's behalf."

"I didn't put you down as a gambler." The detective took his hands from underneath his chin and laid them on the table, sideways and half-curled.

"It's not much of a gamble according to my lawyer."

"All lawyers say that to their clients. If it were true, the jails would be empty." He leaned over the desk toward Danny. "You need to reconsider."

A hot flash whipped through Danny's body. The moment of his arrest was here. He sat erect. "No."

Danny peered over at the door fully expecting the custody sergeant to barge in. Nothing happened. The detective stared at him coldly for twenty seconds.

"If that's your choice." As the detective started to rise, the legs of his chair scraped against the tile floor. "I have to say I expected more of you, Danny."

"Am I under arrest?"

"You're free to leave." He came round the desk toward him. "We had to try."

It was over. He could scarcely believe it. Feeling as if the tiniest scrape of the chair's legs against the floor could provoke the detective to rescind his freedom, Danny rose slowly. It felt very awkward crossing to the door and leaving the room knowing the detective was watching him.

The flickering fluorescent tube at the end of the corridor seemed miles away. His heels resounded monstrously against the corridor tiles. A door creaked open behind him but he didn't look back.

As he reached the turn, the detective called out, "Hey, Danny." His mind urged him to bolt the ten yards to the reception and beyond to the exit, but he stopped and looked over his shoulder. "Be seeing you around, I'm sure."

Authority always made a final threat whether justified or not. He'd learned that when dealing with his father. He passed by the reception without making eye contact with the policewoman.

When he came out onto the sun-washed street Julia was waiting, leaning against the brick wall of the station as she puffed on a cigarette, her dangling pearls beautiful and utterly ridiculous.